THE BLUE ICE

The setting of *The Blue Ice* is the fjords and mountains of Norway, which enables Hammond Innes to combine within one book the sailing adventures of *Maddon's Rock*, the mining excitement of *The Killer Mine*, and the ski-ing thrills of *The Lonely Skier*.

What makes a man love certain metals more than anything else in the world? What makes a man commit every offence against the civil and moral codes when he is on the trail of mineral wealth? What makes a man throw love away, asks the girl in this story, for something a woman can't understand?

Hammond Innes supplies the answer in one word: excitement. In this story he tells of a mining engineer who had found evidence of valuable mineral deposits among the desolate mountains of Norway; in an unshakable pursuit of his belief that precious metals lie beneath the rock and ice, he commits every known crime in turn, including murder. But not only are the police on his track; the representatives of rival industrial concerns are deeply involved in the chase to find the man and extract from him his secret.

Hammond Innes imparts to the reader the same excitement which actuates his characters, the cold terror of the Blue Ice and the driving urge to find the mineral wealth that lies beneath it.

Hammond Innes

THE
BLUE ICE

COLLINS
8 GRAFTON STREET, LONDON

First published 1948
This reprint 1984

ISBN 0 00 221074 6

Made and Printed in Great Britain by
William Collins Sons & Co Ltd, Glasgow

To

FRIENDS IN NORWAY

One of a writer's problems is always the authenticity of background. In the case of this book it was necessary for me to go over the entire ground covered by George Farnell, including the long trek from Aurland to Finse over the Sankt Paal glacier.

In this connection, I should like to thank all those friends in Norway who did everything possible to assist me. The details of the whaling factory, in particular, were made possible by the kind hospitality of my friends at Blomvaag Hval.

In addition, the yachting sequences were greatly assisted by the owners of *Theodora*, who invited me to join their crew for that Grand National of ocean racing —the Fastnet Race.

CONTENTS

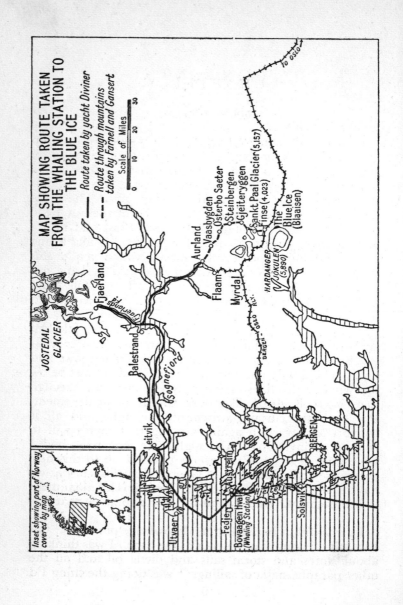

MAP SHOWING ROUTE TAKEN
FROM THE WHALING STATION TO
THE BLUE ICE

—— Route taken by yacht Diviner
--- Route through mountains
taken by Farnell and Gansert

Scale of Miles
0   10   20   30

Inset showing part of Norway
covered by map

JOSTEDAL
GLACIER

Fjaerland

Balestrand

Sognefjord

Leitvik

Utvaer

Fedjen

Bovaagen Hva
(Whaling Station)

BERGEN

Solsvik

Gjeilo

Aurland

Vaasbygden

Osterbo Saeter

Steinbergen

Gjeiteryggen

Sankt Paal Glacier (5,157)

Finse (4,023)

The
Blue Ice
(Blaaisen)

HARDANGER
JOKULEN
(5,890)

Flaam

Myrdal

BERGEN — OSLO RLY.

TO OSLO

CHAPTER 1

A LUMP of rock stands on my desk. It is a dull, grey lump of metallic rock no bigger than my fist and it rests on the blueprints of a great new enterprise. Beside it is a newspaper cutting with the picture of a grave and a little Norwegian church in the background. The blueprints belong to the future. The lump of rock and the newspaper cutting belong to the past. Past and future are a part of George Farnell, for his story is like a fine thread binding together the events which made this project possible. What he dreamed is taking shape out there by the frozen lake. If I switch off my table lamp and pull back the curtains, I can see the half-constructed buildings humped under their canopy of snow. Beyond them, towering white in the cold night, is the Jökulen. And on the glacial flank of the mountain, the *Blaaisen*— the Blue Ice—catches the moonlight in its icy jaws and grins. It is a wild and terrible place. And yet just below my window the lines of the railway that came through here in 1908 gleam like twin swords of achievement. Put back the curtain, switch on the light, and all is comfort and warmth again, proving that man's will to conquer is invincible. The nights are long now, and I have time to write of the events that led up to this new enterprise and of as much of George Farnell's story as we have been able to piece together. For this is his monument of achievement. And I want the world to know that it is his.

I came into it because of my knowledge of metals. But I wasn't thinking about metals at the time. I was thinking about stores and storm sails and diesel oil and all the other paraphernalia of sailing. I was doing the thing I'd

9

always wanted to do. I was going foreign in my own ship.

I can remember that morning so clearly. It was early April and a cold wind whipped the muddy water of the Thames into little angry whitecaps. Across the river the stone battlements of the Tower stood out very white against a sky of driven scud. Above us Tower Bridge rumbled with heavy dock traffic. Little groups of city workers crowded the parapet, gazing down at us as we bent on a new mainsail. The air was full of the thick smell of malt. The gulls wheeled and screamed incessantly. And all about us was the urgent movement of ships.

It's not easy to describe the feeling of exhilaration and impatience that possessed me. The gulls seemed screaming at us to hurry. There was an urgent note in the wind's rattling of the rigging and in the chatter of the wavelets against out newly painted hull. The tugs hooted impatiently. The long search for the right boat, the months of stripping and refitting, the days spent scrounging stores —all now seemed condensed into this one day. This was the period of waiting. To-morrow, before it was properly light, we should be slipping down-river with the outgoing tide—outward bound for the Mediterranean.

A month ago this moment had seemed no more than a dream. Shortages of materials and labour, export targets, foreign markets, man-management—that had been my life. Production manager of B.M. & I.—Base Metals and Industries—that was the job I'd been doing. I'd climbed to that big office in the concrete block outside Birmingham by drive and energy, and because I'd discovered and developed a nickel mine in Canada. All through the war I'd held that job. And I'd enjoyed it. Not because I like war. But because I wielded an industrial weapon and used the last ounce of energy that was in it to get guns and tanks rolling across the deserts of Africa and the fields of Normandy. But now I was through with all that. You'll say at thirty-six I'd no business to get out, the country being in the mess it was then. Well, I'm half Canadian and a scrapper by nature. But I like to know what I'm fighting. You can't fight controls and restrictions. The war gave free rein to my initiative. The peace cribbed it.

Dick Everard's an example of what I mean. He represents the best that Britain produces—tall, freckled, with a shock of fair hair and an honesty and strength of purpose that is a legacy of naval discipline. At twenty he was a naval rating. At twenty-four he was a lieutenant in charge of a corvette, with men and equipment worth the better part of a million under his command and untold responsibility. And now, at twenty-eight, he's regarded as of no more value than a machine-minder. All that training thrown away ! The other two members of the crew, Wilson and Carter, are different. They're paid yacht hands. It's their job. But Dick has no job. He's coming for the hell of it—because he's got nothing better to do and wants to look over the possibilities of other countries.

As I leaned on the boom, watching his deft fingers securing the peak of the sail to the main gaff, I couldn't help thinking what a loss men like he were to the country. So many were getting out. His eyes met mine and he grinned. " Okay, Bill," he said. " Hoist away."

With Carter on the peak halyard and myself on the throat we ran the mainsail up. The canvas was snowy white against the dark background of the warehouses. It slatted back and forth in the wind. We manned the peak and throat purchases. " She's going to set nicely," Dick said.

I looked along the deck. Everything was neatly coiled down. The deck planking was scrubbed white. Brasswork gleamed in the dull light. She was a lovely boat. She was a gaff-rigged ketch of fifty tons and she'd been built in the days when ships were expected to go anywhere. I'd had her stripped out inside and refitted to my own design. A new main mast had been stepped. The rigging was all new, so were the sails and I'd had her auxiliary replaced by a big ex-naval engine. For the first time since the war ended I felt the world at my feet. I'd stores and fuel and a crew—there was no place in the world *Diviner* wouldn't take me.

Dick sensed my thoughts. " With a fair wind we'll be in the sun in a week's time," he said, squinting up at the grey clouds scudding past our burgee.

I looked up at the envious faces lining Tower Bridge. " Yes," I said. " Algiers, Naples, the Piraeus, Port Said . . ."

And then I saw Sir Clinton Mann coming across the wharf. Sir Clinton is chairman of B.M. & I.—a tall man with stooping shoulders and an abrupt manner. He'd come into the business by way of the City. He represented money and statistics. He was as remote as a cabinet minister from the sweat and toil of production. He looked strangely incongruous in his City hat as he climbed down on to the deck.

" Good morning, Sir Clinton," I said, wondering why he had come. His eyes regarded me coldly as I went forward to meet him. I was conscious of my dirty jersey and corduroys. I'd never met him anywhere outside of a boardroom. " Would you care to look over the ship? " I asked.

" No," he said. " I'm here on business, Gansert." I took him down to the saloon. " When do you sail? " he asked.

" To-morrow," I said. " On the morning tide."

" For the Mediterranean ? "

I nodded.

" I want you to change your plans, Gansert," he said. " I want you to go to Norway instead."

" Why ? " I asked, puzzled at his suggestion. And then, quickly, in case he should take that as an indication that I would : " I'm sorry, Sir Clinton. But I'm leaving to-morrow for——"

He held up his hand. " Listen to me first, Gansert,"

he said. " You're no longer connected with B.M. & I.—
I know that. But you can't give eight years of your life
to a concern without something of it sticking to you. Those
thorite alloys, for instance. You started that. They were
developed as a result of your efforts. And if we could get
into full production——"

" That's a pipe dream," I told him. " And you know
it. Thorite costs dollars. And even if you'd got all the
dollars in the world, there just isn't enough of the stuff.
American output is negligible, and that's the only known
source."

" Is it ? " He fished a small wooden box from the
pocket of his overcoat and pushed it across the table at
me. " Then what's that ? " he asked.

I lifted the lid. Inside, resting on cotton wool, was a
lump of metallic-looking ore. I lifted it out and with
sudden excitement took it over to the window. " Where
did you get this ? " I asked.

" First, what is it ? " he asked.

" I can't be certain until tests have been made," I
told him. " But I'd say it's thorite."

He nodded. " It is thorite," he said. " We've been
through all the tests."

I looked out of the window at the smoke and dirt of
London's river. I was thinking of long assembly lines
pouring out thorite alloy equipment, stronger than steel,
lighter than aluminium, rustless and bright. If we could
mine thorite in quantity then Britain would no longer
lose ground to America. " Where was this mined ? " I
asked.

He sat back in his chair again. " That's what I don't
know," he said.

" But surely," I said, " you know where it came from ? "

He nodded. " Yes, I know where it came from." His
voice was dry and unemotional. " A fishmonger in
Hartlepool sent it to me."

" A fishmonger in Hartlepool ? " I stared at him. I
thought he was joking.

"Yes," he said. "He found it in a case of whale meat."

"You mean it came from the stomach of a whale?" I was thinking of the untold mineral wealth that was supposed to be hidden under the Antarctic ice.

"No," he replied. "The whale meat came from Norway. And that lump of ore hadn't been absorbed into the digestive organs of a whale. It had been placed in a fold of the meat when it was packed." He paused, and then said, "We've checked up as far as we can from this end. The meat was part of a consignment dispatched to Newcastle by one of the Norwegian coastal stations." He leaned forward. "Gansert, I want your opinion. Who's the best man for us on Norway?"

"You mean for metals?" I asked.

He nodded.

I didn't have to stop and think. I knew them all. Most of them were friends of mine. "There's Pritchard," I said. "Einar Jacobsen's good, and there's that Swedish fellow, Kults. Oh, and Williamson. But for our purpose, I'd I'd say Pritchard."

"That's no good," he said. "We're not the only people who know about this. Det Norske Staalselskab are on to it, too. Jorgensen's over here now, purchasing equipment. He's also angling for a tie-up with either ourselves or Castlet Steel. He says he possesses all the necessary information, but he's asking us to go into it blind. I've told him that's impossible and he threatens to approach the Americans. We've no time to waste sending Pritchard out there. He could search for months and find nothing. What we need is somebody who could advise us out of his own knowledge."

"There's only one man who could do that," I said. "And he's probably dead by now. But if he weren't he could give you the answers you want. He knew Norway——" I stopped then and shrugged my shoulders. "That was the trouble," I added. "He spent too much time in Norway—his own time and other people's money."

Sir Clinton's gaze was fixed on me and there was almost

a glint of excitement in his eyes. "You mean George Farnell, don't you?" he said.

I nodded. "But it's ten years since he disappeared."

"I know." Sir Clinton's fingers drummed a tattoo on the leather surface of his brief case. "Two weeks ago our representative in Norway cabled from Oslo that there were rumours of new mineral discoveries in the central part of the country. Ever since then I've been trying to trace George Farnell. His mother and father are both dead. He seems to have had no relatives and no friends. Those who knew him before his conviction haven't heard from him since he disappeared. I had a detective agency on the job. No luck. Then I put an advertisement in the personal column of *The Times*."

"Any luck there?" I asked as he paused.

"Yes. I had several replies—including the fishmonger. Apparently fishmongers now read *The Times*."

"But what made him connect that lump of ore with your advertisement?"

"This." Sir Clinton produced a filthy slip of paper. It was stained and stiffened with the congealed blood of the whale meat and had split along the folds. Through the dark bloodstains spidery writing showed in a vague blur. Two lines of what looked like poetry—and then a signature.

Ten years! It seemed incredible. "I suppose it is his signature?" I asked.

"Yes." Sir Clinton passed a slip of paper across to me. "That's a specimen," he said.

I compared the two. There was no doubt about it. Blurred and half obliterated by the blood, the signature on the scrap of paper had the same flourishing characteristics as the specimen. I sat back, thinking of George Farnell—how he'd flung himself out of an express train and had then completely vanished. He'd worked with me once on some concessions in Southern Rhodesia. He'd been a small, dark man with tremendous vitality—a bundle of nerves behind horn-rimmed glasses. He was an authority on base metals and he'd been obsessed with the idea of untold mineral wealth in the great mountain mass of Central Norway. "This means that he's alive, and in Norway," I said slowly.

"I wish you were right," Sir Clinton answered. He produced a newspaper cutting from his brief case. "Farnell's dead. This was published a fortnight ago. I didn't see it at the time. My attention was drawn to it later. There's a picture of the grave. And I've checked with the Norwegian military authorities that he did, in fact, join the Kompani Linge under the name of Bernt Olsen."

I took the cutting. It was headlined—ESCAPED CONVICT IN HERO'S GRAVE. The letters of the name—Bernt Olsen—stood out black against the plain white cross in the picture. In the background was a small wooden church. The story recalled how Farnell had been convicted of forging the name of his partner, Vincent Clegg, and swindling him out of nearly £10,000, how he had escaped from the lavatory window of a train whilst being transferred to Parkhurst and had then completely vanished. That was in August, 1939. Apparently Farnell, trading on his knowledge of Norwegian, had then enlisted in the Norwegian Forces under the name Bernt Olsen. He had joined the Kompani Linge and had gone on the Målöy raid in December, 1941. He was reported missing from this operation. There followed a paragraph marked with blue pencil :—

"Recently the body of a man, later identified as Bernt Olsen, was discovered on the Boya Brae. He had attempted a lone crossing of the Jostedal, Europe's largest glacier. Presumably he had lost his way in a snowstorm. He must have fallen over a thousand feet on to the Boya Brae, a tributary of the main glacier above Fjaerland. He had with him divining rods and other metallurgical instruments. Papers found on the body proved the connection between Bernt Olsen, the hero, and George Farnell, the convict."

The story finished sententiously : *And so another of Britain's sons has found glory in the hour of his country's greatest need.*

I handed the story back to Sir Clinton. "That happened a month ago ? " I asked.

He nodded. "Yes. That's been checked. The body was found on March 10th. The grave is at Fjaerland, which is at the head of the fjord running right up under the Jostedal. Have you read the lines above the signature on that piece of paper ? "

I looked at the bloodied scrap again. The lines were too blurred.

" I've had it deciphered by experts," Sir Clinton went on. " It reads : *If I should die, think only this of me . . .*"

" *This* presumably being the sample of thorite ? " I said. " How does it go ? *If I should die, think only this of me—That there's some corner of a foreign field that is forever England.*" An open invitation ? But the fool hadn't said which corner. " Who was this addressed to ? " I asked.

" That's the trouble," Sir Clinton replied. " The fish-monger destroyed the wrapping. He said it was sodden with blood and quite unreadable anyway."

" Pity," I said. " If we'd known that . . ." I was thinking of all the people who'd like to get their hands on deposits of thorite. B.M. & I. wasn't the only concern that had produced new alloys based on thorite.

" It's almost as though he had some premonition," Sir Clinton murmured. " Why else should he quote those lines of Rupert Brooke ? "

" Why, indeed ? " I said. " And why go and die on the Jostedal ? " That was what really puzzled me. Most of his life Farnell had spent in the mountains of Norway. He'd gone there as a boy on walking tours. By the time he was twenty he knew the mountains better than most Norwegians. All through that hot summer in Southern Rhodesia he'd talked of little else. Norway was his El Dorado. He lived for nothing else but the discovery of minerals in the ice-capped fastnesses of Scandinavia. It

was to finance prospecting expeditions to Norway that he
had swindled his partner. That had come out at the trial.
I turned to Sir Clinton. " Isn't there something strange,"
I said, " about a man who survives a jump from an
express train, goes through the Målöy raid, does resistance
work—all things he's never done before—and then gets
himself killed in the one place in which he's really at
home ? "

Sir Clinton smiled and got to his feet. " He's dead," he
said. " And that's all there is to it. But before he died he
discovered something. When he went to the Jostedal he
knew his life was in danger—hence the thorite sample and
the note. Somewhere in England there's somebody who's
expecting that sample." He folded the newspaper cutting
and thrust the wooden box with the thorite sample back
into the pocket of his coat. " What we need to know is
what he had discovered before he died." He paused.
" See—to-day's Monday. I'll have Ulvik—that's our
Norwegian representative—up at Fjaerland from Friday
onwards. Find out all you can about how Farnell died—
why he was on the Jostedal—and above all where that
thorite sample came from. Needless to say, you'll find
our representative has authority to meet all expenses you
may incur in Norway. And we shan't forget that you'll
be acting for the company as a free-lance in this matter."

He seemed to take it for granted that I'd switch my
plans. That got me angry. " Look, Sir Clinton," I said.
" I'm not in need of money, and you seem to have
forgotten that I'm leaving for the Mediterranean
to-morrow."

He turned in the doorway of the cabin. " The Mediterranean or Norway—what's it matter to you, Gansert ? "
He gripped my arm. " We need somebody over there we
can trust," he said. " Somebody who knew Farnell and
who's an expert on this sort of metal. Above all, we need
somebody who understands the urgency of the matter.
Farnell is dead. I want to know what he discovered before
he died. I'm offering you a purpose for your trip—and

the necessary foreign exchange." He nodded and turned again towards the door. " Think it over," he said.

I hesitated. He was climbing the companion. " You've left your paper," I said.

" You might like to read it," he answered.

I followed him up on to the deck. " Good luck ! " he said. Then he climbed the iron ladder to the wharf. I stood and watched his tall, stooping figure till it disappeared between the warehouses. Damn the man ! Why did he have to interfere with my plans ? To hell with him—I was going down into the sunshine where there was warmth and colour. And then I thought of Farnell and how he'd discovered that seam of copper when every one else had thought the mine worked out. Why in the world should he go and get himself killed on a glacier ?

" What did the old boy want ? " Dick's voice brought me back to the present.

Briefly I told him what had happened. " Well ? " he asked when I had finished. " Which is it to be—the Med. or Norway ? " There was a bitter note in his voice as though he were resigned to disappointment. Norway was to him a cold, dark country. He wanted the sun and opportunity.

" The Mediterranean," I said with sudden decision. " I'm through with the scramble for metals." The wind howled joyfully in the rigging. Soon we'd be wallowing through the Bay of Biscay. Then we'd lie out on the deck and swim and laze and drink wine. " Go and check that that water tender's coming alongside before the tide leaves us on the mud," I said, and turned and went back to the saloon. I crossed over to the porthole and stood there idly watching a barge drift down with the outgoing tide. But why had Farnell died on the Jostedal ? That's what I couldn't get out of my mind. During the war he'd probably lived up in the mountains. He knew all the glaciers. I glanced down at the table. The paper that Sir Clinton had left was still there. I read the headlines without recording them. I was thinking of Farnell's note : *If I should die* . . . Why quote that ?

A story ringed in blue pencil caught my eye. It was headed—METAL EXPERT TO VISIT CONVICT'S GRAVE. I picked up the paper. The story was quite short. It read : —

" Recent reports of mineral discoveries in Central Norway have aroused fresh interest in the death of convict hero, George Farnell, whose body was discovered a month ago on the Jostedal Glacier in Norway. Farnell was an expert on Norwegian minerals. Castlet Steel and Base Metals & Industries are the firms chiefly interested. Sir Clinton Mann, chairman of B.M. & I., said yesterday, ' It is possible that Farnell may have discovered something. We intend to investigate.'

" ' Big ' Bill Gansert, until recently production chief at B.M. & I.'s metal alloy plant at Birmingham, is the man chosen for the job. He leaves for Norway to-morrow, sailing his own yacht, *Diviner*, and postponing a planned Mediterranean cruise. If any one has any information that may assist Gansert in his investigations, they are asked to get in touch with him on board his yacht which is moored at the wharf of Messrs. Crouch and Crouch, Herring-Pickle Street, London, close by Tower Bridge."

I threw the paper down angrily. What right had he to put out a story like that ?—trying to force my hand ? I thought of all I'd read about the ruins of Greece and Italy, the pyramids, the primitive islands of the Aegean, the hill towns of Sicily. I suppose I've been almost everywhere in the world. But I've seen nothing of it. I've always been chasing some damned metal, rushing from place to place, a little cog in the big machine of grab. I've never had a chance to stop off where I like and laze in the sun and look around me. All I knew of the world was cities and mining camps. I picked up the paper and read the story through again. Then I went up on deck. " Dick ! " I shouted. " Any reason why we can't slip out on this tide ? "

" Yes," he answered, surprised. " We've just grounded. Why ? "

" Read that," I said and handed him the paper.

He read it through. Then he said, " It looks like Norway, doesn't it ? "

" No," I said. " No, it doesn't. I'm damned if I'll be thrust into the thing like this."

" What about Farnell ? " he murmured.

" What about him ? "

" You want to know how he managed to kill himself on that glacier, don't you ? " he suggested.

I nodded. He was right. I did want to know that. " I wonder if any one will come forward with information," I murmured.

" Four million people take the *Morning Record*," Dick said. " Some of them will come to see you."

He was right there. Within the next hour I had three journalists, several cranks, an insurance salesman and two fellows wanting to come as crew. In the end I got fed up. I wanted to see the Customs and there were other calls I had to make. " See you for lunch at the Duke's Head," I told Dick and left him to handle any more visitors himself.

When he joined me for lunch he handed me a large envelope. " A B.M. & I messenger brought it," he said. " It's from Sir Clinton Mann."

" Anybody else been pestering you ? " I asked as I slit open the envelope.

" A couple of reporters. That's all. Oh, and Miss Somers here." He turned and I saw a girl standing close behind him. She was tall and fair haired. " Miss Somers, this is Bill Gansert."

Her grip was firm as she shook my hand. She had grey eyes and there was a curious tenseness about her that communicated itself even in that atmosphere of a crowded bar. " What are you having ? " I asked her.

" A light ale, please," she said. Her voice was soft, almost subdued.

" Well," I said when I had given the order, " what can we do for you, Miss Somers ? "

" I want you to take me to Norway with you." The tenseness was in her voice now.

" To Norway ? But we're not going to Norway. Dick should have warned you. We're going to the Mediterranean. I suppose you've been reading that damned newspaper story ? "

" I don't understand," she said. " I haven't seen any newspaper story. Sir Clinton Mann phoned me this morning. He told me to come along and see you. He said you were sailing for Norway to-morrow."

" Well, he's wrong." The sharpness of my voice seemed to jolt her. " Why do you want to get to Norway ? " I asked in a gentler tone.

" Sir Clinton said you were going over to investigate the death of—of George Farnell." Her eyes had an expression of pain in them. " I wanted to come, too. I wanted to see his grave and—and know how he died."

I was watching her face as I passed over her beer. " You knew Farnell ? "

She nodded her head. " Yes," she said.

" Before or after he went on the Målöy raid ? "

" Before." She gulped at her drink. " I was working for the Kompani Linge."

" Have you heard from him since ? "

She seemed to hesitate. " No."

I didn't press the point. " Did you know him as George Farnell, or as Bernt Olsen ? " I asked.

" Both," she answered. Then suddenly, as though she couldn't stand the suspense any longer, she said, " Please, Mr. Gansert—I must get to Norway. This is the only way I can do it. I want to know what happened. And I want to—see where he's buried. Please—help me, won't you ? Sir Clinton said you were going to Norway. Please, take me. I won't be in the way. I promise. I've done quite a lot of sailing. I'll work on deck, cook—anything. Only let me come."

I didn't say anything for the moment. I was wondering what was behind her plea. There was something driving her—something that she hadn't stated. Had Farnell been her lover? But that alone wouldn't account for the urgency of her tone. "Why did Sir Clinton phone you this morning?" I asked her.

"I told you—to tell me to get in touch with you."

"No," I said. "I meant, how did he come to know you were interested?"

"Oh. He put an advertisement in *The Times* some time back. I answered it. I went up and saw him. He thought I might know something of George's activities since the war."

"And do you?"

"No."

"Did you know he was a metallurgist and an expert on Norway?"

"Yes. I knew that."

"But you didn't know whether he might have made some important discovery in Norway during the last few months?"

Again that momentary hesitation. "No."

A silence followed. Then Dick suddenly said, "Bill—I suggest we make for Norway when we leave the Thames to-morrow." I glanced at him. He must have guessed what was in my mind, for he said quickly, "I mean, I'm getting curious about this man Farnell."

So was I. I glanced at the girl. Her features were on the long side with straight nose and determined chin. It was a strong face. She met my gaze in a quick movement of the eyes and then looked away again. I picked up the envelope and shook the contents out on to the bar. There was a little gasp from the girl. Photographs of George Farnell stared up at me from the bar top. I shuffled quickly through them. There was one of him in an open-necked khaki shirt, looking just as I'd known him out in Rhodesia. There were full length pictures of him looking very awkward in a business suit, copies of passport

photographs and one of him at work with a divining rod.
I turned to the passport photographs. They showed a
strangely intense face—long, almost æsthetic features,
short, clipped moustache, thin, dark hair, rather promi-
nent ears and eyes that glinted behind horn-rimmed
glasses. The date on the back—10 Jan., 1936. Then
there were police records, full-face and side-face studies
of him after his conviction, and pictures of his finger-
prints. Sir Clinton had certainly been thorough.

Clipped to the photographs was a note. *These may be
of use. I have telephoned two people who answered my* Times
*advertisement. They both want to go with you. The girl could
be helpful if you gained her confidence. A Norwegian has been
in touch with me this morning. He knew Farnell in Norway
during the war. I told him to see you about six this evening. Also
I have seen Jorgensen again. I said I must have detailed information before presenting his proposals to my board. He talked of
nickel and—uranium! He gave me twenty-four hours to make
up my mind. He flies to America on Saturday. Please keep me
informed of all developments.* It was signed—*Clinton Mann*.

I passed the note across to Dick and finished my beer.
Then I swept the pictures of Farnell back into the envelope
and stuffed it in the pocket of my jacket. " See you
later," I told Dick. " And keep Miss Somers with you."
I started to move for the door and then stopped. " Miss
Somers," I said, " were you by any chance at Farnell's
trial ? "

" No," she answered. " I didn't know him then." Her
tone was genuinely surprised.

I nodded and left them there. I took a taxi to the
offices of the *Morning Record*. There I got the inquiry
people to dig out from the library the file of the *Record*
for the month of August, 1939. The trial of George
Farnell was covered very fully. There were pictures
of Farnell and of his partner, Vincent Clegg, a picture
of Farnell with his father and one of Farnell working
with a divining rod—the same picture that Sir Clinton
had included in the batch he'd sent me.

But though I searched through every paragraph of the reports I could get no line that could conceivably have a bearing on his death. No extraneous characters had appeared as witnesses on either side. It was a simple, straightforward story. Farnell and Clegg had set up as mining consultants in 1936. They had operated successfully for three years. Then Clegg, who handled the business side, found that certain cheques had been cashed of which he had no knowledge. The signature on the cheques appeared to be his. The amount involved was nearly £10,000. Farnell pleaded guilty to the forging of his partner's signature. In evidence he stated that prospecting work in Norway, not on behalf of the firm, had involved him in considerable expenditure. He was convinced that valuable minerals did, in fact, exist in the mountains of Central Norway. His partner had refused to finance him. He had, therefore, acted on his own in the matter. In mitigation, his counsel said that he honestly regarded the money spent as being in the form of an investment. Apart from Farnell and Clegg, the only witnesses called were members of the office staff and Pritchard, who was called in as a metallurgist to give his views on Norway's mineral potentialities. The judge in his summing up described Farnell as a " man obsessed with an idea." Farnell was sentenced to six years.

That was all. I closed the file and went out into the chill bustle of Fleet Street. I jumped on a bus going west and as we moved along the Strand I wasn't thinking about the trial. I was thinking about the girl. *Could be helpful if you gained her confidence.* Maybe Sir Clinton was right. Maybe she did know something. I got off at Trafalgar Square. At the offices of the Bergen Steamship Company, I talked with a man I'd met several times at public functions. He gave me introductions to men in Bergen and in the Norwegian Government which might prove useful. Then I went out and got a complete set of Admiralty charts and sailing directions for the Norwegian coast.

It was late afternoon before I took a bus up to the City and walked across Tower Bridge. I paused for a moment by the parapet and looked down at *Diviner*. The tide was in now and she lay with her decks almost flush with the wharf. To me she looked very beautiful with her tall masts and blue hull. I could understand how all the City people had felt who stood where I was standing, gazing down at her. Up the river the light was fading and the sun, setting in a livid streak, gave an orange glow to the cold, damp air. Lights were still on in some of the big office blocks. Clocks began to strike and I looked at my watch. It was six o'clock. I hurried on then.

As I turned in between the tall warehouses, a taxi passed me and stopped at the wharf. A man got out and paid the driver off. As I came up he was looking uncertainly about him. "Excuse me, please," he said. "Can you tell me if that is the yacht, *Diviner*?" And he nodded towards the slender clutter of spars that towered above the wharf. He was a slim, neatly dressed man. He looked like an American business man. And he spoke like one, except for a peculiar preciseness and the trace of what seemed to be a Welsh accent.

"Yes," I said. "Who do you want?"

"Mr. Gansert," he answered.

"I'm Gansert," I told him.

His rather heavy eyebrows rose slightly, but his leathery features remained entirely expressionless. "Good," he said. "My name is Jorgensen. You have heard of me, perhaps?"

"Of course," I said, and held out my hand.

His grip was limp and perfunctory. "I wish to talk with you," he said.

"Come on board, then," I invited him.

Carter poked his head up out of the engine-room hatch as I stepped down on to the deck. His face was smeared with grease. "Where's Mr. Everard?" I asked.

"Doon in the saloon, sir," he answered. "There's Miss Somers an' a man wi' him. The man came aboord wi' a suitcase as though he were planning to stay for the week-end."

I nodded and dived down the main companionway. " Mind your head," I warned Jorgensen. When I entered the saloon I found the girl seated opposite Dick in the half light. Beside her stood a heavily-built man with red hair. I knew him at once. " Curtis Wright, isn't it ? " I asked.

" So you remember me, eh ? " He sounded pleased. " You know, you were one of the few industrialists I enjoyed visiting," he added, seizing my hand in a powerful grip. " You knew what we wanted and got things moving." At one time he'd been responsible for testing our artillery equipment. He'd been in and out of the works quite a bit. He was regular army.

" Is this a social call ? " I asked. " Or are you here about Farnell ? "

" I'm here about Farnell," he answered. " Sir Clinton Mann telephoned me this morning."

" You knew Farnell ? " I asked him.

" Yes. Met him during the war."

I suddenly remembered Jorgensen. I introduced him and asked Dick to get Carter to give us some light. What was puzzling me was the reason for Jorgensen's visit. " Did you come to discuss Farnell too, Mr. Jorgensen ? " I asked.

He smiled. " No," he said. " I came to discuss rather more important matters—privately."

" Of course," I said.

Dick came in again at that moment. " There's a rather strange-looking specimen up top," he said. " Says he has an appointment."

" What's his name ? " I asked.

" My name is Dahler." The voice came from the doorway. It was low pitched and foreign. I saw Jorgensen jerk round as though somebody had pressed something into the small of his back. A small, awkward-looking person stood in the saloon doorway. I hadn't noticed him

enter. He just seemed to have materialised. His dark
suit merged into the shadows. Only his face showed, a
white blur under his iron grey hair. He came forward and
I saw that he had a withered arm. The lighting plant
started with a shrill whirr and the saloon lights came
on. Dahler stopped then. He had seen Jorgensen. The
lines on his face deepened. His eyes flared with sudden
and violent hatred. Then he smiled and a chill ran
through me. It was such a crooked, twisted smile.
" *God dag, Knut,*" he said and I realised he was speaking
Norwegian.

" What are you doing here ? " Jorgensen answered.
The suaveness of his voice was gone. It was angry,
menacing.

" I am here because I wish to talk with Mr. Gansert
about Farnell." The cripple was peering up at Jorgensen.
Then he turned to me. " Did you know Farnell ? " he
asked. His lips were still set in that crooked smile and
I realised suddenly that half his face was paralysed too.
He had difficulty in forming some of his words. The
paralysis produced a slight hesitation and a little froth
of spittal bubbled at the corner of his mouth, catching the
light.

" Yes," I said. " I worked with him once."

" Like him ? " His eyes were watching me as he put this
question.

" Yes," I answered. " Why ? "

" I like to know whose side people are on," he replied
softly, and looked again at Jorgensen.

" Why have you come here ? " Jorgensen barked the
question out as though he were speaking to a subordinate.

Dahler said nothing. He didn't move. He remained
staring at Jorgensen so that the very silence made the
atmosphere electric. It was as though the two men had
things between them that could be communicated
without speech. It was Jorgensen who broke the silence.
" I would like to speak to you privately, Mr. Gansert,"
he said, turning to me.

"You are afraid to make your proposals openly, eh?" Dahler said, and there was a venomous note in his voice. "It's a pity Farnell isn't here to advise Mr. Gansert."

"Farnell is dead."

"Is he?" Dahler leaned suddenly forward. He was like a spider darting from the corner of its web. "What makes you so sure he is dead?"

Jorgensen hesitated. Any moment now he would pick up his hat and walk off the ship. I could see it coming. And I didn't want that. If I could hold Jorgensen on on board. . . . And at that moment I heard the warning bell on Tower Bridge ring. I knew then what I was going to do. I edged towards the door. Jorgensen said, "I did not come here to talk about Farnell." I slipped out and hurried on to the deck.

A tramp steamer was edging out from the neighbouring wharf. The traffic on Tower Bridge had stopped. Carter and Wilson were standing by the rail, talking. I went over to them. "Carter," I said. "Is the engine warm? Will she start up first go?"

"Ye dinna ha' to fash yersel' aboot the engine, Mr. Gansert," he said. "Ah've got her so she'll go when I click me fingers."

"Get it going then," I said. "And make it quick." As he dived down the engine-room hatch, I ordered Wilson to let go the warps. "And do it quietly," I told him.

He climbed over the rail and in a few seconds both warps were on deck. I slipped aft and took the wheel. The engine coughed twice and then roared into life. "Full astern," I called down to Carter. There was a bubbling froth under our stern and we began to move. As we slid clear of the wharf, I ordered "Full ahead" and swung the wheel. The engine roared. The propellers frothed and gurgled under the water. The long bowsprit swung in a wide arc until it pointed straight for the main span of Tower Bridge.

Dick came tumbling out from the companionway. Jorgensen was right behind him. "What is happening?" Jorgensen demanded. "Why are we moving out into the river?"

"We're changing our berth," I told him.

"Where to?" he asked suspiciously.

"To Norway," I answered.

CHAPTER 2

THE GYBE

When I told Jorgensen we were on our way to Norway, he was furious. He brushed past Dick and came aft to where I sat at the wheel. "Put back at once," he said. "I demand to be put ashore."

I said nothing. The centre span of Tower Bridge was above us now. The two uplifted sections of roadway threw back the sound of our engine. We were through just ahead of the tramp steamer. Beyond our bowsprit, the river lay like a dark road winding to the sea. On either side the warehouses stood like shallow cliffs. And behind us London glowed, reflecting the light of its millions on the low cloud that covered the city.

"You can't get away with this, Gansert," Jorgensen shouted. I thought for a moment he was going to try and seize the wheel. I didn't say anything. I was filled with a crazy feeling of elation. Of course, I couldn't get away with it. I just couldn't kidnap the man. But if I could bluff him into staying on board . . . if I could get him so worried that he didn't dare go ashore for fear of missing something. . . . I had three people with me who all knew something about Farnell. Cooped up in the narrow confines of the ship I'd get their stories out of them. And with Jorgensen on board, instead of on his way to America, I didn't have to worry about the time factor. "For the last time, Mr. Gansert," he said in a quieter tone, "will you kindly put me ashore."

I looked up at him then. "Are you certain you want to be put ashore, Mr. Jorgensen?" I asked.

"What do you mean?" There was genuine surprise in his voice.

"Why did you come to see me this evening?" I asked.

" Because I wanted you to use your influence with Sir
Clinton—to persuade him to agree to operate with
us in the development of the mineral resources of my
country." For the first time I noticed that he had a
slight lisp. But it didn't make him sound effeminate.
Rather the reverse, for his struggle to pronounce his r's
gave his speech added emphasis.

" I don't believe you," I said bluntly. " You came to see
me because you wanted to know what we'd found out
about George Farnell."

" That is absurd," he answered. " Why should I be
interested in this man Farnell ? Perhaps he was good once.
But ten years is a long time."

" He spent most of those ten years in Norway," I
reminded him. And then I said," Why did you come to
see me precisely at six o'clock ? "

He seemed to hesitate. Then he said, " I had a con-
ference at Norway House. I could not come earlier."

" Are you sure you didn't come because Sir Clinton
told you I'd be meeting some people who knew Farnell
at six o'clock ? " I asked. It was a shot in the dark.
And when he didn't reply, I added, " You wanted to
know who was sailing with me to Norway, didn't
you ? "

" Why should I ? "

" Because you are as interested as we are in George
Farnell," I answered.

" That is ridiculous," he replied. " What is all this
about Farnell ? The man is dead."

" Yet I've had a message from him."

I was watching his face and in the light from the open
door of the chartroom I saw his eyes narrow.

" When ? "

" Quite recently," I told him. Before he could ask any
further questions I stood up. " Dick. Take the wheel,
will you," I said. And then : " You don't need to worry,
Mr. Jorgensen," I told him. " I'll not take you to Norway
against your will. But come below a moment and hear

what I have to say." I turned and went down the companionway.

In the saloon I found Curtis and Miss Somers seated where I had left them. Dahler was pacing up and down. He swung round as I came in. "Why are we going down the river, Mr. Gansert? I wish to be put ashore, please."

"Sit down," I said. Jorgensen appeared in the doorway. I pulled up a chair and thrust him into it. "I'll set any one ashore who wants to go," I told them. "But first listen to what I have to say." Dahler sat down at the table, resting his weight on his withered arm as he peered up at me. "For one reason or another we're all here because of one thing," I said, looking round at their faces. "Because of George Farnell's death." I had their attention then. They were all looking at me. I felt like the chairman of some incredible board meeting—the sort of board meeting one could only imagine in the moment of waking up with a hangover. They were such an odd assortment. And the undercurrent of emotion was so violent. It was in the air, like some electrical disturbance. On the surface they were just four individuals. But I was convinced that in some strange way they were all linked— and George Farnell was the link. "For myself," I said, "I'm not satisfied about George Farnell's death. I want to know how it happened. And I'm going to Norway now to find out." I turned to Curtis Wright. "Since you brought your things with you, I take it you want to come?"

His glance went to the girl. Then he said, "Yes. I'd like to."

"Why?" I asked him.

He grinned. "For one thing I've got three weeks' leave and this seems as good a way to spend it as any. For another, I too want to find out more about Farnell's death. There are messages I have to deliver. You see, I was with him on the Målöy raid."

"Why didn't you deliver the messages after the raid when you heard he was missing?" I asked.

"Because I knew he wasn't dead," he replied. "No reason why you shouldn't know about it, I suppose. I should have reported it at the time. But I didn't. One doesn't always do what one is supposed to do when one's on active service. And afterwards—well, there seemed no point."

He paused. Nobody spoke. Every one was watching him. He had taken a gold watch from his pocket and was toying with it. The girl gazed at it fascinated. "I was acting as liaison between the Kompani Linge and our own crowd on the Målöy raid," he went on. "When we were going in to the assault, Olsen came to me and asked me to give messages to various people. 'But only when you're certain I'm dead,' he said. 'I shall be reported missing on this raid.' I asked him what he meant by that, and he replied,' I'll do the job we're ordered to do. But when I've got my men back to the beach, I'll leave them there. I'm going into Norway on my own. There's something I've got to do—something I'd started before the war. It's important.' I argued with him—ordered him, as an officer, to report back with his men. But he just smiled and said, 'I'm sorry, sir. One day perhaps you'll understand.' Well, I couldn't put him under arrest when we'd be in action in five minutes' time. I just had to leave it at that."

"And what happened?" It was Jorgensen who put the question.

Curtis shrugged his shoulders. "Oh, he did as he said he would. He brought his men back to the beach. Then he told them he was going back for a man who was missing. They never saw him again and we left without him. If I thought he'd deserted, I'd have reported the matter. But I'm convinced he didn't. He wasn't the type that deserts. He was tough—not physically, but morally. You could see it in his eyes."

I leaned forward. "What was it he had to do over there in Norway?" I asked.

"I don't know," he answered. "It may not have been

important. But I know this. It was important to him."

I glanced at Jorgensen. He was leaning forward, his eyes fixed on Curtis. Opposite him, across the cabin, the cripple sat back in his chair and smiled softly. "What about you, Mr. Dahler?" I said. "Why have you come to see me?"

"Because I also wish to know more about Farnell's death," he said.

"Then why do you want to be put ashore?" I asked. "The answer surely is to come with us to Fjaerland?"

"I should like to," he replied. "But unfortunately——" he shrugged his shoulders.

"You say you'd like to?" I was puzzled.

His fingers plucked at the cloth of the half-empty sleeve. "There are difficulties, you see." His face was working. His whole body looked taut.

"What difficulties?" I inquired.

"Ask Jorgenson." His voice was violent.

I turned. Jorgenson's face was white. The rather leathery skin remained an impassive mask, but his blue eyes were narrowed and watchful. "Suppose you tell them yourself," he said.

Dahler jumped to his feet. "Tell them myself!" he cried. "No. Why should I tell them that I can no longer enter my own country?" He thrust back his chair and took a step towards Jorgensen. Then he turned abruptly about. A few agitated paces and he was brought up by the door to the galley. He swung round and faced us. "Never will I tell them that," he said. His brown eyes fastened themselves on me with a strange intentness. "I'll come, Mr. Gansert. I owe Farnell a debt." He glanced at Jorgensen. "And I believe in paying my debts," he added.

"What sort of a debt?" I asked.

"He saved my life," he answered.

"You are making a mistake, Mr. Dahler," Jorgensen said quietly. "In Norway you will be liable to arrest."

"And which one of your employees will you get to

inform against me this time, eh ? " Dahler asked with a sneer. " Or will you do your own dirty work ? " He moved slowly across the room, his head thrust out towards Jorgensen and twisted slightly to one side. " Haven't you done enough already ? "

" Sit down, Mr. Dahler please," I said and put my hand on his shoulder.

He spun round on me and for a moment I thought he was going to bite my hand, there was such a look of venom on his face. Then suddenly he relaxed and sat down. " Excuse me," he said.

I looked towards Jorgensen. " Finally there is you, Mr. Jorgensen. You came here, you say, to discuss the possibilities of a B.M. & I. tie-up with your own organisation." I leaned towards him. " As I've already told you, I don't believe you. You came here because you're as interested in Farnell as we are. You talked to Sir Clinton about nickel and uranium deposits. You were just guessing. You don't know what metal has been discovered in Norway." I paused and then said very deliberately, " But I do—and it isn't either nickel or uranium. As for knowing where the deposits are located, you haven't the faintest idea. Your visit over here is nothing but bluff."

" So you know what metal it is that has been discovered, eh ? " His eyes were without expression. It was impossible to read his thoughts. " Was it Farnell who told you that ? "

" Yes," I answered

" When did you hear from him ? "

" The message was received after his death," I said.

The girl started forward with a little cry. Dahler was watching Jorgensen.

" I'll set you ashore if you like," I said. " But re-member—here in this cabin, I am convinced, is collected all the truth about Farnell—or as much as we require to know. And whilst you're in the States—I shall be in Norway." I paused, watching him. Then I crossed over

to the door. " Think it over," I said. " If you like, I'll
put you ashore at Greenwich. Only make up your mind
quickly. We'll be passing the landing stage in about
five minutes."

I closed the door on them then and went up on deck.
It was very dark after the glare of the cabin. All about us
was a litter of lights. The air was cold on my face. The
deck throbbed under my feet. The swish-swish of water
slipping past us was exhilarating. We were on our way.

I went aft to where Dick sat, a still, dark figure behind
the wheel, the slender mizzen mast outlined like a spear
against the glow of London. " I'll take her now," I said.
" You go down and get our passengers sorted out.
Allocate cabins, issue blankets, sheets, clothes, anything
they need. Keep them occupied, Dick, and separate
Jorgensen from Dahler. Introduce the Somers girl to the
galley and have her get a meal together. Don't give any
of them time to think. I don't want anyone, least of all
Jorgensen, coming up to me and asking to be put ashore."

" Okay, skipper," he said. " I'll do my best."

" Oh, and tell them to write down any messages they
want sent," I added as he moved off. " Explain we've got
transmitting as well as receiving sets."

" Right," he said and disappeared down the companionway.

I slipped into a duffle coat and took my place behind
the wheel. Wilson was coiling down the warps. I called
to him and he came aft. He was a Cornishman, not
young, but a fine seaman. " Get Number One jib and
stays'l from the sail locker," I said. " And the jib-
headed tops'l. If the wind doesn't increase we'll be able
to carry them."

" Aye, aye, sir," he said. His seamed, weather-beaten
face showed ruddy in the glow of the port navigation
light. He paused. " Is there any truth in what Mr.
Everard was saying, sir, that we're bound for Norway ? "

" Quite true," I said. " Make any difference to you ? "

His rugged features spread into a grin. " There's better

fishing in Norway than in the Mediterranean." He spat
over the lee rail as though to emphasise the uselessness of
the Mediterranean and went for'ard. My gaze wandered
to the masthead. The light, signifying that we were a
sailing vessel under power, shone on the bare rigging.
I settled myself down to the long vigil of conning the ship
down to the mouth of the estuary. I didn't need the
chart. I'd been up and down the Thames under sail
so often. I knew every turn and twist, the buoy lights and
the landmarks. Going down under power was compara-
tively straightforward. The only thing that worried me
was whether Jorgensen would stay aboard.

It was with a sigh of relief, therefore, that I watched
the Royal Naval College at Greenwich slide past in the
darkness. He was not the sort of man who couldn't make
up his mind. I'd said I'd set him ashore at Greenwich
if he wanted me to. Since he hadn't requested me to,
the odds were he had decided to stay. But I wouldn't be
happy till I picked up the Nore. After that there'd be
no turning back.

Half an hour passed and then Dick came up. " Well,
I've got them all sorted out," he said. He glanced over
his shoulder and in a mock whisper said, " Believe it or
not, Jorgensen, the great Norwegian industrialist, is
helping Jill get grub."

" Jill I take it is Miss Somers ? "

" That's right. She's a pippin. Got stuck into it right
away. Knows her way around already."

" Where's Dahler ? " I asked.

" In his cabin. I've given him the single one for'ard
of the saloon on the starb'd side. The girl's got the port
one. Jorgensen's in with you and Curtis Wright's sharing
with me." He produced a sheaf of papers. " Shall I
send these off right away ? "

" What are they ? "

" Messages for transmission."

" Leave 'em in the chartroom," I told him.

" They're quite straightforward," he said. " Three

from Jorgensen, one from Dahler and one from the girl."

"I'd still like to look them over," I replied. "And get below again, will you, Dick. I don't want them left on their own till we're at sea."

"Okay," he said, and went below.

It was cold, sitting there at the wheel, and the time passed slowly. I was impatient to be out of the river. Gradually the lights of the docks and warehouses on either side thinned out until black areas of darkness marked open countryside and mud-flats. We passed a big freighter moving slowly upstream. Her deck lights slid quickly by and in a few minutes she was swallowed up by the night. At full ahead we made a good eight knots. Add to that a four knot tide and we were going downstream at a fair rate. At a call from Dick, Wilson went below and returned with mugs of steaming coffee and sandwiches for Carter and myself. By eight we were running past Tilbury and Gravesend and half an hour later we could see the lights of Southend. We were out in the estuary now and the ship was beginning to show a bit of movement. The wind was south-east and piling up a short, steep sea that hissed angrily in the darkness as it broke against our sides.

Dick joined me just as I picked up the Nore light, blinking steadily far ahead. "Dirty looking night," he said. "When are you getting the sails on her?"

"We'll run out to the Nore," I answered. "Then we'll be able to steer our course with a good reaching wind. How's everything below?"

"Fine," he said. "Dahler went straight to bed. Said he's a bad sailor. Wright and Jorgensen are talking skiing over a bottle of Scotch. And the girl's changing her clothes. What about to-night—are we splitting into watches? Wright's done some sailing and Jorgensen says he can handle small boats."

That was better than I'd hoped. The boat was an easy one to handle and the four of us could have managed her quite comfortably. But if there were much sail changing

to do, we'd soon tire ourselves out and then we'd have to
heave-to for sleep. And I was anxious to get across to
Norway as quickly as possible. " Right," I said. " We'll
split into watches. You take the starboard watch, Dick,
with Carter, Wright and Jorgensen. For the port watch
I'll have Wilson and the girl."

That choice of watches was made without thought. Yet
it was of vital importance to what followed. Almost
any other split-up would have made the difference. It
would have put Jorgensen in my watch. But how was I
to know then the violence that would be bred in the close
confines of the ship.

I handed the wheel over to Dick and went into the
chartroom to work out our course. I read the messages
through and transmitted them. They were simple
notifications of departure to Norway—Jill Somers to her
father, Dahler to his hotel and Jorgensen to his hotel and
to the London and Oslo offices of Det Norske Staalselskab.
When I emerged I found Wright, Jorgensen and the girl
all sitting in the cockpit. They were talking about sailing.
The Nore Tower was quite close now, illuminating the ship
each time the powerful beam swept over us.

" Take over the wheel, will you, Miss Somers," I said.
" Keep her head to the wind." As soon as she had
relieved Dick, I called to Carter and we got the mainsail up. The canvas cracked as the boom slatted to and
fro in the weird red and green glow of the navigation
lights on either side of the chartroom. As soon as peak
and throat purchases were made fast and the weather
backstay set up I had the engine stopped and I ordered
Jill Somers to steer up Barrow Deep on course north
fifty-two east. The mainsail filled as the ship heeled
and swung away. In an instant we had picked up way
and the water was seething past the lee rail. By the
time we had set jib, stays'l and mizzen the old boat was
going like a train, rocking violently as she took the steep
seas in a corkscrew movement that brought the water
gurgling in the scuppers at each plunge.

I sent Dick and his watch below. They were due on at midnight. Wilson was stowing gear down below. I was left alone with the girl. Her hand was steady on the wheel and she eased the boat over each wave with a sure touch, keeping steadily to her course. The light from the binnacle was just sufficient to show her features in silhouette against the howling darkness of the sea. Her fair hair blew free about her head. She was wearing a polonecked sweater under a rainproof windbreaker. " You're quite at home on a ship," I said.

She laughed. And by the way she laughed I knew she was enjoying the wind and the feel of the ship under her. " It's a long time since I've done any sailing," she said. And then a shade wistfully : " Nearly ten years."

" Ten years ? Where did you learn ? " I asked.

" Norway," she answered. " My mother was Norwegian. We lived in Oslo. Daddy was a director of one of the whaling companies at Sandefjord."

" Is that where you first met Farnell ? " I asked.

She looked up at me quickly. " No," she said. " I told you. I met him when I was working for the Kompani Linge." She hesitated and then said, " Why do you suppose poor Mr. Dahler queried George's death ? "

" I don't know," I said. It was a point that had been puzzling me. " Why do you speak of him as—poor Mr. Dahler ? "

She leaned forward, peering into the binnacle, and then shifted her grip on the wheel. " He has suffered so much. That arm—it quite upset me to see him like that."

" You've met him before ? " I asked.

" Yes. Long, long ago—at our home." She looked up at me, smiling. " He doesn't remember. I was a little girl in pigtails, then."

" Was he a business contact of your father's ? "

She nodded and I asked her what sort of business he had been engaged in.

" Shipping," she replied. " He owned a fleet of coastal steamers and some oil tankers. His firm supplied us with

fuel. That's why he came to see my father. Also he had
an interest in one of the shore whaling stations, so they
liked to talk. Father enjoyed being with any one who
was prepared to talk whaling."

"Why is Dahler scared to go back to Norway?" I asked.
" Why does Jorgensen say he's liable to be arrested ? "

" I don't know." She was frowning as though trying
to puzzle it out. " He was always such a dear. Each time
he came he brought me something from South America.
I remember he used to say that's what he kept tankers for
—to bring me presents." She laughed. " He took me
skiing once. You wouldn't think it now, but he was a
fine skier."

We fell silent after that. I was trying to visualise
Dahler as he had been. She, too, I think was lost in the
past. Suddenly she said, " Why doesn't Major Wright
deliver those messages he talked about ? " She did not
seem to expect any reply for she went on, " All these
people on board your ship going to look at his grave ;
it's—somehow it's frightening."

" Did you know him well ? " I asked.

She looked at me. " George ? Yes. I knew him—
quite well."

I hesitated. Then I said, " Does this mean anything
to you—*If I should die, think only this of me* ? "

I wasn't prepared for the jolt my question gave her.
She sat for a moment as though stunned. Then, like a
person in a trance, she murmured the remaining two
lines—" *That there's some corner of a foreign field—that is
forever England.*" She looked up at me. Her eyes were
wide. " Where did you hear that ? " she asked. " How
did you know——" She stopped and concentrated on
the compass. " Sorry. I'm off course." Her voice was
scarcely audible in the sound of the wind and the sea.
She put the wheel over to port and the ship heeled again
till her lee scuppers seethed with water and I could feel
the weight of the wind bearing on the canvas. " Why did
you quote Rupert Brooke to me ? " Her voice was hard,

controlled. Then she looked up at me again. " Was that what he said in his message ? "

" Yes," I said.

She turned her head and gazed out into the darkness. " So he knew he was going to die." The words were a whisper thrown back to me by the wind. " Why did he send that message to you ? " she asked, suddenly turning to me, her eyes searching my face.

" He didn't send it to me," I replied. " I don't know who it was sent to." She made no comment and I said, " When did you last see him ? "

" I told you," she answered. " I met him when I was working for the Kompani Linge. Then he went on the Målöy raid. He—he didn't come back."

" And you never saw him after that ? "

She laughed. " All these questions." Her laughter trailed away into silence. " Don't let's talk about it any more."

" You were fond of him, weren't you ? " I persisted.

" Please," she said. " He's dead. Just leave it at that."

" If you wanted it left at that," I answered, " why did you come along this morning, all packed and ready to go to Norway ? Was it just a sentimental desire to see the grave ? "

" I don't want to see the grave," she said with sudden heat. " I don't want ever to see his grave."

" Then why did you come ? " I insisted.

She was about to make some angry retort. But suddenly she changed her mind and looked away from me. " I don't know," she said. She spoke so softly that the wind whipped her words away into the night before I could be sure of what she said. Then she suddenly said, " Will you take the wheel now, please. I'm going below for a moment." And that was the end of our conversation. And when she came up on deck again she stood out in the wind by the port navigation light, a tall, graceful figure, even in a duffle coat, moving rhythmically to the dip and climb of the ship. And I sat on at the wheel, talking to Wilson who had sat himself down in the cockpit and wondering how much she knew and what Farnell had meant to her.

We were nearing the Sunk Lightship now. I altered course for Smith's Knoll Lightship. An hour later we called the starboard watch and I took the log reading and marked up our course on the chart. Since setting sail we'd made a steady eight and a half knots. " Course is north thirty-six east," I told Dick as I handed the wheel over to him.

He nodded vaguely. He was always like that first day out. In the six years he'd been in the Navy he'd never been able to conquer sea-sickness. Wright was feeling bad, too. His face looked green and sweaty and in contrast his hair flamed a brighter red in the glare of the chartroom light. Jorgensen, on the other hand, attired in borrowed sweaters and oilskins, was as unaffected by the movement of the ship as Carter, who'd acclimatised himself by many years in the stoke-holes and engine-rooms of aged freighters.

My watch was called again at four in the morning. The wind had strengthened to about Force 5, but the ship was riding easier. They had taken a tuck in the sails. Nevertheless, the movement was considerable. The sea had increased and *Diviner* was plunging her bowsprit like a matador's espada into the backs of the waves. All that day the wind held from the south-east, a strong, reaching wind that sent us plunging on our course across the North Sea at a steady seven to eight knots. By dusk we were 155 miles on our way to Norway. Watch and watch about, and with every bit of sail we could carry, it was like real ocean racing. I almost forgot about the reason for the trip to Norway in the sheer exhilaration of sailing. The weather forecasts were full of gale warnings and shortly before midnight we had to shorten sail again. But the next day the wind lessened slightly and backed to the north east. We shook out one

of our reefs and, close hauled, were still able to steer our
course.

During those two days I got to know Jill Somers
pretty well. She was twenty-six—tall and active, and very
calm in a crisis. She wasn't beautiful in the accepted
sense of the word, but her boyish ease of movement and
her zest for life gave her a beauty of her own. Her charm
was in her manner and in the way her rather wide mouth
spread into a smile that was slightly crooked. And when
she smiled her grey eyes smiled too. She loved sailing and
in the excitement of the wind's driving force we forgot
about George Farnell. Only once was his name mentioned. She was telling me about how she and her father
had got out of Norway just before the German invasion
and how after some months in England she had got in
touch with the Kompani Linge through the Norwegian
military authorities in London and arranged to work for
them. " I just had to do something," she said. " I
wanted to be in it with everybody else. Daddy wangled
it. He was in the Norwegian Shipping and Trade
Mission in London. I went up to Scotland and began
work right away at their headquarters—I and five other
girls kept a twenty-four hour radio watch. That was how
I met Bernt Olsen."

" Did you know his real name was George Farnell ? "
I asked.

" Not then. But he was dark and short and one day I
asked him if he was really Norwegian. He told me his
real name then."

" Did he also tell you he was an escaped convict ? "
I asked.

" Yes," she said, smiling quietly to herself. " He told
me everything there was to tell me about himself then."

" And it made no difference to you ? " I inquired.

" Of course, not," she answered. " We were at war.
And he was training for one of the first and most desperate
raids into what was by then enemy territory. Three
month later he went into Norway on the Målöy raid.

" He meant a lot to you, didn't he, Jill ? " I asked.

She nodded. She didn't speak for a moment and then she said, " Yes—he meant a lot to me. He was different from the others—more serious, more reserved. As though he had a mission in life. You know how I mean ? He was in uniform and training hard for a desperate job—and yet he wasn't a part of it all. He lived—mentally—outside it."

It was this description of Farnell before the Målöy action that intrigued me. Farnell's interest in life was metals. In this respect he had been as much an artist as a painter or a musician. War and his own life were small matters in the balance against the excitement of discovering metals. Curtis Wright's description of Bernt Olsen at the moment of going into Målöy and Jill's account of him prior to embarkation all added up in my mind to one thing—Farnell had been after new metals in the mountains of Norway.

Farnell wasn't mentioned again. On watch our minds were fully occupied with the sailing of the boat, and keeping awake. Unless you have done any passage-making it is difficult to realise how completely one becomes absorbed in the operation of a ship. There is always something to concentrate on, especially for the skipper. When I wasn't at the wheel there were log readings to take, the dead reckoning to work out, position to be fixed by shooting the stars or the sun whenever opportunity offered, radio watch to be kept at certain times, forecasts to be listened to, sails to be checked. And over everything was the dead weight of sleepiness, especially in the early watches.

And there was little chance to get to know Jorgensen or Wright. Certainly no opportunity to discuss Farnell with them. As long as the wind held it was watch and watch about. The watch on duty went below as soon as it was relieved by the other watch. And during the day there were meals to get and the other chores to be done. And every now and then the watch below had to be called to help change sails. All I had time to notice in those first two days was that Jorgensen was a first-rate sailor and seemed to be literally enjoying the trip and that Curtis Wright settled down quickly.

The third day out the wind veered back to sou'-sou'-east. We were able to take out our last reef, set main tops'l and yankee. The sea lessened to a steep swell. We were nearly four hundred miles on our way by then and the sun was shining. We began to sight some of the trawlers of the Aberdeen fleet. There were gulls about and occasionally a stormy petrel skimmed low over the tumbled water like a flying fish.

That was the morning on which things began to develop. We were able to relax, and think of other things besides sailing. At noon I handed the wheel over to Jorgensen. Dick had taken both watches for'ard to get the main tops'l down and replace a jammed swivel shackle. For the first time since we'd started I was alone with the Norwegian. " Course north twenty-five east," I told him as I climbed stiffly out of the wheel seat.

He nodded and took the wheel, peering forward at the compass. Then he raised his eyes to the group busy on the halyards round the mainmast. Finally he looked up at me. " Just a moment, Mr. Gansert," he said, for I was going for'ard myself to lend a hand. I stopped then and he said, " My health is benefiting greatly from this little trip. But I do not think my business will—unless we can come to some arrangement."

" How do you mean ? " I asked.

He leaned back, holding the wheel easily in his strong fingers. " I admit that I was not being honest with you when I said I was not interested in Farnell. I am—and particularly now that I know he has communicated with you recently. He told you, I suppose that he had made important mineral discoveries in Norway ? "

There was no point in denying it. " His message implied that," I answered.

" Did he tell you what metals he had discovered ? " he asked.

I nodded. " Yes," I said. " And sent samples."

" By post, I suppose ? " His eyes were watching me narrowly.

I smiled. " His method of dispatch was rather more unorthodox," I said. " However, I imagine it's sufficient for you to know that I got the samples safely."

" And you know where the mineral is located ? " he asked.

I saw no reason to disabuse his mind of what was a natural supposition. " The samples wouldn't have been of much use to us without that information," I pointed out.

He hesitated and then said, " I think we could come to some sort of an arrangement. Suppose we make straight for Bergen ? I can then put specific proposals before you and you can get Sir Clinton——"

His voice died away. He was gazing past me. I turned. Dahler was standing at the top of the companionway. I hadn't seen him since we left the Thames, except once when I'd stumbled into him in the half darkness as he made his way to the afterheads. Jill had been looking after him. The sun emerged from behind a cloud and his lined face looked grey in the bright light. He had on a sweater of Dick's that was several sizes too large for him and a pair of old grey trousers turned up twice at the bottom. He was looking at Jorgensen. Once again I was conscious of the latent enmity of these two men. Dahler weaved his way awkwardly across the pitching deck. He must have heard what Jorgensen had been saying for he said, " So it's reached the stage of specific proposals, has it ? "

" What is that to do with you ? " Jorgensen snapped.

" Nothing," the cripple replied with that crooked smile of his. " I am interested, that is all. You are like a dog worrying over a bone. You have buried it, but you are afraid some other dog will come along and dig it up. You were even questioning Miss Somers."

Jorgensen said nothing. He was watching the other

with a strange intentness. The man's nerves were plucking at a little muscle in his jaw.

"I told her to tell you nothing," Dahler added.

"Since when have you become her guardian?"
Jorgensen asked with a sneer.

"I was a friend of her father," the other answered.
"Fortunately you got nothing out of her—or Major
Wright." He smiled. "Yes, you didn't know my cabin
door was not properly shut, did you?" He turned to
me. "Before you discuss specific proposals, Mr. Gansert,
I suggest you find out what he knows about George
Farnell."

Jorgensen's knuckles were white as his grip on the wheel
tightened. "Why are you so interested in Farnell?" he
asked Dahler.

The cripple leaned on the chartroom roof to steady
himself against the pitch of the ship. "Bernt Olsen
smuggled us out of Finse." He thrust his head suddenly
forward. "Also he told me who had instructed the
Germans to raid my house that night. You didn't know
I knew about that, did you?"

"Your house was raided because you talked too much
about what you pretended you were doing."

"Mueller, your Bergen representative, had nothing to
do with it, I suppose?"

"If he did, then he's paying for it with a six-year
sentence for aiding the Germans."

"For doing what you ordered him to do."

"*Det er lögn.*" In his excitement Jorgensen dropped
into Norwegian. His face was flushed with anger.

"It is not a lie," Dahler answered.

"Prove it then."

"Prove it?" Dahler smiled. "That is why I am
here, Knut. I am going to prove it. I am going to prove
that you ought to be doing the sentence that Mueller is
serving now. When I've found Farnell——"

"Farnell is dead," Jorgensen cut in, his voice sharp and
controlled again.

Dahler didn't say anything after that. The curt reminder that Farnell was dead seemed to bring him up with a jolt. He turned and started to move back towards the companionway. But he stopped and looked round. " Before you discuss his proposals, Mr. Gansert," he said quietly. " Remember that he worked for the Germans till the tide turned, just as hard as he worked for the British later." And with that he disappeared down the companionway.

There was a sudden shout from Dick—" Watch your course." The boat's head was right up into the wind and canvas everywhere was slatting madly. Jorgensen paid her off on to course. Then he sighed. " That is what happens, Mr. Gansert," he said quietly, " in a country that has been occupied."

I made no comment and after a moment, he went on : " Before the war Jan Dahler and I did business together. His tankers supplied my metal plant. Now"——He shrugged his shoulders. " He was foolish. He helped some British agents and then went and talked too freely about it. And because Mueller was pro-German and informed against him, he blames me. And his escape from Finse." He looked up at me. " A German officer has admitted that the price of his escape was certain information they wanted. The information concerned new types of marine engines planned by my engineers. The plans were " lost " when Norway was occupied. But Dahler knew about them because I'd promised to fit his tankers before accepting any other orders. And—well, there was a leakage and the plans were extracted from us."

" And Dahler was responsible ? " I asked.

" There's no proof—apart from the German officer who broke down under cross-examination by our Intelligence. But the demand for the plans was made just after Dahler's escape from Finse. That is why the authorities do not want him back in Norway."

" What was he doing up at Finse ? " I asked.

" Forced labour," he answered. " The Germans had

some fantastic scheme for an ice drome on the Jökulen."
He pulled out a cigarette and lit it. " You see how it is,
Mr. Gansert. To cover himself, he must make counter-
allegations. And "—he hesitated—" the trouble is
that a man in my position is awkwardly placed under an
occupation. I had to carry on, publicly showing friend-
ship for the Germans, in order to work for the liberation
of my country. If they did not trust me, then I should
have ceased to be useful. Many people who do not know
what I did secretly are prepared to believe that I was
pro-German. That is why it makes me angry to hear a
man like Dahler make wild accusations. I know how
vulnerable my work has made me." He smiled a trifle
sadly. " I thought it better that you know," he said.
And then he added, " Now, what about running straight
into Bergen and arranging things ? "

I hesitated. Two things were occupying my mind. One
was the information that at some period of the war
Farnell had been up at Finse. The other was that Jorgensen
was no longer dictating terms to B.M. & I., but seeking
them. I glanced for'ard for an excuse to break off the
conversation. Dick was hoisting the tops'l again and it
was jammed. " Hold it," I called out to him. " You
haven't cleared the topping lift. We'll talk about this
later," I said to Jorgensen and hurried for'ard to give
them a hand.

As soon as the tops'l had been set and everything made
fast I took my watch below for food. I needed time to
think over Jorgensen's change of attitude. Dahler was
seated in the saloon when we came down. Jill poked her
head in from the galley. " Four is it ? " she asked.

I nodded. I was looking at Dahler. He was rocking
gently backwards and forwards with the movement of
the ship. "Bit hard on Jorgensen, weren't you?" I
said.

" Hard ? " He gave a mirthless laugh. " Knut
Jorgensen is——" He hesitated and then said, "He's a
business man." He leaned towards me across the rocking

table. " I tell you, Mr. Gansert, the only dangerous
Norwegian is a Norwegian business man. I'm a Norwegian
and a business man. I know. We're an open air, easy-
going, comfortable people—until it comes to business."

" And then ? " I asked.

He fastened on to my sleeve with his sound hand.
" And then—anything is possible," he replied. The way
he said it made me feel cold inside. Jill came in then and
immediately everything seemed normal. But after the
meal, when I had gone to my cabin to sleep, the scene
between Dahler and Jorgensen came back to me. I lay
with my eyes open, listening to the movement of the ship,
sensing the violent antagonism of the two Norwegians,
and wondering what the hell to do about it. To keep
them apart was out of the question on a small ship. To
let them come together . . . They'd have to be watched,
that was all. I swung myself out of my bunk and went up
on deck to find Jorgensen at the wheel and Dahler seated
in the cockpit watching him. Jorgensen looked paler than
usual under his rather leathery skin. His gaze alternated
between the binnacle and the burgee at the masthead—
anywhere but in the direction of Dahler. The tension
between them was noticeable, even up there on deck
with the wind blowing and *Diviner* lifting and surging
with each wave.

" Mr. Dahler," I said. " Now you've recovered, you'll
join my watch, please."

" Good," he said.

" We're the watch below now," I added pointedly.

He smiled. " I like it very well up here," he answered.
" My stomach is happier."

So I, too, stayed up on deck. But I knew it was useless.
If Dahler wanted to sit and watch Jorgensen he could do
it any time the starboard watch was on duty. If only I'd
arranged it so that they were both in my own watch. I
could have kept my eye on them then. As it was I had to
sleep sometime.

That night my watch came off duty at midnight. The

forecasts were of gale warnings on practically all coasts of the British Isles. The wind had already veered to the sou'-west. We had gybed in the course of our watch and for the first time since we left the Thames estuary we were leaning our starboard scuppers under. I had stowed the mizzen to avoid it blanketing the mainsail. "Watch it," I told Dick. "I don't think the wind will back, but if it does suddenly, you'll have to gybe. And keep an eye on the wind force. If it blows much harder that yankee will have to come off."

I left him then and went below. Dahler had already gone to his cabin. I could see the light on under the door. Jill and Wilson were drinking tea laced with rum. She filled a mug for me. "Rum?" she asked and poured it without waiting for my reply. Her face was very pale and her eyes looked bright, almost feverish. She handed me the mug. "Cheers!" I said, watching her over the rim of it.

As soon as Wilson had gone for'ard to the foc's'le she said, "Are you doing a deal with Mr. Jorgensen, Bill?" Her voice was jerky and pitched a shade high.

"How do you mean?" I asked.

"That's what Mr. Dahler told me," she said. "He said you and Jorgensen were joining forces—against George Farnell."

"Against George Farnell?" I didn't get it. "George Farnell's dead," I reminded her.

She nodded. "That's what I told Mr. Dahler. But he only said, 'Don't lose Gansert—that's all.'"

"Did he ask you to have a talk with me?"

"Not exactly. But——" She hesitated. Then she took a step towards me and caught my arm. "Bill. I'm scared. I don't know why. There's something about this boat to-day. Everybody's on edge. Everybody's asking questions."

"Who's been asking you questions?" I asked.

"Oh, Jorgensen this morning. Curtis this afternoon. You're about the only person who hasn't." She suddenly laughed. "Instead, I'm asking you. What about Jorgensen?"

"I'll decide that when I get to Norway," I said. "Right now you'd better turn in and get some sleep."

She nodded and downed the rest of her drink. I waited till she'd switched her cabin light on, then I turned off the saloon light and went aft to my own cabin.

I was dead tired and fell asleep on my bunk with my clothes on. The movement of the ship was like the rocking of a cradle. I was conscious of it whilst I slept and it added to the sense of deep luxury. I dreamed of soft things, of deep purples and velvets, and of the rocking, swaying, lurching of the tree tops. Then the motion changed. It became slower, heavier. It shook with the crash of each onslaught. It leaned more steeply, more terribly. I clawed at the blankets, clutched at the side of the bunk at each roll. And suddenly I was awake, and I knew that I had to go up on deck. Down there in my cabin I could feel it. I'd sensed it in my sleep. The wind was holding her down. She was carrying too much canvas. I slipped into my sea boots. As each wave slid under her I could feel her reluctance to lift to the next.

I opened the cabin door. There was a light on in the saloon. At the foot of the companionway, I paused. I could hear voices raised in altercation. I turned and peered through the crack of the half-open door. Jorgensen and Dahler faced each other across the saloon table.

"*Så det er det De tenker å gjöre, hva?*" Jorgensen's voice was low pitched and violent. The ship heaved and he clutched the centre support. Behind him Jill's cabin door opened. She was fully clothed. Presumably their argument had woken her. "*De får ikke anledning,*" Jorgensen continued, still speaking in Norwegian. "*Så fort vi kommer til Bergen skal jeg få Dem arrestert.*"

"Arrested?" Jill cried, and he spun round. "Why will you have him arrested? What has he done?"

"Sold secrets to the enemy during the war," Jorgensen answered.

"I don't believe it," she replied hotly.

I threw open the saloon door. "On deck, please, Mr. Jorgensen," I called. "We're going to shorten sail." I didn't wait for his answer, but hurried up the companionway. Out on deck the night was a howling wilderness of water. I dived for the weather rail and scrambled aft to the dim shapes gathered in the cockpit. The wind would soon be reaching gale force. I could sense the growing weight of it as gust after gust buffeted me. "Dick!" I shouted, "Time you shortened sail. That yankee's far too much for her."

"I was just going to," he answered. His voice betrayed his anxiety. He knew he'd left it later than he should. Jorgensen came out on deck, followed by Jill. Then Dahler emerged. I cursed the cripple for coming up. But I hadn't time to worry about it. If he got swept overboard it would be his own fault. Curtis was at the wheel. "Keep her running before the wind," I ordered him. "Dick. You and Carter out on the bowsprit. Jorgensen. You work with me."

We scrambled for'ard. The ship was pitching violently. Dick and Carter stepped over the bows on to the bowsprit strands and worked their way out. Jill eased off the sheets and, as the yankee emptied itself of wind and began to flap, Jorgensen and I let the sail down with a run. Dick and Carter out on the bowsprit gathered it in and passed it aft to us. We set the ordinary jib and then, began to get the main tops'l in. With a following wind and the main boom swung right out we were still carrying far too much canvas. The wind was driving us into the sea. You could feel it.

In the light of the spotlight I had switched on in the rigging for'ard we manned the halyard and sheet of the tops'l. But she jammed as we ran her down. The weight of the wind was pressing the sail against the gaff of the mainsail and the canvas had caught. As we worked to free it, I felt the wind shift and saw the clew of the mainsail lift as the wind got behind it. "Curtis," I shouted.

" Port your helm or you'll gybe her. Wind's shifting."
But he'd already seen the danger and swung the wheel
over. " Don't worry about course," I told him. " Just
keep her running before the wind."

" Okay," he called back.

That's the danger with a following wind, especially at
night. The main boom is swung right out. If the
wind changes or you get off course without noticing it
and a sudden gust swings in behind your canvas, then
your boom comes across with a rush, sweeping the ship,
and fetching up with a crash on the other tack that's
enough to rip the mast out of her. That's gybing the
way it shouldn't be done.

We tried setting the tops'l again. But she wouldn't
budge. We needed more weight to clear her. " Curtis,"
I called. " Hand over the wheel to Jill. And come for'ard."
With his extra weight we managed to clear the jam at the
expense of the canvas. With a ripping sound the sail
came down with a run. " Hold it," I yelled. " Jorgensen.
Take the jackyard as it comes down, will you." He went a
little further aft and, standing on the main hatch, reached
up for the yard. " Right," I called. " Lower away."

The sail came down then, a flapping, billowing bunch
of canvas that lashed at us as we gathered it in. And in
that moment I sensed rather than saw the swing of the
boat. I pulled the canvas aside just in time to see the wind
get behind the leach of the mainsail. The great pile of
canvas filled from the other side. The boom began to
swing inboard. " Gybe-ho ! " I screamed. " Jorgensen !
Down ! Get down ! "

I saw him glance to starb'd. " Duck ! " I shouted.
" Everyone." Jorgensen raised his hand as though to
ward off the blow. Then suddenly he dived full length
on to the hatch cover. I felt the ship straighten up as
the weight lifted from the starb'd side. I seized canvas
and jackyard, slung it over my head and rolled on to the
deck. Next instant it was torn away from me as the
great mainsail boom came swinging inboard. I felt the

weight of it fling past me and heard Jill scream. The ship heeled and then plunged into a wave in a burst of spray as the boom roared out to port. There it fetched up with a crash that shook the ship to her keel and brought crockery clattering down in the galley below. There was a splintering of wood and the port backstay was ripped out of the bulwarks and catapulted into the rigging with a clang of metal.

Jorgensen picked himself up. He was white. I pulled the tops'l clear of Dick, Curtis and Carter, wondering whether any of them had been hit by the boom. Only Curtis was hurt. He seemed to have caught his shoulder. I left him to Dick and went aft. Jorgensen was before me though. Dahler was at the wheel. His face was a pallid mask. Jorgensen took hold of him by the collar of his coat and pulled him out from behind the wheel.

I thought for a moment he was going to fling the cripple overboard. I shouted to him. Instead he smashed a vicious right into the man's face. Dahler ceased to struggle. His muscles went slack and Jorgensen dropped his inert body back across the wheel.

"Stand back, Jorgensen!" I ordered. "You've no right to do a thing like that. It wasn't Dahler's fault. He's not a sailor. Curtis shouldn't have handed the wheel over to him."

"Not Dahler's fault!" Jorgensen laughed unsteadily. "That wasn't an accident," he said. "Ask Miss Somers."

I looked at Jill. "What happened?" I asked.

But she seemed too frightened to speak. She just stood, staring down at Dahler's inert body.

CHAPTER 3

THE VOICE OF "HVAL TI"

WHETHER THAT gybe was intentional or an accident I
didn't know. And I hadn't time to think about it then.
Dahler's body was crumpled over the wheel, jamming it.
The mainsail, still overweighted with canvas in the howling wind, was dragging at the mast. With the port
backstay gone and the starboard backstay slack the
massive timber of the mast was bending to each gust. I
could hear it groaning above the thunder of the seas
breaking inboard over the bows. I hauled Dahler's body
off the wheel and thrust it into the cockpit. Then I put
the helm hard to starb'd and brought the ship up into
the wind. "Haul in on the mainsheet, Jorgensen," I
shouted as the boom began to swing loosely inboard.

Somehow we got the boat close-hauled and the starboard
backstay set up. Then I handed the wheel over to Jill
and went for'ard with Jorgensen to get a reef in the mainsail and repair the port backstay. Curtis wasn't badly
hurt, but he'd a nasty cut on his shoulder and I sent him
below as soon as Wilson arrived on deck. "Take Dahler
with you," I told him. And then suddenly remembering
that he'd originally been at the wheel, I said, "Why did
you hand the wheel over to Dahler and not to Jill as I
ordered?"

"Jill wasn't in the cockpit," he said. "I saw you were
in a jam and as I got up from the wheel, Dahler stepped
in right beside me. He'd been at the helm once during the
day, so I thought it would be all right. It left Jill as a
gash hand. I didn't realise——"

"All right," I said. "You get on below and see to that
cut. Put Dahler on his bunk. I'll see him later."

It took us the better part of an hour to get things sorted

58

out and the boat properly trimmed. I took in two reefs
to be on the safe side. The damage didn't appear great,
but only daylight would reveal what had happened aloft.
The strain as the full weight of the mains'l had swung
across had been terrific. Masthead fittings might be
torn out or loosened. When the ship was at last riding
easily, I sent Jill below to fix Curtis's arm and put
Jorgensen on the wheel. Dick and the two hands were
stowing sails for'ard. I entered up the log and then
checked our course on the compass. The binnacle light
threw a faint glow on Jorgensen's face. "Why did you hit
Dahler?" I asked him. He didn't answer and I said,
"The man's a cripple. He should never have been
allowed to take the wheel in this wind. He couldn't hold
it." Still Jorgensen said nothing. "Do you think he did
it on purpose?" I demanded.

"What do you think?" he asked.

I remembered how Jorgensen had been standing on the
hatch cover, reaching up for the jackyard. If I hadn't
sensed the gybe coming and yelled a warning to him,
the boom would have swept him overboard. It would
have smashed his ribs and sent him hurtling over the life
lines. If Dahler had wanted to get rid of Jorgensen . . .
"It was an accident," I said angrily.

"An accident?" He laughed. "Dahler has been
sailing boats all his life. That was no accident, Mr.
Gansert. You heard what was said between us in the
saloon just before we came on deck."

"You were threatening to have him arrested," I said.
"But that doesn't prove that he tried to—to involve you
in an accident."

"To murder me I think you were going to say." He
shifted his grip on the wheel. "Let us call things by their
proper names," he added. "What Dahler did was
attempted murder." The way he said it, it sounded ugly.

"I'll go down and have a word with him," I said, and
left him sitting there at the wheel.

It seemed incredible that Dahler should have meant to

kill him. And yet, sitting there at the wheel and seeing
Jorgensen standing on that hatch, the means of killing
was right there in his hands. He had only to turn the
wheel and the gybe was bound to happen. An accident.
Nobody would have been able to prove that it wasn't an
accident. And there would have been no chance of
picking Jorgensen up with the ship a tangle of sails and
broken rigging. It was understandable if he were a novice.
Only a little while before he took the wheel Curtis had
almost done the same thing by accident. But if he'd been
sailing boats all his life . . .

I pushed open the saloon door. Curtis was pulling on
his jersey. Jill was in the galley sweeping up broken
crockery. " How's the shoulder ? " I asked Curtis.

" All right," he said. " Bit stiff, that's all."

" Dahler in his cabin ? "

" Yes. He's come round. Cut lip and bruised cheek-
bone, that's all. What did Jorgensen want to go and hit
him for ? There's something funny about those two. They
hate each other's guts."

I went into Dahler's cabin. The light was on and he was
sitting propped up in his bunk, dabbing at his lip, which
was still bleeding. I shut the door. He turned at the
sound, holding his handkerchief to his face. " Well ? "
he asked. " How much damage have I done ? "

" Quite enough," I said. " Why did you take the
wheel if you didn't know how to sail ? "

" I was right beside Wright when you told him to give a
hand for'ard," he replied. " I couldn't help. Jill Somers
could. So I took Wright's place at the helm. And I do
know how to sail, Mr. Gansert. Unfortunately I haven't
done any sailing since—since this happened." He waved
his withered arm at me. " The ship heeled to a gust of
wind and the wheel was torn out of my hand."

" Jorgensen thinks you did it purposely," I told him.

" I had gathered that." He dabbed at his lip. " Is
that what you think ? " His dark eyes were watching me.
The cabin lights were reflected in the over-large pupils.

" I'm prepared to take your word for it," I told him.

" I asked you, Mr. Gansert, whether you thought I had done it purposely ? "

I hesitated. " I don't know," I answered. " He had just threatened to have you arrested. And you don't exactly conceal your hatred of him."

" Why should I ? " he answered. " I do hate him."

" But why ? " I asked.

" Why ? " His voice rose suddenly. " Because of what he's done to me. Look at this." He thrust the withered claw of his arm at me again. " Jorgensen," he snarled. " Look at my face. Jorgensen. Before the war I was fit and happy. I had a wife and a business. I was on top of the world." He sighed and sank back against his pillow. " That was before the war. It seems a long time ago now. My interests were shipping. I had a fleet of coasters and four tankers that supplied Det Norske Staalselskab. Then Norway was invaded. The tankers I ordered to British ports. Some of the coasters were sunk and a few got away, but the bulk of the fleet continued to operate. And whilst Jorgensen was entertaining the German commanders in Oslo, I worked for the liberation of my country. My house at Alverstrummen was a refuge for British agents. My offices in Bergen became a clearing house for boys slipping out of the country. Then suddenly my house was raided. A British agent was captured. I was arrested and imprisoned in Bergen. That was not so bad. My wife could come and see me and I passed the time binding books. But then the Germans drafted us for forced labour. I was sent to Finse. The Germans planned to build an aerodrome on top of the Jökulen. Did you ever hear of that monumental piece of German folly ? "

" Jorgensen mentioned it to me——" I began.

" Jorgensen ! " he exclaimed. " What does Jorgensen know about it ? He was much too clever."

He leaned out of his bunk and got a cigarette from his jacket pocket. I lit it for him. He took several quick puffs.

His fingers shook. The man was wrought up. He was talking to steady himself. And I listened because this was the first time I'd got him talking and up there at Finse he had met George Farnell.

" So you didn't know about the Jökulen project ? Nobody in England seems to have heard about it. So many strange things happen in a war and only a few people outside the countries where they happen ever hear about them. In Norway everybody knows about the Germans and the Jökulen. It is a big joke." He paused and then added, " But it was not a joke for those who had to work on it." He leaned over towards me and grabbed at my arm. " Do you know the height of the Jökulen ? "

I shook my head.

" It is the highest point on the Hardangervidda. It is 1,876 metres high—a glacier, perpetually covered by snow. They were crazy. They thought they could make an airfield up there. The snow was blown into waves by the wind. They drove tractors with heavy iron rollers up to the top. And when they found circular rollers packed the snow up in front of them, they made octagonal rollers. There were crevasses. They tried filling them with sawdust. Oh, it is a hell of a fine joke. But we had to work up there and in the winter on the Jökulen there is sometimes as much as 50 degrees of frost." He had been talking fast. Now he suddenly leaned back against the pillow and shut his eyes. " Do you know how old I am, Mr. Gansert ? "

It was impossible to put an age to him. " No," I said.

" Just over sixty," he said. " I was fifty-four then. And I'd never have come down from Finse but for Bernt Olsen. He got six of us away. Packed us into areo engine crates—the Germans were testing engines under ice conditions up by Finse lake. From Bergen the resistance people got us away to the island of Fedje by boat. And a few days later we were taken off by a British M.T.B."

It was an incredible story. I suppose he noticed my surprise, for he said, " This came later." He indicated

the withered arm. " After I got to England. Delayed
reaction. Paralysis. My wife died that year I was at
Finse." He struggled on to his elbow. " All that, Mr.
Gansert, because Jorgensen wanted my shipping fleet. It
was a family business started by my father. After my
arrest the Germans confiscated it. Jorgensen formed a
company and bought it from them. And you ask why
do I hate the man." He lay back as though exhausted,
drawing on the cigarette. " Remember what I told you ?
The only dangerous Norwegian is a Norwegian business
man."

" What about Farnell ? " I asked. " What was he doing
up at Finse ? "

His eyelids flickered open and he stared at me.
" Farnell ? " He suddenly laughed. " You English—
you are like bulldogs. You never let go. You can ignore
anything and concentrate on the one thing that matters
to you. You don't care about what I have been telling
you. It doesn't mean anything to you, eh ? " His voice
had risen to sudden passion. " I tell you a story of
injustice, of the destruction of one man by another. And
all you think about is——" His voice dropped again.
" All right," he said. " I'll tell you. Farnell worked on
the Bergen railway. He worked at the railway yards at
Finse under the name of Bernt Olsen. He was working
for the resistance. He risked his life to get us out. Now
I would like to help him—if I can."

" How can you help him when he's dead ? " I asked.

" If he's dead—then that's that. But if he's not . . .
My life's finished. I have no future—nothing. When you
have reached that stage, Mr. Gansert, you can afford to
take a little risk here and there."

" Such as—trying to kill somebody," I suggested.

He smiled. " You are still wondering whether that
gybe was an accident or not—eh ? Jorgensen thinks I did
it on purpose, does he ? " He chuckled. " All his life now,
until I'm dead, he'll be wondering—wondering what the
noise at the window is, wondering whether he'll die a

sudden death." He began plucking nervously at the blankets. " Farnell knew a lot about Jorgensen. If only I could find Farnell. Is Jorgensen sure Farnell is dead ? " He closed his eyes.

The door opened then and Jill came in with a cup of beef tea. " How is he ? " she asked me.

Dahler sat up in his bunk. " I'm quite well, thank you," he said sharply.

She handed him the cup. " Drink that," she said. " And then try to get some sleep."

I followed her out and shut the door. " We must always see that somebody else is with him when Jorgensen is about," I said.

She nodded.

" Was it an accident or not ? " I asked her.

" I don't know." She turned quickly towards the galley.

I caught her arm. " You saw what happened. Or Jorgensen thought you did. What was it—accident or—attempted murder ? "

She winced at the ugliness of the word. " I don't know," she said again.

I let her go then. " He seems to have reason enough for his hatred," I said. " Anyway, from now on I'm taking no chances."

She went into the galley. I turned and climbed the companionway to the deck. The weight of the wind hit me as soon as I hauled myself through the hatch. I staggered to the weather rail and looked out into the darkness. Broken wavetops hissed hungrily each time the ship lifted. The sea was a roaring waste of heaving water. Each wave was a tussle between ship and sea and sometimes the sea won, breaking inboard with a crash and seething out through the lee scuppers. Jorgensen was still at the wheel. Dick was huddled beside Curtis in the shelter of the cockpit. " What are we making by the log ? " I asked him.

" About seven," he answered.

" Have you seen Dahler ? " Jorgensen asked.

" Yes," I said.

" What does he say ? "

" He says it was an accident," I replied. " The wheel was too heavy for him."

" He's lying."

" Possibly," I said. " But you wouldn't convince a jury of it. The fact remains that the man's a cripple and only has one hand." I turned to Dick. " Time for my watch to take over," I said.

Jorgensen handed over the wheel to me without a word. I watched him cross the green glow of the starb'd navigation light and disappear down the main hatch. " Keep your eye on him, Dick," I said. " If we don't watch out we'll have one of them overboard."

" They don't love each other, do they ? " he said.

" Not so as you'd notice," I answered. " Would you mind bunking in the saloon for a couple of nights ? "

" Watchdog, eh ? Okay. But I warn you, Bill, when I close my eyes a regiment of killers could trample over me and I wouldn't bat an eyelid."

He went below then and I was alone in the thundering, pitching night. Seated there at the wheel I could feel *Diviner* tearing forward through the water at the surge of each wave. Then she'd slip back, stern foremost, into the trough and wallow till the next wave lifted her and the wind drove her on into the darkness. It was a weird scene. The red and green navigation lights illuminated the canvas of the sails with an unearthly glow, a sort of demon phosphorescence. The music of *The Damnation of Faust* drifted through my mind. The weird descent into Hell . . . If Berlioz had included a scene with Charon crossing the Styx, then this was the lighting he'd have used. What a setting for something horrible ! I thought of those two men—Jorgensen and Dahler—hating each other and fearing each other at the same time. I laughed out loud. And I'd been so damned pleased with myself when I'd bluffed Jorgensen into sailing down the Thames

with us. And right now I'd have given a lot to be able to
set him ashore at Greenwich.

The macabre turn my thoughts had taken was
interrupted by the arrival of Jill. " How's Dahler ? " I
asked her as she seated herself in the cockpit.

" Sleeping," she said. " He's quite exhausted."

" And Jorgensen ? " I asked.

" Gone to his cabin. And Dick has settled himself in
the saloon." She sighed and settled her back against the
chartroom. I could just see the pale oval of her face in
the light of the binnacle. The rest of her was a dark
bundle of sweaters and oilskins. Every now and then a
burst of spray swept across us, stinging my eyes with salt.

" Tired ? " I asked.

" A bit," she answered drowsily.

" Why not go below ? " I suggested. " There'll be no
more sail changing to do this watch."

" I'd rather stay up here," she answered, " in the fresh
air."

Wilson came up shortly after that with mugs of scalding
coffee. After we'd drunk it the remaining three hours of
the watch dragged. Once we sighted the navigation lights
of a drifter. The rest of the time the boat was plunging
through a void of utter darkness. Sleep weighed on our
eyes. It was a constant fight to keep awake. At four in
the morning we called the starboard watch. A faint grey
light percolating the low cloud and the tumbled outline of
the waves marching up behind us was just visible.

That was to be our last full day at sea. The wind
lessened and the sea dropped. Daylight revealed no real
damage aloft and we piled on sail again. By midday a
watery sun came out and I was able to obtain a fix. This
confirmed out postition—about 30 miles due west of the
Norwegian port of Stavanger. I altered course to north
eleven east.

All that day Dahler kept to his cabin. Jill reported
that he was in a state of nervous exhaustion and suffering
from sea-sickness and lack of food. I went to see him

just after the midday meal. The cabin smelt stale and airless. Dahler was lying with his eyes closed. His face looked grey under the dirty stubble except for a livid bruise on his cheek and the red line of his cut lip. I thought he was asleep, but as I turned to go he opened his eyes. "When will we be in—Norway?" he asked.

"Dawn to-morrow," I replied.

"Dawn to-morrow," he repeated slowly. The way he said it made me realise what it meant to him. He hadn't seen his country for a long time. And when he had last been there it had been as a prisoner, a slave labourer working for the Germans over 4,000 feet up in the mountains. And he had left it as a fugitive. I thought of the awful trip he must have had down the railway to Bergen hidden in a crate that was supposed to contain German aero engines. Then the trip out to the island and then the final journey by M.T.B. And now he was going back for the first time, and he was threatened with arrest. I suddenly felt very sorry for him.

"There's a chance we may sight a steamer off Bergen, bound for Britain," I said. "If so, shall we signal it to take you on board?"

He sat up suddenly. "No," he said violently. "No. I'm not afraid. I'm a Norwegian. Neither Jorgensen— nor any one else—will stop me from going back to my country." His eyes had a wild look. "Where are you making for?" he asked.

"Fjaerland," I said.

He nodded and sank back. "Good! I must find Farnell. If I can find Farnell—he knows the truth, you see. There were records. The resistance people kept records of what went on between the Germans and suspected Norwegian civilians."

I couldn't remind him that Farnell was dead. In his overwrought state it would have done no good. He had closed his eyes again and I went out, closing the door gently behind me.

I had told him that Fjaerland was our destination.

But something happened that evening which altered things. We kept radio watch on ultra-short wave at seven in the morning and seven in the evening. We had from the hour to ten minutes after in which to transmit or receive and either Dick or myself, whoever was on watch at the time, tuned in to our wavelength. Dick was on watch that evening and shortly after seven he burst into the saloon where Jill and I were having a quiet drink, " Message for you, skipper," he said excitedly.

" What is it ? " I asked, taking the sheet of paper.

" They've traced the consignment of whale meat Farnell smuggled that message out in," he answered. " It came from a company called Bovaagen Hval."

" Bovaagen Hval ? " Jill exclaimed.

I glanced across at her, mentally cursing Dick for blurting out the contents of the message. " What does Bovaagen Hval mean to you ? " I asked.

" It's a whaling station out on the islands of Nordhord-land, north of Bergen," she answered quickly.

" Do you know it ? " I asked her.

" No. But——" She hesitated. She seemed puzzled, and excited at the same time.

" Well ? " I asked.

" That was the whaling station Mr. Dahler was interested in."

" Dahler ? " I glanced down at the message. It began : *Whale meat consignment traced Bovaagen Hvalstasjon, Bergen, Norway.* Was that why Dahler had come on the trip ? Was that why he'd queried Farnell's death ? I suddenly remembered something. I looked across at Jill. " Jorgensen bought up Dahler's shipping interests," I said. " Did he also acquire the interest in Bovaagen Hval ? "

" I don't know," she answered.

I turned to Dick, a sudden suspicion in my mind. " Where was Jorgensen when you took this message ? " I asked him.

His face fell. " Good God ! " he said. " I never

thought about it. He was sitting in the chartroom, right beside me."

"And heard every word that came over," I said.

"Well, I couldn't throw him out, could I?" he demanded.

"I suppose not," I answered resignedly.

He pushed the paper towards me again. "Have a look at the dates," he said. "That's what's really interesting."

I looked down at the sheet of paper. *Date of dispatch March 9th.* March 9th! And Farnell's body had been discovered on March 10th. *Proceed Bovaagen and find out how Farnell was able dispatch message from Hvalstasjon on 9th and be killed on Jostedal following day. Report by radio daily on arrival Bovaagen. Mann.* "Get the map of Norway," I told Dick.

When he had gone I read the message through again. He could, of course, have got someone else to smuggle the parcel into the consignment of meat. That seemed the only explanation. "Bill." Jill's voice interrupted my train of thought, "What's the rest of the message say?"

I hesitated. Then I passed the message across to her. Jorgensen knew it. No harm in her knowing it too. Dick came back with the map and we spread it out on the table. Jill pointed Bovaagen out to us. It was on Nordhordland, one of the larger islands about thirty-five miles up the coast from Bergen. Bovaagen Hval. There it was on the end of a long finger of land pointing northwards. And twenty miles away, at the southern end of the island, I saw the name Alverstrummen. "Is that where Dahler had a house?" I asked Jill.

"Yes. Alverstrummen. That's the place." She looked down at the message and then at the map again. "Was the message you received from George smuggled out in a consignment of whale meat?" she asked.

"Yes," I said. My eye was following the line of the Sognefjord up to Fjaerland.

"Whale meat for export has to be got away pretty

quickly," Jill said. " If the consignment was dispatched to England on the 9th, it means that it was either packed that day or on the 8th. It couldn't possibly have been packed earlier."

" Exactly," I said. " That doesn't leave Farnell much time to get up to the Jostedal."

" He could do it by boat," Dick said.

" Yes," I agreed. " But he'd have to be in an awful hurry to get there." I traced the route with my finger. It would be north for twenty miles or so from Bovaagen and then east up the long cleft of Norway's largest fjord. The better part of a hundred miles to Balestrand and then another twenty up the tributary fjord to Fjaerland. " It's a day's journey by boat," I said. " And after that he'd got to climb the 5,000 feet to the top of the Jostedal and then fall on to the Boya Glacier. He'd be running it a bit fine." I turned to Jill. " There's a steamer service, is there ? "

" Yes," she said. " But from Bergen. He'd have to pick the steamer up at Leirvik and then stay a night at Balestrand. He couldn't possibly reach Fjaerland till the evening of the 10th—not by the ordinary steamer service."

" That's no good," I said. " He must have had a boat. If so we'll find out whose when we get to Fjaerland. The only other alternative is that he was never at Bovaagen. In which case we ought to be able to get hold of the man who sent the message for him." I turned to Dick. " What was the reaction from our friend Jorgensen when this message came through ? " I asked.

" Can't say I noticed," he replied. " Afraid I wasn't thinking about Jorgensen."

" Then I'll go up and find out," I said.

Carter was at the wheel as I came out on deck. The wind was dying away and we were gliding over a long, oily swell. The sun had set and against the darkness of the eastern horizon was the darker line of Norway. " Dinna think we'll get much wind the nicht," Carter said to me.

I glanced at the speed of the water slipping past the lee rail. "We're still doing about four knots."

"Aye," he replied. "She's a fine boat in a light wind. Slips along easy as a swan."

"Where's Mr. Jorgensen?" I asked.

He nodded towards the chartroom. "Doon there, sir," he said.

I stepped down into the cockpit and entered the chartroom. Curtis was lounging on the chartroom bunk. Jorgensen was seated at the table. He looked up as I entered. "Just been checking the distance," he said, nodding towards the chart. "If the wind holds we should be in by dawn."

"In where?" I asked.

He smiled. "I am presuming, Mr. Gansert, that you are obeying orders and proceeding to Bovaagen."

"You heard the message then?" I asked.

"I could not help it," he answered. "I was sitting right beside Mr. Everard. I was very intrigued to know just how George Farnell had contacted you. As you said, his method was a shade unorthodox. Does that suggest anything to you?"

I said, "Yes. It suggests he was scared to use the more normal postal methods."

"I find it very hard to believe that a man who had made a vital mineral discovery should communicate his information by this means." His voice betrayed his curiosity. "Did he give any reason? How was he to know where his message would finish up?"

"I know only this, Mr. Jorgensen," I said. "He was scared to use any normal method. And," I added, speaking deliberately, "he had a premonition he was going to die."

His hand was on the heavy brass chart ruler. He began to roll it slowly back and forth across the table. His face was, as always, expressionless. But his eyes avoided mine and I sensed his agitation. In some way the information he had acquired was worrying him. "What do you

intend to do now, Mr. Gansert ? " he asked suddenly.
" You will presumably go to Bovaagen Hval. But what
then ? "

" I shall try and find out how Farnell, who sent off
this message from Bovaagen on the 9th of March,
managed to be lying dead on the Jostedal on the 10th,"
I replied.

" But why ? " he asked. " Why is that important to
you ? This is something I have been meaning to ask you,
Mr. Gansert, since we left the Thames : Why is your
company so interested in Farnell when, according to you,
they have the vital information—the nature of the metals
and their location. One would have surely supposed that
you would go straight to the location and check the
information for yourself. You are an expert in base
metals. That would be your natural course. Yet your
interest is in Farnell. Your company, too. It is almost as
though——" He pasued with a lift of his eyebrows.

" Well ? " I said.

" I was going to say—it is almost as though you had
less information than you pretend to have." All the time
he had been speaking almost causally. But I was conscious of his eyes watching me closely. " I have an
idea," he went on, " that an arrangement between
our two organisations might yet be of benefit to both
sides."

" I personally am not interested," I replied. " That is
between you and the B.M. & I. The object of my visit
to Norway is to find out what happened to Farnell."

" And what he discovered—and where." His voice was
suddenly harsh. " This is Norway, Mr. Gansert. And the
metals are in Norway. My object is to see that the
development of my country's mineral resources is not
dominated by foreign capital. We're a small country and
we cannot develop them without some help. I offered
Sir Clinton a 40 per cent participation. That offer is still
open."

" But do you know where the minerals are ? " I said.

" Or what they are ? You're in no position to make an offer till you have that information."

" And you have it ? " He laughed. " No, Mr. Gansert. If you had you wouldn't be chasing the ghost of dead Farnell. You'd be up in the mountains with metallurgical instruments, and the whole weight of the British Foreign Office would be supporting applications for concessions. But I do not wish to be regarded as discourteous to the representative of a big British industrial organisation. You may count on me to give you every assistance in your search, Mr. Gansert. May I use your transmitter at eight this evening ? "

" Why ? " I asked.

" As Dahler may have told you I took over his interests after the war. One of them was Bovaagen Hval. I own a controlling interest in the company. At eight o'clock the catchers report back to the whaling station. I can contact the manager then and arrange for water and fuel for your ship and for him to make a preliminary investigation into who smuggled that message into the consignment of whale meat. That is what you want to know, isn't it ? "

There was no point in refusing. I'd have Jill in the chartroom at the same time so that I'd know what he was saying. " All right," I said. And then I remembered the cripple lying in his bunk down below. " What about Dahler ? " I asked.

" What about him ? " he inquired.

" You threatened to have him arrested," I reminded him.

He was fiddling with the ruler again. " I don't think there is much point," he said slowly. " The man is not quite right there, you know." He tapped his forehead. " Provided he causes no trouble, I shall do nothing. I suggest you try and persuade him to stay on board at Bovaagen Hval. His word was law there before the war. There is no knowing how it will affect him, seeing the place again now when he is—nothing."

That queer way of his of emphasising words out of all proportion to their value. *Now when he is—nothing.* Nothing to Jorgensen was a man who had no power over other men. Power was what he loved more than anything. Power over men, possibly women, too. The sleek smoothness of the man ! Even in borrowed clothes he achieved a sort of bourgeois respectability. And yet behind it all was this violent delight in power. It was there in his eyes, in the quick down-drawn frown of his thick eyebrows. But never exposed, never revealed. The iron claw in the velvet glove. I'd seen it all my life. This man belonged to the ranks of the controllers of the machine of grab.

I suddenly saw that he was watching me as though he knew what was in my mind. He smiled. " You could make a lot of money out of this, Gansert," he said, " if you played your cards right."

He got up and paused at the chartroom door with his hand on my shoulder. " You've been in this game long enough to know what the scramble for new minerals means. And you're your own master. Think it over."

" What's he mean by that ? " Curtis asked as the Norwegian went for'ard.

I looked at him then and realised that as a regular army officer he was mentally incapable of thinking of himself in terms of a single unit. He was part of a team and as such never stepped outside the safe confines of the organisation. " It means I've indirectly been offered a very large amount of money—if I deliver the goods."

He looked surprised. " Bribery—eh ? "

" Well, shall we say, inducement," I amended. I suddenly had an impish desire to shake his indifference. " Any idea of the money involved in this metal business if it's big enough, as this may be."

" None whatever, old boy," he answered without interest.

I said, " It could mean a few millions for somebody who handled it right."

He laughed. "It's no good talking to me about millions. My pay is about fifteen hundred a year. Oh, I realise that you really meant millions. But I just wouldn't know what to do with that sort of money if I had it. Nor would you," he added. "Here you are with a fine boat, the freedom of the seas and a reasonable amount of money. A few millions would just complicate your life."

"It depends on what you want," I said. "At the moment this is the life I want—just sailing. But once you've known the thrill of opening up a mine—well, it gets you. It isn't the money. It's the sheer excitement of handling the thing. I did it once, out in Canada, where I struck lucky in nickel. It's the sense of power, the fun of seeing problems coming at you from every direction and mastering them."

He nodded. "Yes, I can understand that," he said slowly. Then he frowned. "What puzzles me," he went on, "is how Farnell was able to produce samples of ore. I can understand that a good metal diviner can locate a seam. But to produce samples—I should have thought that would have required machinery."

It was a good point. "That puzzled me at first," I said. "I can only suggest that the ore itself has been uncovered by ice erosion. His samples may even have been found in the rubble at the foot of a glacier."

"I see," he said. "But it still seems to me that you and Jorgensen are placing too much reliance on discoveries that are quite unproved."

"No," I said. "No, I don't think so. Farnell was in a class by himself. Before dispatching samples he would have taken into account the geological nature of the ground as well as his own divining results. He won't have slipped up on anything. Jorgensen knows that. If we combined, he and I could clean up a lot of money."

He looked at me with a lift of his eyebrows. "You don't mean to say you're going to accept his offer?"

"No," I said, laughing. "But the choice is not as

clear cut as it would be in your case. I don't owe
allegiance to anyone. I'm my own master."

" What will you do, then ? "

" Oh, I'll play the hand in my own way—if my cards
are good enough." I got up and went out on deck. I'd
let my thoughts run away with me. I stood by the rail
and looked out across the darkening sea towards
Norway. Go west, young man. Well, I'd been west
and found nickel. Now I was looking east and wondering whether this cold, snow-clad country might not be
the land of opportunity. Farnell had had that urge.
He'd let nothing stand in his way—he'd stolen and deserted and fought because of the call of the minerals there
under the mountains. The same urge was in me—the
same thrill of excitement. And I had something more than
Farnell—I had the ability to organise and develop the
mineral when I found it.

I was still standing by the rail in this mood of elation
when Jorgensen came up from below. " It's eight
o'clock," he said. " I'll get Bovaagen Hval now. Doubt-
less you'll want to have Miss Somers up to check on
what I say." He smiled and went down into the chartroom.

He was right. I certainly did want to know what he
said. I called Jill up from below and we settled ourselves
in the chartroom. Jorgensen had already tuned in and a
voice was speaking what I presumed was Norwegian.
But suddenly it concluded with—" Twa bloody baskets,
an' that's all, Johnnie."

" Scotch trawlers," Jorgensen said. And then, " Here
we are." A deep voice had suddenly broken in across the
fainter voices of the trawlermen : " *Ullo-ullo-ullo-ullo-
ullo. Ul-lo Bovaagen Hval. Ul-lo Bovaagen Hval. Dette er
Hval To. Ullo-ullo-ullo—Bovaagen Hval.*" There followed
a double whistle and then another voice came in : " *Ullo-
ullo-ullo Hval To. Bovaagen Hval her.*" The double whistle
again and the first voice came back with a stream of
Norwegian.

"Whale Two—that's one of the catchers—reporting a seventy-foot whale," Jill whispered.

When he had finished another voice came in—Whale Five. "He's seen nothing," Jill murmured in my ear. "He says the weather's still bad up there—that's about two hundred miles farther north, I think."

As soon as Whale Five had signed off, Jorgensen switched on to the transmitting set and holding the mike close to his mouth said, "*Ullo-ullo-ullo-ullo Bovaagen Hval. Det er direktör Jorgensen. Er stasjonmester Kielland der?*" The double whistle and then a voice on the loudspeaker: "*Ullo-ullo-ullo direktör Jorgensen. Det er Kielland. Hvor er De nå?*"

"*Jeg er ombord på den britiske yachten* Diviner," Jorgensen answered. "*Vi ankrer opp utenfor Bovaagen Hval imorgen tidlig. Vaer så snild å sörge for vann og dieselolje. Og nå har jeg——*"

"What's he saying?" I asked Jill.

"He's arranging for water and oil for the boat on our arrival," she whispered back. "Now he's explaining about the message in the consignment of whale meat. He's asking the station manager, Kielland, to make inquiries and report on how the message got into the whale meat when we arrive."

"*Javel, herr direktör,*" replied the manager's voice. "*Jeg skal ta meg ar saken.*"

"*Utmerket,*" answered Jorgensen. He gave the signing-off whistle and then turned to us. "To-morrow we will know the answer to this little mystery—I hope," he said.

And then our attention was called back to the radio with a voice calling, "*Ullo-ullo-ullo. Hval Ti anroper direcktör Jorgensen.*"

Jorgensen picked up the microphone again, "*Ja, Hval Ti. Det er Jorgensen her.*"

"*Dette er kaptein Lovaas,*" replied the voice.

Jill gripped my arm. "It's the captain of the catcher, Whale Ten. I think he knows something."

The conversation went on in Norwegian for a moment

and then Jorgensen turned to me. " Lovaas sounds as
though he has some information. He wants a description
of Farnell." He thrust the microphone towards me. " He
understands English."

I leaned down to the microphone and said, " Farnell
was short and dark. He had a long, serious face and wore
thick-lensed glasses. The tip of the little finger of the
left hand was missing."

Jorgensen nodded and took the microphone. " Now
what's your information, Lovaas ? " he asked.

" I speak English now." There was a fat chuckle over
the loudspeaker. " She is not very good, my English. So
please excuse. When I leave Bovaagen Hval two days
before one of my man is sick. I take with me another man
—a stranger. His name, he said, is Johan Hestad. He is
very good to steer. But he has magnetise the compass and
when I think I am near the whales I find I am off the
Shetlands. He offered me many monies to go to the
Shetlands. He says to me that he was with a man called
Farnell seeking minerals on the Jostedal and that an
English company will pay him money for his discoveries.
I remember how this man Farnell is discovered dead on
the Boya glacier and I lock him in a cabin. When I
search his clothes I have found papers showing his real
name to be Hans Schreuder. Also some little pieces of
rock."

At the mention of the man's real name, Jorgensen's grip
on the microphone tightened. " Lovaas," he interrupted.
" Did you say—Schreuder ? "

" *Ja, herr direktör.*"

" Put about at once and return to Bovaagen Hval at
full speed," Jorgensen ordered.

Again there was the fat chuckle over the loudspeaker.
" I have done this six hours before," Lovaas replied. " I
thought you will be interested. See you to-morrow, *herr
direktör.*" The double whistle as he signed off was almost
derisive. Silence settled on the chartroom. The fat,
jovial voice with the sing-song intonation of Eastern

Norway had left me with the impression of a big man—a big man who enjoyed life and was also a rogue. I was to get to know that voice too well in the days that followed. But I was never to revise my first impression.

"Who was Schreuder?" I asked Jorgensen.

He looked up at me. "I do not know," he said.

But he did know. Of that I was certain.

CHAPTER 4

THE WHALING STATION

THAT NIGHT I hardly slept at all. The voice of Captain Lovaas and the information he had broadcast dominated my mind. Why had he wanted a description of Farnell? Why had he spoken in English and not Norwegian? Above all who was Hans Schreuder? These questions kept hammering at my tired brain. Jorgensen had recognised the name Hans Schreuder. I was certain of it. And if he recognised the name—recognised the significance of it in the mystery of Farnell's death—then he had known that Farnell was not alone on the Jostedal. Had Farnell been murdered? Had this man Schreuder killed Farnell for the information he had? How else explain those " little pieces of rock " Lovaas had discovered among the man's things. I had no doubts about what those little pieces of rock would prove to be. They would be samples of thorite. As soon as Jorgensen obtained those from his whaling captain, then he would know as much as I knew.

My watch took over at four in the morning. The ship was heeling to a warm sou'-westerly breeze. The moonlight showed a long, flat swell marching northwards and the surface of the sea ruffled and corrugated by the new direction of the wind. Dahler came up with us. He sat on the chartroom roof gazing out towards Norway. He sat there without moving, a little, hunched-up figure, watching the moonlight fade and the dawn come up out of the east, waiting for the first sight of his homeland. Jill was silent. She, too, had her face turned to the east and I wondered again what Farnell had meant to her.

I began to feel a sense of excitement. It was a mood that increased as the pale, cold light strengthened. Jill

put her hand on my sleeve. " There," she said. " Do you
see it, Bill ? It's nearer than I expected."

A low, dark line emerged on the edge of visibility. It
grew rapidly sharper and blacker. From a vague blur
it took shape and became small hills and rock-bound
inlets. It was the islands of Norway about five miles
away on our starboard beam. And then behind, in great
serried lines emerged the shape of Norway's mountains.
The light strengthened and then we saw that the huddled
masses of the mountains were topped with snow.

The light grew from ghostly grey to cold blue and then
changed to an orange glow. The hot rim of the sun rose
and for a moment the mountains were a sharp black line
like a cross-section marked on a map. Then the sun was
up, the snow was pink, rimmed with crimson, and I could
see the white-painted, wooden houses on the islands.

I glanced at Dahler. He hadn't moved. He sat perched
there like a little troll, his gaze fixed on the coastline.
In the early sunlight it seemed to me his face had softened.
The lines were not so deep and the set of his mouth was
kinder.

Curtis came on deck and stood for a while by the rail,
gazing out towards the land. A ship was steaming along
the coast—a little, painted thing, trailing a wisp of smoke.
A fjord had opened up—a long rift between the islands.
A small town gleamed fresh and clean on a headland. It
was Solsvik. Beyond lay the Hjeltefjord and the way to
Bergen. Curtis came aft. " First time I saw Norway,"
he said, " was from the deck of a destroyer."

" Where was that ? " I asked.

" Farther north," he answered. " Andalsnes." He was
gazing out again to the islands. He sighed and shook his
head. " It was a bad business. The Norwegians had
nothing. We weren't properly equipped. Jerry had it all
his own way in the air. They hadn't a hope. But they
kept on fighting. We were driven out. But they wouldn't
give up. We gave 'em help up in the north, in Finnmark,
and they started to fight back. We got as far as Tromso,

pushing Jerry back all the way, then the break-through in France came and we had to go. All that effort wasted." He was still staring out towards Norway. " Still," he said, " there were sixty thousand less Germans."

" You came back later—after the war, I mean—didn't you ? " Jill asked.

He turned and looked at her steadily for a second. " Yes," he said. " I was in Norway from the beginning of 1945 until the middle of the following year. In Bergen," he added.

They stared at one another for a moment. And then Jill looked away. She picked up the glasses and began sweeping the coast. Curtis turned to me. " When will this Captain Lovaas get in ? "

" I don't know," I answered. " Jorgensen said last night that he'd be able to get in touch again by radio at nine this morning."

" We'll be at the whaling station by then, won't we ? " Curtis said.

" Just about," I replied.

" What is this about Kaptein Lovaas ? " I turned. It was Dahler. He had got down from his perch on the chartroom roof and was standing over me where I sat in the cockpit. His hand was plucking agitatedly at the cloth of his jacket.

" He's the captain of one of the Bovaagen catchers," I said. " He has information for us that may have a bearing on Farnell's death. Why—do you know him ? " I asked.

" Yes, I know him." I watched his hand slowly clench into a fist. " Kaptein Lovaas ! " He hissed the name out between clenched teeth. Then suddenly he caught at my shoulder. " Be careful of him, Mr. Gansert—he is dangerous, you know. He is a violent man, and he is not straight." He turned to Jill. " He worked for your father once, Miss Somers. But not for long. I remember your father saying at the time ' If there was not a *skytter* in all Norway, I would not employ Paal Lovaas.' "

" Why ? " Jill asked.

" For many reasons. But chiefly because he killed a man. Nothing was proved. His crew were all so frightened of him, they said the fellow was washed overboard. But your father was certain Lovaas had killed him. He had his sources of information. Lovaas had violent rages. Once, on a factory ship in the Antarctic, he was said to have chased a man with a flensing knife for bungling the winching up of one of his whales." He gripped my shoulder. " What does Lovaas know about Farnell's death ? "

There was no point in not telling him. " He says he's got a man on board who was with Farnell at the time of his death. This fellow, Hans Schreuder, was trying to get to——"

" Hans Schreuder ? "

I looked up in surprise. "Yes," I said. "Does that name mean anything to you ? "

" Was he a metallurgist ? " he asked.

" Quite possibily," I replied, " if he was with Farnell." Actually I was thinking of the samples of ore Lovaas said he had found among the man's possessions. " Why ? " I asked. " Who was he ? "

I felt him stiffen. His hand relaxed on my shoulder. I looked up. Jorgensen was emerging from the main hatch. His face was tired and grey in the early sunlight and little pouches showed under his eyes. I wondered how long he'd lain awake during the night. " Well ? " I inquired, looking up at Dahler.

" Ask Jorgensen," he replied with a violence that I did not understand. " Ask him who Hans Schreuder is."

Jorgensen stopped at the name. Then he came slowly aft. His eyes were watching Dahler. With a sudden assumption of carelessness, he said, " Good morning, gentlemen. Good morning, Miss Somers. I see we're off Solsvik. We'll be at Bovaagen in time for breakfast." His eyes swept over our watchful faces and then gazed out towards the islands.

" Who is this Hans Schreuder, Mr. Jorgensen ? " I asked.

He swung round on me. " How should I know ? " His voice was angry. Then he turned to Dahler. " What do you know about Schreuder ? "

The cripple smiled. " I would prefer you to tell them about him," he said. " He was your man."

" I have never heard of him. What are you talking about ? " Jorgensen's voice had risen. It was trembling with anger.

" I think you have heard of him, Knut."

Jorgensen took a cigarette out of his case and lit it. " Knocking you out yesterday seems to have upset your mind. The name Hans Schreuder means nothing to me." He flicked the match overboard. The flame made a little hiss as it hit the water. " What speed are we making ? " he asked me.

" About five knots," I answered. I was watching his face. " Jorgensen," I said. " I'd still like to know who Hans Schreuder is ? "

" I tell you I don't know." He emphasised the point by striking the roof of the chartroom with his clenched fist. I waited and in the silence he said, " Don't you believe me ? "

" No," I said quietly. I turned to Dahler. " Who is Hans Schreuder ? " I asked.

" A metallurgist employed by Det Norske Staalselskab," Dahler replied.

I looked at Jorgensen. He was watching Dahler, his body taut and his right hand clenched. Dahler stepped down into the cockpit and seated himself on the further side. He was smiling quietly. " Know anything about him ? " I asked.

" Yes," Dahler said. " He was a German Jew. He left Germany in 1936 and settled in Norway. He became naturalised. When war broke out he was in the research department of D.N.S. After the invasion of Norway he worked for the Germans."

" Where did you meet him ? "

" At Finse."

" What was he doing there ? "

" He was an expert on metal alloys. He was engaged on certain low temperature tests in the German test sheds by Finsevatn."

" Did Farnell meet him up at Finse ? "

Dahler shrugged his shoulders. " I do not know," he said. He looked up at Jorgensen. " What was Schreuder doing up on the Jostedal with Farnell ? " he asked.

But Jorgensen had recovered his ease of manner. " I don't know," he said. " And I must say, Mr. Gansert, that I am surprised that you took the attitude you did just now. I have never heard of this man Schreuder until last night. He may have been a collaborator, as Dahler says. He may work for D.N.S. But you must remember that because I manage the affairs of the company, it does not mean that I know every one who works in the laboratories, workshops and foundries." He turned towards the companionway. " Let me know when we are nearing Bovaagen Hval, please."

I watched him go below with a feeling that I hadn't handled him very well. It was quite possible for Schreuder to have worked for D.N.S. without Jorgensen knowing. And what reason had I to believe Dahler, a man branded as a traitor, in preference to one of the country's industrial leaders ? And then I began to wonder again why Schreuder should have been on the Jostedal when Farnell met his death.

One thing I was now determined to do—I must have a post-mortem carried out on Farnell's body. I must know whether there was any evidence of a struggle. If Schreuder had killed Farnell . . . But why the message in that consignment of whale meat if he worked for D.N.S.—why the desire to get to England ? It didn't make sense.

I must have sat there lost in thought for a long time, for Curtis suddenly emerged from the chartroom and said, " Skipper—this looks like the gap we take for Bovaagen."

I noticed then that we were close in to the islands. They were bare, salt-scored rock without sign of habitation. A narrow gap with sheer cliffs like the Corinth canal cut through to Hjeltefjord. I checked with the chart and then ordered Carter, who was at the wheel, to alter course. As we glided into the gap the wind died away. I took the wheel and sent Carter below to start the engine.

The sea was smooth as glass. The gap was like a street paved with water. The rock cliffs on either side threw back the sound of our engine. We passed a brief inlet with a little *vaag* or wharf. Beside it lay the bones of a barge, weed-grown and slimy. Above, a white wooden cottage, perched precariously under the cliffs. The flag of Norway flew lazily from a flag-pole. Children waved to us, their shrill voices mingling with the sound of the engine. We glided out into the wide thoroughfare of Hjeltefjord. Here, too, the sea was a mirror, broken only by the long ripples of our wash trailing out on either side from the bows. And in the continued absence of any wind we lowered the sails. We turned north then, following the distant wake of a coastal steamer. Dahler touched my arm and pointed to the land over the stern. " That is Herdla," he said. " The Germans built nearly five hundred gun positions round the coast of Norway. The island of Herdla was one of the strongest—sunken batteries, torpedo positions, even an airfield."

" How do you know about Herdla ? " I asked him.

" I worked there," he answered. " For three months I helped to dig one of the gun positions. Then we were moved to Finse." He nodded in the direction in which our bows were pointed. " Straight ahead of us is Fedje. That's the island we were taken to after our escape from Finse. We waited there two weeks for the arrival of a British M.T.B."

He fell silent again. Nobody spoke. The only sound was the throb of the engine and the swish of the water slipping past. The sun was warm in a clear blue sky and beyond the low, rocky islands the mountains stood cool and white in their cloak of snow. We slid diagonally across Hjeltefjord and ran up the coast of Nordhordland. Little landing stages showed here and there among the rock, and above them always a huddle of wooden houses, each with its inevitable flag staff flying the red and blue of Norway. White-painted churches with tall, wooden steeples were visible for miles on the high ground on which they had been built. The tall chimneys of the fish canneries showed here and there in the narrow fjords. Up and down the coast motor fishing boats moved lazily, their hulls white and black and an ugly little wheelhouse aft. "Tock-a-tocks," Dahler said. "That's what your Shetlanders called them." And tock-a-tocks exactly described the sound made by their little two-stroke engines.

We cleared the first northward pointing finger of Nordhordland and under Dahler's direction I turned a point to starboard. We ran past tiny islets white with the droppings of the seabirds that wheeled constantly about us. A fjord opened up, leading, he said, to Bovaagen itself where there was a fish factory. Cairns, chequered black and white, indicated that it was a shipping route.

And then suddenly we saw the whaling station. It was half hidden in a fold of rock and protected from the north by low islands. The corrugated tin of its ugly factory buildings and the tall iron chimneys belching smoke were a black scar in the wild beauty of the islands, as ugly as a coal pit in a Welsh valley. Not another building was to be seen. The fjord leading to Bovaagen was astern of us now, the friendly black and white shipping guides lost behind a jutting headland. We were in a world of rock and sea— not dark granite cliffs topped with grass as in the west of England, but a pale, golden rock worn smooth and sloping in rounded hillocks to the water. It reminded me of Sicily. These rocks had the same volcanic, sunbaked look. And they were bald—bald to the top of the highest

headland—save for wisps of thin grass and big rock plants.
And the sea-birds wheeled incessantly.

A minute later and we had opened up the channel
leading into Bovaagen Hval. I ordered half speed and
we drifted quietly in to the quay. The water became oily
and streaked with a black, viscous excretion. Pieces of
grey, half-decayed flesh slid by. The smell of the place
closed in on us like a blanket. A Norwegian tock-a-tock
moored to the quay was loading cases of whale meat.
Beyond was the slipway leading to the flensing deck.
The place was littered with the remains of the last whale.
Long, straight-bladed steam saws were tearing through the
gigantic backbone, slicing it into convenient sections. A
little group of men stood at the end of the quay, watching
us.

Jorgensen came on deck and stood by the starboard rail,
gazing out towards the factory. I ran up alongside the
quay just beyond the meat boat and we tied up. An elderly
man detached himself from the group of watchers and
came towards us. He was tall and lean with a face that
was the colour of mahogany below thick, white hair.
" *God dag, herr direktör,*" he called to Jorgensen. He had
small, impish features that puckered into a smile and the
corners of his eyes were lined with a thousand little
crinkles.

I climbed over the rail and jumped on to the quay.
" This is Mr. Kielland, the station manager," Jorgensen
said curtly by way of introduction. And then still speaking
English, he said, " Well, Kielland, what have you found
out about that consignment of whale meat for England ?
How did the message get into it ? "

Kielland spread his hands in a gesture of hopelessness.
" I am sorry," he said. " I have found out nothing. I
cannot explain it at all."

" You've questioned all the men ? "

" Yes, herr direktör. They know nothing. It is a
complete mystery."

" What catchers were in at the time ? " I asked.

" Was it *Hval Ti* ? " Jorgensen's voice was sharp, precise. He was dealing with a subordinate now and I suddenly knew I wouldn't like to work for the man.

But Kielland was unperturbed by his director's tone. " Yes," he answered, a shade surprised. " Yes, it was *Hval Ti*. Lovaas brought that whale in. It was the first of the season. How did you know ? "

" Never mind how I knew," Jorgensen answered. " Come up to the office and we will talk." And he went off through the packing sheds.

Kielland turned to me and smiled. " We had better follow," he said.

Jill and Curtis had both come ashore. They joined me as I moved off after Jorgensen. " What a horrible smell," Jill said. She had a handkerchief held to her nose. The delicate scent of it was obliterated by the overpowering stench.

" That is money," Kielland chuckled. " Money always smells on a whaling station."

" Thank God I don't possess much of it then," Curtis said with a laugh. " I've never smelt anything as bad as this—not even in the desert, and the smell was pretty bad there sometimes."

We went through the packing sheds where whale meat was stacked on deep shelves, tier on tier, from floor to ceiling. Then we emerged into the charnel house of the flensing deck. This was a wood floored yard surrounded by the factory buildings. To our left the slipway dropped into the sea. To our right were the winches, their greasy hawsers littering the deck. And opposite us was the main part of the factory with the hoists for raising the blubber to the vats for boiling. Great hunks of backbone, the meat hanging in red festoons from the enormous bones, were strewn all over the deck. Men in heavy boots slithered on the blood-soaked planking as they dragged the sections of bone on long steel hooks to the hoists. The wooden boards were covered in a thick film of oily grease. Jill caught my arm. It was very slippery. We went past the winches and up a cindered slope by the boiler house and the oil storage tanks to a huddle of wooden buildings perched on a flat rock.

In the office the smell was less penetrating. The windows looked out to the smoking chimneys and over the corrugated iron roof of the factory to the sea. " So it was Lovaas who brought that whale in." Jorgensen seated himself at the desk by the radio equipment. " Was that on the 8th or 9th ? "

" The 9th," Kielland answered. He had pulled forward a chair for Jill. Curtis and I seated ourselves on the edge of a desk. " He came in at dawn. The meat was cut out, packed and away on the meat boat by the evening."

" When did Lovaas leave ? " Jorgensen asked.

" Not till the evening. He required water and fuel."

" So the message could have been placed in the meat by any one on the station or any of the crew of *Hval Ti* ? "

" Yes."

" What about your head packer ? Why doesn't he keep an eye on things ? "

" He does. But the packing sheds are too big to watch every one who comes and goes. Besides, there is no reason for him to watch the men coming through from the deck to the quay."

" They might steal meat."

" They have no need. I allow them to take as much as they wish back to their homes."

" I see." Jorgensen stroked his chin, massaging the blue stubble with his fingertips. A gold signet ring glittered as it caught the light. " It could be almost any one on the station then ? "

" That is so."

Kielland, I felt, was not being helpful. It was clear he resented this cross-examination. Jorgensen looked at his watch. " Just on nine," he murmured and turned to the radio. A moment later the familiar " *Ullo-ullo-ullo-ullo Bovaagen Hval* " of the catchers reporting filled the office. Whale Two reported his position and then Whale Five reported whale. Jorgensen lifted the microphone and requested Whale Ten for his position. The voice of Captain Lovaas answered : " *Vi passerer Utvaer Fyr, herr Jorgensen. Vi er fremme klokken ti.*"

" What's Lovaas say ? " I whispered to Jill.

" He says he's just passing Utvaer lighthouse," she answered. " He will be in at ten o'clock this morning."

An hour to go. Just one hour and he would be here in this office. He might tell his story to Jorgensen and myself together. On the other hand, Jorgensen might get him alone and persuade him to keep his mouth shut. " Where's Utvaer Light ? " I asked Jill. " North of Bovaagen ? "

" Yes," she answered. " About twenty miles north."

Jorgensen had switched off. He was sitting, staring out of the window, still rubbing his hand across his unshaven chin. I got to my feet. " Nothing we can do till Lovaas gets in," I said. " We'll go and have breakfast." I gave Curtis a nod to get him moving. Jorgensen glanced up at me. " Will you have yours on board ? " I asked. " Or on the station ? "

" Thank you, I will have it here," he replied.

I turned to Kielland. " By the way, what's this Captain Lovaas like ? Is he a good skipper ? "

" He's a good *skytter*, if that is what you mean," Kielland answered. And then as I looked puzzled he said, " *Skytter* is the same as your word shooter. We call our captains that because they always operate the harpoon gun. I am not interested in anything else. With *Hval To* and *Hval Fem* it is different. They are factory boats and I choose my captains. But *Hval Ti* belongs to Lovaas. He is his own master and sells his catches to us on a royalty basis."

" So he does what he likes ? " I said.

" On board his own ship—yes."

" That explains it," I murmured.

" Explains what, please ? " Kielland was watching me with a puzzled expression.

" Some years ago I gather he was in trouble for killing a man."

He nodded. " I have heard something about it.

" This lady is the daughter of Walter Somers—Petersen and Somers, one of the Sandefjord companies," Jorgensen explained, nodding towards Jill.

" So ! " Kielland's glance moved from Jorgesen to Jill.

" Mind if I use your telephone ? " I asked.

" No—please." Kielland pushed the instrument across to me.

" Jill," I said. " Will you get me Fjaerland. I want to speak to a man called Ulvik—Johan Ulvik. He'll probably be staying at the hotel there." I was watching Jorgensen's face and saw the sudden interest that leapt into his eyes at the mention of our representative's name.

She picked up the receiver and asked for Fjaerland. There was a short silence. Jorgensen began to tap with his fingers on the blotting paper that covered the desk. " *Er det Boya Hotel ?* " Jill asked. " *Kunne De si meg om der bor en herr Johan Ulvik der ? Utmerket. Jeg vil gjeme snakke med ham. Takk.*" As she waited she straightened up and gazed out of the window. Her face was set and firm. This was a different Jill. This was the girl who had worked for the Linge Company during the war. And I realised suddenly that besides being attractive, she was also very efficient. She bent down quickly as a voice crackled in the receiver. " *Er det herr Ulvik ?* " And then in English. " Hold the line, please. Mr. Gansert wishes to speak to you."

As I took the receiver from her, I said, " You and Curtis go down and stir up breakfast. I'll be along in a minute." I glanced at Curtis to make sure he'd got the point. Then I bent to the telephone. " That you, Mr. Ulvik ? " I asked.

" Ulvik speaking." The voice was thick and faint over the telephone.

" This is Gansert," I said. " Sir Clinton Mann has been in touch with you ? "

" Yes. That is why I am at Fjaerland."

" Good. Now listen," I went on. " I want the body of George Farnell, which is buried at Fjaerland, to be exhumed. I want a post-mortem. Is there any difficulty about that ? "

" The police will have to be informed of a reason."

" Tell them we have reason to believe that his death was not an accident." I glanced across at Jorgensen. He was gazing out of the window. But he had stopped drumming with his fingers. He was tense and listening to every word. " Arrange for the exhumation to be carried out as soon as possible. Can you manage that ? "

" It will be difficult," was the answer. " Have you any proof to support the view that it was not an accident?"

" No," I said. " I am hoping that we shall find the proof on the body—signs of a struggle or something."

" From what I have gathered the body was a little damaged when they brought it down."

" Who signed the death certificate ? " I asked then. " A local doctor ? "

" Yes. From Leikanger."

" Then get hold of him. Put the fear of God into him. Get him to support your application for post-mortem. Tell the police that there was another man with Farnell when he fell."

" Have you spoken to this other man ? " Ulvik asked. " The police would be much more likely to view with sympathy our application if they——"

" The name of the man who was with Farnell was Hans Schreuder, a metallurgist at one time employed by D.N.S.," I said. " I haven't seen him yet. But he's alive and he's been trying to get out of the country. Now get hold of that doctor and go to work on the police. I want an exhumation order signed by the time I reach Fjaerland to-morrow evening."

" But Mr. Gansert—such a short time—things do not move so fast."

" I'm relying on you, Mr. Ulvik," I snapped. " I don't

care how you get that exhumation order or what it costs—
but get it. Do you understand?" I put down the
receiver.

"So you are going to have a look at your precious
Farnell, eh?" Jorgensen said, smiling.

"Yes," I said. "If it's murder, God help those who
were behind it." He was still smiling. "Maybe we'll
know more about it when Lovaas gets in." I turned towards the door. "I'm going to get some breakfast now.
I'm damned hungry."

I went out into the sunlight and turned down the cinder
track to the factory. I wanted to hurry. But I knew they
would be watching me from the office window and I
forced myself to walk slowly. Not until I was across the
flensing deck and in the shadow of the packing sheds did
I look behind me. Nobody was following me. Apparently
they didn't suspect anything.

Curtis emerged from the companionway as I vaulted
over the rail. "Breakfast is ready," he said.

"To hell with breakfast," I answered. "Let go the
fore and aft warps." I pushed past him to the hatch.
"Carter!" I called down.

"Yes, sir?"

"Get the engine started—and quick."

"Aye, aye, sir."

Curtis, without waiting to think out the reason for
my order, had jumped on to the quay and tossed the
for'ard warp on to the deck. The after warp followed.
"What's the idea?" he asked as he clambered on board
again.

"Lovaas," I said. "I want to see him before Jorgensen
has a chance to get to work on him."

The engine roared into life. "Half ahead," I ordered
into the speaking tube. The propellers threshed the filthy
water under our stern. The quay began to glide by. I put
the wheel over. The bowsprit swung out towards the
sheltering islands. And then Jorgensen emerged from the
packing sheds. He'd tumbled to my plan. But too late.

Already there was a gap between us and the quay and as he ran forward, it widened. " I'm going to have a word with Lovaas," I called to him. " On my own."

He stopped. His face was dark with anger. He said nothing, but turned on his heel and walked back through the packing sheds. At full ahead we glided out between the islands into the milky haze of the North Ocean and headed for Utvaer Fyr. Right ahead of us two small boats were moored. One was an ordinary Norwegian fishing boat. The other attracted my attention because of its strange appearance. It looked as though it had been clumsily converted into a house boat. Two men were standing for'ard of the square deck house and steps led down into the water. As we passed bubbles broke the surface and the round helmet of a diver emerged. " What's down below ? " hailed Dick, who was leaning against the starboard rail.

Back came the reply in English, " An aircraft engine."

" Does everybody speak English here ? " I asked Dahler, who was in the chartroom where he had remained all the time we had been at Bovaagen Hval.

" Most of them," he replied. " Any man who had a boat, you know, got across to England during the war. They even attempted to cross in rowing boats." He shrugged his shoulders. " Some of them reached the Shetlands. Others were less fortunate. And then, of course, so many have served on English or American merchant ships, you know. Only the old men and the farmers speak no English." He pulled himself up into the cockpit. " So you go to see Lovaas ? " He leaned back and gazed out ahead. " I have met him once. He wished to captain one of my coastal boats. I will stay below," he added. " I do not wish to meet the man."

" What's he like ? " I asked.

" Lovaas ? " He turned his head and stared at me for a moment. " He is an eel." His lips spread into a tight, crooked smile. " But he does not look like one. Oh, dear me, no. He is a short man with a big stomach. He laughs a lot, but his eyes do not laugh and men are afraid of him. He has no wife or family. He lives for himself alone, you know. How much money are you prepared to offer for what Schreuder can tell you ? "

" I don't know," I said. " I hadn't thought about it.

" If Lovaas has the information you and Jorgensen want—then he will ask a great deal."

" Perhaps he won't know the value of the information ?" I suggested.

Dahler laughed. " Lovaas always knows the value of things."

I sat silent after that, wondering how I was going to handle this whaling skipper. And as we glided northward over the flat calm of the sea, the haze gradually increased, until the sun was no more than an iridescent light and it began to grow cold. Visibility was being gradually reduced as the mist formed and I began to fear we might miss Lovaas.

But ten minutes later Curtis hailed me from the bows. " Ship on the port quarter, skipper."

I peered into the opaque void that made sea and sky appear one and saw a vague shape catching the light about a point to port. I put the wheel over and as our bows swung towards it, the shape became a ship. It was not unlike a small Fleet sweeper—high bows dropping to a low deck that ran level with the water to the stern, and a single raked-back funnel. She was cutting through the water at considerable speed, throwing up a high bow wave and trailing a black line of smoke from her funnel. A catwalk ran from the bridge to a level platform set right in the bows. On that platform was a gun—a harpoon gun. I swung *Diviner* farther to port and ran to intercept. When I was almost across her bows, I turned on to a parallel course and hailed her as she came surging past. " Captain Lovaas ! " I called. " Can I come aboard ? "

I heard the engine-room telegraph bell ring and then a man emerged on the catwalk. He was short and fat with a peaked cap set at an angle and a green jacket whose silver buttons twinkled in the strong light. " Who are you, please ? " he roared.

" The man who described George Farnell to you," I answered.

He turned and gave an order. The engine-room telegraph sounded again and the engines of the catcher died away. " Please come alongside," he called across. " Alongside here." And he pointed to the side of his ship.

" I'll handle this alone," I told Curtis as I closed with the other ship. " Keep the others on board." The catcher was so low built, presumably for speed, that when our fenders bumped against her iron sides I could climb on to her deck with ease. Lovaas came down on to the deck to greet me. He was, as Dahler had said, a short man with a big stomach. His bottle green jacket flapped open as he walked and the serge trousers of the same colour were stretched taut. Only a wide leather belt with a silver buckle seemed to hold his huge belly in place.

" My name is Gansert," I said.

He held out a big hand covered with sandy hairs. " I am Lovaas," he said. " We have met before, eh—as voices." He laughed. It was a fat chuckle that rumbled up from his stomach. " Voices," he repeated as though pleased. " You like a little drink, eh ? Come on." He took hold of my arm. " Nobody come on board my boat and not have a little drink." He glanced down at the yacht. " We will tie your boat, eh ? Then we proceed and waste no time while we talk. " *Hei ! Jan ! Henrik ! Fortöy denne båten !* " As the two men doubled to their task, he pushed me for'ard. " Good boat you have," he said. " Good sea boat, eh ? This is mine, too." He waved his hand round the ship. " All mine—very cheap. I could sell her for three times what I give." He chuckled and pressed my arm. " Good profit, eh ? Good profit. Twice I have been with the factory ships to the Antarctic. But no more. This is better. I can do as I wish. I do not work for any damned whaling company. I work for

myself and they pay me for what I bring them. Better,
eh? Better, isn't it?" He had a way of repeating
himself as though pleased over a word. "In here," he
said as we reached the top of the ladder that led to the
accommodation below the bridge. "*Halvorsen!*" he
called up. "*Full fart forover så snart den andre båten er
fortöyet.*"

"*Ja,*" came the reply.

"In here, please." Lovaas pushed open a door. "My
cabin," he said. "Always a dam' disorder. No woman,
you know. Never have a woman on board. Have 'em
ashore, but never on board, eh? Here they are." He
pointed to the photographs pinned to the wall above his
bunk. "Hilda. Martha. Solveig." He slapped his desk.
"I have one whole drawer full. You would not believe
that, eh—a man as big as me?" And he patted his
stomach. "Now. You like *aquavit*, eh? Or brandy?
I have French brandy—no duty, good stuff."

"What's *aquavit*?" I asked. I'd always heard of it
as a Norwegian drink, but I'd never had it.

"Never had *aquavit*, eh?" He roared with
laughter and slapped my arm. "Then you will have
aquavit." He stooped down with a grunt and brought
a bottle and two glasses out of a cupboard below the
desk. Above our heads the engine-room telegraph rang
and the engines throbbed into life. "There," he said,
holding up the bottle. "Real line *aquavit*. See the
inside of the label? The name of the ship it crossed the
Line in, going south, and the name of the ship that brought
it back. All good *aquavit* must cross the equator
twice."

"Why?" I asked.

"Why? Good God! How should I know? That is the
job of the men who make the dam' stuff. All I know is
that it does good to it. Well—*skaal.*" He raised his glass
and drained it at a gulp. "A-ah!" he breathed. "That
is good, eh? Very good if you eat much fat, you know."
And he patted his stomach again and roared with laughter.

I remembered what Dahler said and noticed that his little bloodshot eyes did not laugh. The fat round them creased into wrinkles of laughter, but the eyes themselves were blue and steely and were watching me all the time. " Now, sit down," he said. " Sit down." And he kicked a chair over to me. " You wish to know about Schreuder, eh ? "

" Yes," I said.

He sat on his bunk. " So does herr direktör Jorgensen." The way he said herr direktör it sounded like a sneer. " I was expecting you, you know."

" Expecting me ? Why ? " I asked.

" The radio. Our radio watch, you know, is for half an hour. Jorgensen spoke to me after you had left." I was again conscious of his eyes watching me. " Another drink, eh ? "

" No, thanks," I said.

" I understand you are the representative of some English company ? " The bottle gurgled as he refilled both glasses. " *Skaal*," he said. " What company, Mr. Gansert ? "

" Base Metals and Industries," I answered.

His thick, sandy-coloured eyebrows lifted. " So ! A big concern, eh ? Bigger than D.N.S."

" Yes," I said. I wanted him to do the talking. I wanted to get the measure of the man. But he waited so that at length I said, " Where is this man, Schreuder ? "

" Locked in a cabin," he answered.

" Can I see him ? "

" Perhaps." He rolled the thick, colourless liquid round his glass. Then he looked at me out of his sharp little eyes. He didn't say anything. The vessel's foghorn suddenly blared through the cabin, drowning the steady thrum of the engines. He waited. Again the foghorn blared.

" How much ? " I asked.

" How much ? " He smiled and shrugged his shoulders.

" You wish to buy. But do you know what you are buying, eh, Mr. Gansert ? "

" Do you know what you're selling ? " I answered.

He smiled. " I think so. On board my ship is the man who can give the location of important new mineral deposits. So much herr Jorgensen has tell me. He has also said I must bring this man—Schreuder—to Bovaagen Hval—without letting you speak with him. Now, you see how awkward it is for me, Mr. Gansert. Herr Jorgensen is direktör of the whaling station I sell my whales to. He is a hard man. If I do not deliver him Schreuder, the station will no more take my whale. You see, there are only three whaling stations in Norway. Each station is allowed only three catchers. If Bovaagen Hval is closed to me I cannot take my whale elsewhere. Then how do I live ? How do my men live ? And my ship—it will lie in Sandefjord and rot. But first we will talk with Jorgensen. If he does not offer too much and you offer more—well, maybe I come to live in England, eh ? Then how do I keep my stomach fed ? " He patted the protruding bulk which shook with laughter. " Perhaps there is a good black market restaurant in your Soho, eh ? But first we talk with Jorgensen."

He heaved himself up and peered for'ard out of the port-hole. Then he glanced at his watch. " In five minutes we arrive at Bovaagen Hval. Then we will see. Now we have another drink, eh ? " He refilled my glass. " Skaal." Then as I did not pick up my glass, he said, " Please, Mr. Gansert, when I say skaal you must drink. If you don't drink I cannot drink. That is our custom in Norway. And I like to drink. Skaal." I raised my glass and knocked back the liquor. It was sharp and fiery.

" Why did Schreuder want to get to the Shetlands ? " I asked.

" Maybe he kill someone. I do not know. But he nearly make a dam' fool of me—magnetising my compass." He was watching me again. " That description of Farnell

—you said the tip of the little finger of the left hand missing, eh?"

"That's right," I said. "I know about that because it happened when I was with him in Rhodesia. Caught it in a crushing plant. Why?"

His eyes were back on his drink. "O-oh. I just wondered, that is all. This man Schreuder did not say nothing about it. His description was correct from what you say, but he did not say about the little finger of the left hand."

The engine-room telegraph rang and the engines slowed. I got up and peered out ahead. The fog was thickening. But out of it emerged the vague shape of one of the small islands masking Bovaagen Hval. "We're almost in, I think," I said. He made no reply. I imagine he was considering how best to handle negotiations involving both Jorgensen and myself. I wondered why he had brought up the matter of Farnell's little finger and how much he knew about the whole business.

And then suddenly pandemonium seemed to break loose. There was a shout. Then an iron door slammed and feet pounded down the iron-plated length of the after-deck. There followed a splash. Then shouts and more feet running on the deck plating. The engine-room telegraph rang again and the ship shuddered as the engines were set to full astern.

At the first shout Lovaas, with surprising speed for a man of his bulk, had leapt to his feet and reached the door. "*Hvar er hendt?*" he roared.

Over his shoulder I caught a glimpse of a man who's face was running in blood looking up from the rail below. "*Det er Schreuder,*" he shouted back. Then he pointed over the starboard rail. "*Han unnslapp og hoppet overbord.*"

"*De fordomte udugelig idiot!*" Lovaas roared and swung himself on to the bridge ladder.

"What's happened?" I asked as I followed him.

"Schreuder," he answered. "He's escaped and dived

overboard." He flung open the door to the bridge. The
mate was there, peering through binoculars. "*Kan De se
ham ?*" Lovaas demanded.

"*Nei*," the mate answered. And then suddenly : "*Jo,
jo—der borte.*"

I followed the direction of his arm. On the edge of the
mist's visibility a black blob showed for an instant on the
colourless surface of the sea. Then it was gone. "*Full
fart forover babord motor. Full fart akterover styrbord motor.*"
Lovaas was peering into the opaque void. "*Roret hardt
over til babord, Henrik !*" Again I saw the black blob as
our bows swung. It turned and looked back and I saw
then that it was a man's head. He raised his arms out of
the water. He was struggling to get clear of his clothes.
Then the head vanished. I had no idea what the temperature of the water was. But I knew it must be pretty cold.
No man would try such a swim in these waters unless he
were desperate. And at the moment that he had disappeared he had been heading out to sea. The poor wretch
must have lost his sense of direction. From where I stood,
balancing myself to the heel of the ship as she turned, I
could see the vague shape of the island. But from water-
level it was probably invisible.

I glanced quickly at Lovaas. He was peering into the
mist at the point where the man's head had disappeared.
The fierce grip of his hand on the edge of the bridge
betrayed his impatience at the slowness of the turn. I
glanced down at *Diviner* straining at the warps that
secured her to the catcher. If we could pick Schreuder
up and not Lovaas . . . I was down the ladder in a
flash. "Dick ! Curtis ! " I shouted. " Cut her clear.
Quick ! "

I heard Lovaas bellowing in Norwegian to his crew as
I slipped across the engine-room hatches and down the
ladder to the main deck. Somebody tried to bar my way
at the foot of the ladder. I lashed out with my foot and
then jumped straight over on to *Diviner's* deck. Dick
and Wilson each had an axe. Two blows severed the

warps and as I picked myself up off the deck, the engines started and we drew clear of the catcher.

Lovaas was out on the catwalk. He shook his fist at me as he hurried down to the bows to act as lookout. I saw his hand touch the heavy harpoon gun and then he glanced across at us. " Hard a'port ! " I shouted to Jill who was at the wheel.

" Hard a'port it is," she answered and we swung away. I wanted to get well clear of the catcher. The rage of the man was obvious even though the distance between us was rapidly widening. I wondered what he would do if we succeeded in picking up Schreuder.

But we didn't succeed. And nor did Lovaas. The two of us cruised back and forth over that little area of sea a hundred times.

But we saw no sign of Schreuder—only his discarded jacket floating half submerged with the sleeves held out like a man drowned. There was not a breath of wind. The sea was like glass. And the mist was so thick we were often out of sight of the catcher. I had a bucket of sea water brought up and dipped my hand in. It was as cold as ice. No man could live for long in water that cold. After half an hour I gave it up and followed the catcher as it made off slowly through the mist to Bovaagen Hval.

As we left the spot I saw Jill gazing back over the stern. " If only we could have saved him," she said. " He could have told us so much. I'm sure he could." She turned suddenly to me. " What do you think happened up there on the Jostedal ? "

" I don't know," I said. The less she thought about it the better.

" But something must have happened," she murmured. " He was there with George. And then after—the accident—he tries to make for England. He's afraid to stay in Norway. So afraid that he's willing to take a chance in that icy water. And those samples of ore. He must have taken them from George's body. Bill ! " She caught at my arm and her voice was tense. " Do you think—do you think he killed George ? "

" I don't know what to think," I replied. I didn't look at her. I didn't want to see that hurt expression in her eyes.

" Well, whatever he did," Curtis said, " the poor devil's dead now. And we'll never know the truth of what happened." He turned and gazed aft. " Hallo ! Mist's lifting a bit. I wonder what happened to those two boats ? "

" What two boats ? " I asked.

" You remember—the diver who was after an aero engine. Maybe they were farther out. Difficult to tell in this mist. But I thought they were just about here. I remember that island was just where it is now when Dick hailed them." He nodded in the direction of the island we were approaching.

" That's right," Dick agreed. " This is about the spot."

Curtis glanced up at the burgee. It was fluttering. " There's a breeze sprung up. Look, the mist is clearing now."

" Pity it didn't do that earlier," Dick said. " Might have saved Schreuder's life." The mist was clearing fast. The sun shone through. " Not a sign of the divers," he added.

" Probably packed up for the day," Curtis suggested.

But Dick shook his head. " No. They wouldn't do that. I don't expect they often get a sea as calm as this up here. This is just right for diving. And it's early, too. They'd only just started the day's operations."

I looked at him. I think we all had the same idea. " Do you think Schreuder could have swum to the divers' boats and persuaded them to take him ashore ? " I asked.

Dick shrugged his shoulders. " We didn't find his body. And we didn't find the boats. And if they had moved off we wouldn't have heard their little engines above the sound of ours. Nor would Lovaas on the catcher. But how could he persuade 'em to up anchor and get away as quickly as that?"

"I don't know," I said. "But it's just a chance that he did." I ordered Carter to stop the engine and jumped down into the chartroom. I cleared the litter of pencils and rulers from the chart and stared at the outline of Nordhordland. The others crowded round peering over my shoulder. "Curtis," I said. "This is your sort of problem. Schreuder for some reason was desperate. He wanted to escape. Now if you were Schreuder and you'd persuaded those divers to help you, where would you get them to take you?"

He leaned forward over the chart and studied it. "He wanted to get away from Lovaas," he murmured. "And to him Lovaas would be Bovaagen Hval. In that case I'd steer clear of any place on the same stretch of land as Bovaagen. And I wouldn't go out to the islands, however much I wanted to get across to England. I'd feel cut off out there. No. I think I'd get them to take me to the next island to the north of here and land me at some quiet inlet near Austrheim. From the other side of the island I could probably get a fishing boat to take me across Fensfjord to Halsvik on the mainland. And from there I could get up into the mountains and lose myself until the hue and cry had died down."

"Or he could stop one of the steamers going to Sognefjord," Jill put in. "They'll always take on passengers from boats that hail them."

"Fine," I said. "We'll make for Austrheim then. If we're right, we should meet the divers coming back to their work here."

Shortly afterwards a breeze sprang up and the mist cleared to bright sunshine. But we saw no sign of the divers' boats. They weren't in Austrheim, nor was there any sign of them in any of the inlets along the coast. Reluctantly we put about.

On the way back to Bovaagen Hval something occurred

which, in a strange way upset me. Austrheim was disappearing in the haze astern. I went down to the saloon to fix drinks for the crew. But outside the door, I stopped. It was not properly shut and through the crack I could see Jill and Curtis standing close together. Jill's eyes were wet with tears. Curtis held a watch in his hand —the same gold watch that I had seen him with when he first came aboard. " I'm sorry," he was saying. " I should have given it to you before. But I wasn't certain he was dead. Now I am certain. So "—he thrust the gold timepiece into her hands—" It was his father's. When he gave it to me, your address was inside the back. I opened it foolishly in the assault craft. The wind swept the piece of paper with your address overboard. Only your picture remained. That's why I recognised you at once."

She had clutched hold of the watch. " You—saw us, that time in Bergen, didn't you ? "

" Yes."

" That was the last time I saw him." She turned away. She was crying quietly. " Was there any message—when he gave you this ? "

" Yes," Curtis answered. " A line from Rupert Brooke——"

I turned quietly away then and went back on deck. Why was she crying ? Was she still in love with him ? I took the wheel from Carter. I didn't want to think about her being in love with Farnell.

It was midday by the time we got back to the whaling station. Two catchers lay at the quay. And as we landed the winches were clattering and a huge whale was being dragged up the slipway by its tail. We stood and watched for a moment. It was all strange and exciting. When the winches stopped, the great animal stretched the whole length of the flensing deck. Its gigantic tail lay by the winches. Its mouth, wide open to show the finners and the huge pink tongue, overhung the slipway. In an instant half a dozen men, armed with flensing knives set to work. The winch hawsers were attached to the flaps of the hide cut out from either side of the head behind the jaw. Then flensing began, the winches tearing at the blubber whilst the flensers cut it clear with their knives. This exposed the meat along the backbone. Then the winch hawsers were refixed, run through blocks and the whale was winched over to expose the grey-white belly of the animal to the flensing knives.

Kielland came up as we stood watching. He was dressed in ex-German jackboots and an old khaki shirt. " Ah, you have returned, eh ? " He shouted instructions to one of the men and then said, " I hear this man, Schreuder, jumped into the sea. You did not recover him, eh ? "

" No," I said. The workmen were swarming round the whale now. The meat was being hacked out in great chunks and hooked on to trolleys to be carried to the packing sheds. " Where's Jorgensen ? " I asked.

" He has gone to Bergen in the meat boat." There was a jauntiness about Kielland that suggested he was glad to see the last of his director.

" And Lovaas ? "

He smiled, crinkling the corners of his eyes. " He is sick with himself."

" What about Schreuder's possessions ? " I asked. " What happened to them ? "

" Kaptein Lovaas handed them over to Jorgensen to deliver to the police."

" Did you see what they were ? Did they include any pieces of what would look like dull, grey rocks ? "

His brows lifted. " So that was why you were all so interested in Schreuder, eh ? What was it—gold, silver, something valuable ? "

" Yes," I answered. " Something valuable." No wonder Jorgensen had hurried off to Bergen. He would be flying those pieces of rock down to the D.N.S. laboratories and within a day he would know as much as I did.

" I'm going back to the boat," Jill said. " I can't—I

can't stand this any longer." She had her handkerchief to her nose.

"But please—you will feed with me and my wife?" Kielland said. "Everthing is ready. I have been expecting you. You will not disappoint my wife, will you now? She likes English people." He shook my arm. "We are all very pro-British out here on the islands. We get on fine, eh? We are fishermen and sailors like your people. Peace or war, we fight the same battles. So you will stay for food, eh?"

"It's very nice of you," I said.

"Not at all, my dear fellow. Not at all. And there are beds for you if you have had too much of the ship. Come. We go and have a drink, eh? We always have a drink before food." He chuckled and nodded at Jill, still holding her handkerchief to her nose. "Mrs. Gansert does not like the smell, eh? But we like it. To me it smells of money. That is what I always say to people. It smells of money. Look at that whale now. I have just measured him—seventy-three feet. That is about seventy tons. He has over a thousand pounds worth of oil in his blubber and the same value in meat. That is why I like the smell." He patted Jill's hand. "My wife says it smells like a new dress. Every time a whale comes in over seventy feet I promise her a new dress. And now she likes the smell, too. Come on, We will go and have a little drink."

He led us up the cinder track to the office. Behind the office was a long, low house. I caught Jill's eyes as we went in. She was bubbling over with laughter. We were shown into a tastefully furnished lounge. Mrs. Kielland came in as her husband was pouring out large cognacs. She was a jolly woman with twinkling eyes and an elegance that was delightfully unexpected out on a whaling station. Kielland introduced us   Jill explained that she was not my wife. "You poor girl," laughed Mrs. Kielland. "Albert has such a tidy mind. And he knows nothing about anything—except whale. You'll find if you stay here long enough that there is nothing but whale talk in this house." She turned to her husband. "Albert, what was the length of the whale Nordahl has just brought in ? "

" Seventy-three feet, Martha," he replied, grinning like a kid.

" Seventy-three." She gave a gurgle of delight. " Look ! This is the frock I have from the last whale that was over seventy feet." It was a flame-coloured silk and as she twirled round the skirt flared out. " Now," she said. " We drink to your health." She raised her glass. " *Skaal*," she said.

We all drank. And then the door opened and a little man with dark hair and sharp, creased features came in. " Ah, here is Mr. Sunde," said Mrs. Kielland. " Come in and have a drink, Mr. Sunde. I wish you to meet some nice English people."

I couldn't quite place him as he was introduced to us. He was quite a tough looking man and he seemed a little embarrassed at drinking with us as though he felt out of place. I put him down as an artisan. Yet he, too, seemed to understand English.

" What do you do on the station ? " I asked as he stood beside me.

" Oh, Mr. Sunde is not on the station," Mrs. Kielland said. " He's another little venture of Albert's."

" What do you do then ? " I asked him.

" Gor' blimey, Oi'm a diver," he said.

The sudden outburst of pure Cockney took me by surprise. " A diver ? " I said.

" That's roight."

I caught Dick's eye and then said, " Are you diving for the station ? "

" That's roight," he repeated and concentrated on his drink.

" What are you diving for ? "

" Aerer engines," he answered. " A Jerry plyne was shot da'n just off the stytion. Oi'm gettin' the engines up."

"Then yours were the boats we saw this morning, just off the outer islands," I said. "A diving boat and a little fishing boat?"

"That's roight."

"Where are your boats now?"

"The divin' boat's lyin' just ra'nd the 'eadland."

"And the other—the fishing boat?" I asked.

His grey eyes looked up furtively at me over his drink. "Me mate's gorn inter Bovaagen for somefink," he muttered and gulped down his glass of cognac.

CHAPTER 5

DON'T FORGET THE DIVER

I watched the little Cockney diver as he sipped a second glass of cognac and I was certain he was hiding something. The others had the same idea. They were watching him, too. He glanced quickly in our direction and edged away towards the station manager. Jill gripped my arm. " Bill ! " she whispered. " Do you think he could have picked Schreuder up this morning ? " Her voice was tense and strained.

" I don't know," I answered. " It's possible. What do you think ? "

" I felt——" She hesitated and then looked up at me. " Bill, I felt close to him this morning—terribly, strangely close. It was as though——" She stopped and then said, " I don't know. I just felt as though I were close to him, that's all."

" To Farnell ? "

She nodded.

I looked across at the dark haired little diver. He was talking to Kielland. He was talking fast as though he had to keep on talking. I caught snatches of his conversation. It was about depth of water and oxy-acetylene cutting. " He's nervous," I told Jill quietly. " I'll get him alone as soon as I can and see what I can find out."

But I didn't get him alone before lunch and at lunch something happened that made me even more anxious to talk to the man privately. The meal was laid in a long, low room branching off from the steward's big kitchen. Windows looked out across ridges of bare rock to a black cutting where the sea lay still in the hot sunshine like a piece of glass. The meal—*middag* they called it—was a colossal affair. It began with big steaks of whale meat

111

served with tomatoes and potatoes. This was followed by *koldtbord*—there were innumerable tins of fish treated in different ways, smoked salmon, pickled hake, pressed whalebeef and a whole assortment of different meats, salad and several types of cheese. There was milk and a light Norwegian Pilsner to wash it down.

Lovaas was there, and Captain Nordahl of *Hval To*. The talk was mainly of whale. Sunde kept his eyes on his plate and when he spoke it was only to ask for something to be passed to him. If Dick had let him be, I might have found out what I wanted and Lovaas might never have come into the picture again. But Dick asked him how it was he spoke such good English, and with a Cockney accent.

The little diver looked up. "Me muvver was Cockney," he answered, tucking his food into his cheek. "She never could get on wiv the Norwegian language, so roight from the time Oi first opened me ma'f she talked ter me in English."

"Who were the men working with you this morning?" Dick asked.

"Me partner an' a fisherman."

There was a lull in the general conversation and Lovaas looked across at him. "What are you fishing for?" he asked.

The Cockney Norwegian grinned. "Fer aerer engines, Kaptein Lovaas," he answered. "Oi'm a diver. Started yesterday."

"He is getting up the engines of that old Junkers 88 that was shot down off Skarv Island," Kielland explained.

"Off Skarv Island?" The sudden interest in Lovaas's voice hit me like a punch. I could see it coming and I couldn't stop it. I began to talk about salvage operations in British harbours. But only the Kiellands were interested. Lovaas had stopped eating and was watching the diver. "Were you out there this morning, Mr. Sunde?" he asked.

I kept on talking. But all around me was a heavy

silence. Sunde gave Lovaas a quick, scared glance and then his eyes fell to his plate. He toyed nervously with his knife and fork. But he didn't eat. " That's roight," he said. And then hurriedly : " Oi went da'n ter examine the engins. When Oi sees they're okay Oi sends me mate inter Bovaagen fer an acetylene cutter."

Lovaas was on him like a hawk. " To Bovaagen, eh ? "

" That's roight," Sunde replied. But the way he said it lacked conviction and he fumbled with his knife as he spread thin layers of cheese on top of meat.

" Who are you working with ? " Lovaas went on.

" Peer Storjohann," Sunde replied. " He and Oi is partners. We own the boat an' the equipment."

" And the fisherman ? "

" Oh, he's a local man," put in Kielland. " Old Einar Sandven from Nordhanger."

" From Nordhanger, eh ? " Lovaas seemed chewing this information over in his mind. Then he said, " What time was it when you ceased work this morning ? "

Sunde looked across at me and then at Lovaas. He seized his glass and took a gulp of beer. I leaned forward across the table and said, " Can you tell me more about these engines ? Presumably the plane was shot down several years ago. Surely the engines will be rusted beyond use ? "

Sunde seized on to my new line of conversation with evident relief. " Lor' bless me soul, no," he answered. " They'll be all roight. Metal don't rust right under the water, see. It's air and water what rusts metal. You see ships rusted 'cos you see 'em after the air's bin at 'em. But you sink a ship right under the sea an' then go da'n an' take a look at 'er—well she's all roight, see."

He paused, and in that pause, Lovaas said, " How long were you out off Skarv Island this morning, Mr. Sunde ? "

" Oh, Oi dunno," Sunde replied quickly. " An hour— maybe two. Why ? " He looked across at Lovaas, but somehow he wasn't able to hold the other's gaze. His eyes dropped to his plate again.

" What time did you start work ? " Lovaas persisted.

" Oh, Oi dunno. 'Ba't eight."

" Then you would still be out there about ten this morning ? "

" Couldn't say what time we was a't there till. Ask me partner. 'E's got a watch."

" When will he be returned, eh ? "

" 'Ow should Oi know ? Depends 'ow long 'e takes ter get the oxy-acetylene plant. Mebbe 'e'll 'ave ter go inter Bergen fer it ? "

Lovaas leaned towards Sunde. There was something almost menacing in the solid, squat bulk of him. " Were you out off Skarv Island when we were searching for Schreuder ? " he asked.

" Was that the name of the man wot fell overboard from *Hval Ti* ? " Sunde asked, trying hard to cover up his nervousness.

" Yes," Lovaas answered abruptly.

" Well, we weren't there, see. We didn't 'ear nuffink."

Mrs. Kielland patted Lovaas's arm. " I'm sure Mr. Sunde would have said at once if he'd been there, Kaptein Lovaas."

Lovaas said nothing. He sat watching Sunde. The silence at the table became uncomfortable. Mrs. Kielland said, " It is so terrible. It is the first man we have lost at Bovaagen Hval. And so close to the station—it does not seem possible."

" Is this the first man you've ever lost ? " I asked Kielland.

He nodded. " We have accidents, you know. Men cut themselves on flensing knives. And then we had a man's leg badly torn by the winches. But that is all at the factory. Never have we any accidents on the ships. This is the first."

I looked across at Lovaas. " But it's not your first, is it, Captain Lovaas ? " I said.

" What do you mean ? " His eyes flared with sudden anger.

" I seem to remember hearing that you killed a man once."

" Who tell you that, eh ? "

" A Mr. Dahler."

" Dahler." His eyes narrowed. " What did he say about me ? "

" Only that you were sacked from the command of a catcher for killing a man."

" It's a lie."

" Maybe," I said. " But how will you explain this man Schreuder's death to the police ? "

" Explain ? Schreuder jumped overboard."

Lovaas was crumbling a piece of bread and suddenly I felt on top of him. " What about my evidence ? " I said.

" But the man jump over the ship," Mrs. Kielland said. " Surely that is right ? All the men say he jump straight over. You and Kaptein Lovaas search for him together."

" The man was desperate," I said. " That's why he jumped. I wonder what you had done to make him so desperate, Captain Lovaas ? Had you threatened him as you did that other man ? "

Lovaas thrust back his chair and got to his feet. He was red with anger. " I am not to stay here to be insult," he cried, losing his English in his excitement. " You are a guest here. If you were not you would get hurt for that. Now I go back to my ship. But be careful, Mr. Gansert. Be careful. This is dangerous talk." He turned to Mrs. Kielland and said, " *Takk for maten.*" Then, with a quick glance at me, he left the room.

I had overplayed my hand. I should have kept quiet. But I'd wanted to get his mind away from Sunde and those two diving boats. I glanced round the silent table. Kielland was watching me. His eyes had lost their good-humoured twinkle. " Will you please tell me what happened on board *Hval Ti* ? " he asked.

I told him. And when I had finished, he said, " You were interested in this man Schreuder for the same reason that Jorgensen was interested, eh ? "

I nodded.

He didn't say anything, but sat slumped in his chair as though lost in thought. "Will there be an inquiry into the man's death?" I asked him.

He looked up. "No," he said. "No. I do not think so."

"But surely——" I began.

He held up his hand. "You forget," he said, "Herr Jorgensen is a very powerful man. We are like you people. We are hard working, honest and law-abiding. But when a thing is a matter of high politics and big business—then——" He hesitated. "Then it is best left in the hands of those who understand it. Come. We will go and have a little drink with our coffee, and we will forget all about this, eh?"

We had our coffee and drinks in the Kiellands' sitting-room. Sunde sat himself next to Mrs. Kielland. I had no opportunity of getting him alone, and after our coffee, Kielland insisted on taking the four of us round the station. He took us through the boiler-rooms where the steam for the oil vats was generated and on into a roofed-in space piled high with the rotten-smelling remains of whalebone. There were great sections of backbone the size of big drums that had had all the goodness steamed out so that they were like huge loaves of areated bread, as light as a feather. This refuse scraped from the bottom of the oil vats was being crushed and packed in sacks as guano for agriculture. Then we went down into the main part of the factory where the vats stood like huge blast furnaces, six aside in two long lines. We walked down the narrow space between them. The heat was terrific. On each side of us a scalding hot gutter carried a thin, yellow stream of whale oil to big, open tanks. "From these tanks it goes to be cooled," Kielland said. "Then it is packed in oil drums. It goes all over the world—for soap, candles, cosmetics, margarine."

I tried to show interest, but I was impatient to get back to Sunde before Lovaas had a chance to talk to him alone.

But Kielland's life was the whaling station and he was determined to show us everything. He took us to a vat that was being cleared of slag, all the oil having been extracted. Two men, stripped to the waist, were hauling out the filth with iron scrapers from an open door at the base of the vat. It piled up on the floor, a mass of decayed-looking rubbish that might have been the sweepings of an incinerator. " More guano," Kielland said. " It is all money. Every little bit of whale is money. Nothing is waste. Even the finners are used. They go to England to be made into brushes. Come. I show you how we cut and pack the meat."

We went out on to the flensing deck. The sun was hot and bright. The steam saws hummed. The men slid along the slippery deck with great, star-shaped sections of bone ; all that was left of the great monster we had seen being dragged up the slipway that morning was a long, ragged, bleeding backbone. The meat had all been cleared. They were hosing down the deck. Kielland noticed our surprise and said, " We do not waste time, eh ? I have forty men here and we can handle three whales a day if necessary."

" Three whales a day ! " Curtis said. " But that never happens, surely. You've only three catchers."

" Oh, not early in the season," Kielland answered. " But later the whale comes south. In September we may be catching them just off the islands. Then quite often we have all three catchers in day after day. It is hard work. But we do not mind. It is good money for every one then."

We crossed the deck and went into the packing sheds. Whilst Kielland was talking to the others, I strolled through on to the quay. And then I stopped. Captain Nordahl's *Hval To* was lying there, but there was no sign of *Hval Ti*. I turned back. " Kielland," I called. " Where's Lovaas's boat ? "

He turned, a large hunk of red whale beef in his hand. " *Hval Ti* ? He should be there."

" It's not there," I told him. " Has Lovaas gone back to the whaling grounds, do you think ? "

But he shook his head. " No. He has to have water and fuel. Perhaps he has gone to Bovaagen." His eyes creased to a twinkle. " He has a girl at Bovaagen. And the mate has his wife staying at the *Skjaergaardshotelet*. Most of his men have a woman of some sort there. I think you will find he has gone to Bovaagen. He has more whale than the other boats. He is in no hurry. Also it is no good out in the *Norskehavet* now—*Hval Fem* reports bad fog. Now look at this, Mr. Gansert. What do you think of this for meat, eh ? " He held the slab of red meat out to me. It looked like real beef. " Not all of the whale is like this, you know," he went on. " The meat is all graded. This is the best. This will go to Bergen or Newcastle for the restaurants. Then there is other meat which goes to make sausages. The worst meat goes for the foxes. We have big fox farms here in Norway." He tossed the piece of beef back on to one of the packing shed shelves and glanced at his watch. " Now we go up to the house, eh ? There is the radio at four and then, after, we have tea— just a cup, but it is very good because my wife always insists on a little drink with it." He chuckled and patted my arm as he led the way back across the flensing deck.

I was in a hurry to get back. I wanted to see Sunde. Mrs. Kielland was alone in the sitting-room. She put her knitting down as she rose to greet us. " Well, has Albert shown you everything ? " She took hold of Jill's hand. " You poor dear. I think you are very brave. The smell is something you have to get used to. But did you see the meat ? " Jill nodded. I think she was quite exhausted with whale. " What did you think ? Is it good ? Is it like your ox beef, eh ? "

" Yes. Very." Jill folded up quietly into a chair.

" Where's the diver ? " I asked.

Mrs. Kielland turned. " Mr. Sunde ? That is very strange. I have not seen him since *middag*."

"Probably he has gone to Bovaagen to help his partner with that equipment," Kielland said.

"Ah, yes," his wife agreed. "That is it. I'm sure that is what he will have done. Why? Did you wish to speak with him?"

"Yes," I said. "I—I wanted to know more about his diving methods. If you'll excuse me, I'll just take a stroll round and see if he's about." I nodded to Curtis and he followed me out.

"He wouldn't have gone to Bovaagen surely," he said as we closed the door. "Not with Lovaas there."

"He might have gone first and Lovaas followed," I answered. "We'll just see if he's on the station."

Curtis, who knew quite a bit of Norwegian from his service in the country, questioned every one we met. But the only person who seemed to have seen anything of Sunde since the midday meal was the steward. He'd seen him going down behind the station towards the cutting where the sea swept in. We walked down to it across the bare rock. The sun was slanting behind the iron chimneys of the station and the rock was a warm, golden colour. We reached the cutting. It was narrow and the sea ran out through it fast as the tide fell. We crossed a bridge and continued on. Men's boots had blazed a trail through the years that led like a white path to the crest of a jagged shoulder of rock. From the top we could see the white spire of Bovaagen church standing like a bright spearhead against the pale, burnished blue of the sky. And in a little backwater to our left a rowing boat lay tied to a rock. It was the sort of boat you find everywhere in Norway—a development of the coracle, pinched out to a point at bow and stern, a miniature Viking's craft that has survived down the ages even to its fixed wooden rowlocks. From a neighbouring rock, a length of rope trailed in the greasy water.

"Perhaps there was another boat there," Curtis suggested. "He may have rowed down to Bovaagen."

"Possible," I said.

"Or he may have walked," Curtis added, gazing towards the little wooden church on the distant hill. " It can't be so very far if the men walk it every day."

" Far enough," I said. " Anyway, their houses are probably this side of the village. Come on. We'll take *Diviner* down there."

We turned back then and walked towards the sun. As we crossed the wooden bridge that spanned the cutting, we met some of the men starting home. They were a small, dark lot with dirty clothes and almost every one of them carried a dripping hunk of red meat. They smiled at us as in a quiet, friendly way and said, " *God dag*," as they passed. Curtis spoke with one or two. Most of them had houses much nearer than Bovaagen. Bovaagen, they said, was over an hour's hard walking.

We got back to the Kiellands' in time for tea and a drink. Immediately afterwards we excused ourselves and went down to the ship. As we walked through the almost deserted station, Jill said to me, " If we don't find Mr. Sunde at Bovaagen, we might try Nordhanger."

" Einar Sandven's cottage ? " I asked.

She nodded. " There's a road to Nordhanger from Bovaagen.

As we passed through the dark cavern of the packing sheds, a ship's siren reverberated through the low island hills. I stopped, listening to the sound of it dying away. Then it came again, a deep, hollow sound. Curtis, who was ahead, ran out on to the quay. Then he turned and called to us. " It's Lovaas," he shouted. " He's coming in."

The slanting sunlight sprawled the shadow of *Hxal To* across the quay. Curtis was pointing across the catcher's bow with its deadly harpoon gun. Through the gap between the islands steamed another catcher. Its siren-puff of steam still hung like a white wreath astern of it. Across the still water came the sound of the engine-room telegraph. The catcher began to swing as it manoeuvred in to the quay. The golden sunlight caught

the side of the bridge. *HVAL 10*. " Come on," I said to
the others. " We mustn't appear too interested."

We went on along the quay, past the pile of fifty-kilo
cases of whale meat awaiting dispatch, past *Hval 2*, whose
men were all on deck watching Lovaas come in, until we
came to *Diviner*. Her deck was deserted. The varnish of
her bare masts shone warm in the slanting sun. We
climbed aboard and went below. Dahler was sitting alone
in the saloon. " Where's Carter and Wilson ? " I asked
him.

" They have gone to look over *Hval To*, and to have a
little drink, I think." He smiled. A bottle of whisky
and a half full tumbler stood at his elbow. " I am glad
you have returned. It is very dull down below here. But
I do not wish to look at the factory." He reached for the
bottle. " Have a drink," he said. " Everybody come an'
have a drink." He suddenly crashed the bottle down on
to the table top. " I do not wish to look at the factory, I
tell you." He pushed the bottle quickly away and raised
his withered arm. " Why d'you bring me here, eh ? " he
demanded of me. " Why did you bring me here ? Was
it to torture me ? Do you think I like to be here—
marooned in your damned yacht—knowing that if I go
up on deck I shall be face to face with the factory—my
factory. Ever since you went to lunch with Kielland I
have been down here. And I have been thinking. I have
been thinking about the ships I owned and the tankers—
and Knut Jorgensen." He slammed his claw-like hand
down on to the table top with a violence that shook the
room. " I do not like to think about such things," he
cried. His voice was slurred and hysterical. " It is not
good to think about them." He stopped and his eyes
narrowed cunningly. He leaned towards me. " What
would you do, Mr. Gansert ? " he asked softly. " What
would you do in my position, eh ? " And suddenly
violent again, he shouted, " You'd do what I'm going to
do. There is no justice—no God. I have lived through
two wars. I have seen evil flourish and the good have

been mown down. I tell you—there—is—no—justice."
Then, speaking faster, so that the saliva was visible at the
corners of his mouth : " But I will make my own justice.
I will fight them with their own weapons, do you understand ? "

Jill went forward and took his hand. " Yes, we
understand, Mr. Dahler," she said. Her voice was quiet
and soothing. " Sit down now. We're all going to have a
drink with you." She picked up the bottle and smiled
at him. " You haven't left us very much, Mr. Dahler."

" No," he said. He swallowed awkwardly and sat
down again. He was suddenly a tired and rather
pathetic old man. He passed his hand wearily over his
face. " I have drunk too much," he whispered. Then,
with sudden renewal of his violence, " But I will not sit
here doing nothing while Knut Jorgensen fills my place.
It was my father built this factory. It was quite small
then. I enlarged it. At his death we had five ships, that
was all. When the Germans invaded Norway, I had a
fleet of fourteen coasters and four tankers. Twenty-three
thousand tons." He seized the tumbler and drank,
spilling the whisky down his chin. " All gone," he
murmured. " Nothing left. Nothing left, damn them—
do you hear ? God ! " He buried his head in his hands.
He was crying openly.

" Go up and get some more glasses, Dick," I said.
" There are several lying about in the chartroom."

As he slid open the door, we could hear orders being
shouted in Norwegian and the sound of the catcher's
engines going astern. Jill looked across at me. " What
are you going to do ? " she asked. " Are you going to
Bovaagen ? "

I hesitated. Dahler lifted his tear-stained face. His
eyes were wild and bloodshot. " Have a drink," he said,
seizing the bottle and pushing it across the table towards
me. He rose unsteadily to his feet. " I want you all to
have a drink with me," he said, raising his glass. " I
want you to drink with me to the—to the damnation of

Jorgensen." He drained his glass and sat down. He looked dazed.

Dick came tumbling down the gangway. " Bill," he called. " Lovaas is coming on board."

" On board *Diviner* ? "

" Yes."

I turned to Jill. " Get Dahler into his cabin. Curtis. Shut him in. He musn't meet Lovaas."

Heavy footsteps sounded on the deck over our heads. "Mr. Gansert ! " It was Lovaas's deep voice. "Mr. Gansert ! Any one below ? "

Jill and Curtis between them had got Dahler out from behind the table. " Yes ? " I called. " Who wants me ? "

" Kaptein Lovaas," came the reply. " May I come down please ? "

I went to the companionway. " What do you want, Captain Lovaas ? " I asked.

" I wish to speak with you," was the reply.

I glanced back into the saloon. Curtis was just shutting the door of Dahler's cabin. " Very well," I said. " Come on down."

A moment later Lovaas's squat bulk filled the companionway. " It is a party, eh ? " he said smiling as he saw the glasses on the table. " That is *god*. I will never refuse a little drink." His face beamed. He was positively genial.

" Whisky ? " I asked, picking up the bottle and one of the glasses.

" Whisky. Yes, that will do very well." His thick, powerful fingers engulfed the glass I handed him. He waited till all our glasses were filled. Then he said, " *Skaal !* "

" *Skaal !* " I replied.

He drained his glass at one gulp and breathed with satisfaction. " That is good whisky, Mr. Gansert."

I refilled his glass. " And why have you come to see me ? " I asked. My tone was not particularly welcoming.

He laughed. " You think I should be angry, eh ? I

have a quick temper, Mr. Gansert. It comes easily. It goes easily. I do not think about what happens at *middag*. There are more important things." He glanced at the others. " Shall we speak alone, Mr. Gansert ? " he asked.

" It's not necessary," I replied sharply.

He shrugged his shoulders. " As you wish." He pulled up a chair and sat himself down. His heavy body in its bottle green jacket seemed to engulf the chair. " I have been to Bovaagen. From there I took a *drosje* to Nordhanger." He pulled a short cigar from his pocket and lit it. " Einar Sandven was not at Nordhanger. Nor was he at Bovaagen. Peer Storjohann was also not at Bovaagen. Both of them have not been to Bovaagen today. Mr. Sunde is a liar." He smiled. It was a fat, roguish smile. But his blue eyes were narrowed and watchful. " But I think you knew that, Mr. Gansert, eh ? "

" Well ? " I said.

He looked around the silent room. " You and your friends are all interested in this man—Schreuder ? You think, as I think, that he is rescued by the divers. He is still alive. In that case he can be traced." He paused and drew on his cigar. " Mr. Gansert,—you are here for a big English metals company. You do not come all this way just to find out about the death of a man who is not even employed by your company. This man, Farnell ; he was an expert on metals. Perhaps Schreuder kill him." He smiled as though at some secret joke. " Perhaps he kill himself. But the man who escape from my boat, he leaves with me those little grey pieces of rock I mention. When I show them to herr direktör Jorgensen, he seize them and is away to Bergen at once. Now I am not a stupid man. I know when a thing is important. When I give them to herr Jorgensen, his eyes light up like my searchlight. Like my searchlight. He is excited, you understand. So I know that this is the clue." He leaned quickly forward, stabbing his cigar at me. " These pieces of rock—they are samples of metal, I think. Is that not so ? "

I said, "You've a right to your own conclusions, Captain Lovaas."

"My own conclusions!" He laughed and slapped his knee. "That is *god*. Very careful. Most diplomatic." Then his voice suddenly hardened. "Please, I do not like long words. Am I right or wrong?"

"You can think what you like," I answered.

"So." He smiled. "I understand. Now, Mr. Gansert. The position is this. You know what this metal is. Herr Jorgensen does not—not yet. By to-morrow he know. But now—at this moment—he does not. You have the advantage of one day. I have thought of this very carefully. This is what I have thought. You know what the metal is. But you do not know where it is. That is why you are here. Now I know something that you do not know."

"What is that?" I asked.

He laughed. "That I keep a secret. Just as you keep seeret the metal. But now, perhaps we talk about business, eh? We can help each other. You are a smart man. Jorgensen is a fool. He take my pieces of metal. But he does not pay me. He only threatens. I could have helped him. But no! He is the great herr direktör. And I am just the best *skytter* in Norway. Now, you are clever. We can work together and when we find this man——"

"How will you find him?" I asked.

"Oh, I have ways of doing things. I will find him all right. Now, what do you say?"

I hesitated. The man was no fool. But what was it he knew that I didn't? And as I hesitated I heard the door of Dahler's cabin open behind me.

"So you will double-cross your master?" Dahler's voice was no longer slurred. It purred.

Lovaas jumped to his feet. "Herr Dahler?" His voice was startled. Then angrily: "Why are you here? What is the little game, eh?"

"You are surprised to see me?" Dahler gripped the

table for support. " Why are you so surprised ? Am I not permitted to visit my own country ? " His voice was suddenly violent. " Who are you to decide whether I shall come here to Bovaagen Hval or not ? Answer me ! What did you do in the war, eh ? I will tell you. You were a collaborator. You went where there was money. You worked for the Germans. You captained one of their——"

" This is enough, herr Dahler," Lovaas roared. " Every one in Norway knows how you sell the secret of the new marine engine—how you arrange the guard up at Finse. Whilst you flee to England, I was working for my country—underground." Lovaas suddenly sat down. He was breathing heavily. " But I do not come here to throw words at you, herr Dahler. I come here to talk to Mr. Gansert."

I glanced up at Dahler. His face was white. He looked utterly exhausted. But there was a strange gleam in his eyes. " Yes. I am sorry." His voice was quieter, almost apologetic. " I talk too quickly. I am upset." He sank down on to the settee beside me. " So Jorgensen has not paid you, eh ? " He laughed softly. The sound was cold, almost gleeful. " And you like money, do you not, Lovaas ? " He leaned quickly forward. " I wonder if you realise what there is in this for the man who knows where the metals are to be found ? I will tell you, Lovaas. There is a fortune. Jorgensen has gone to Bergen with your samples of ore. From there he will fly to Oslo. By to-morrow his experts will be examining those samples. In a day, two days perhaps, he will know. You have realised that. And so you are here to discover what there is in this for you. Is not that right ? "

Lovaas nodded. His eyes were fixed on Dahler. There was a cold, avaricious gleam in them.

" Mr. Dahler," I said. " Will you please leave this to me."

He cocked his head on one side as he peered into my face. " You need not be afraid," he said softly. " I am

finding an ally for you—an ally—for—us—both." He
switched to Lovaas. "Find the man who escapes from
your ship this morning, Kaptein Lovaas. That is all you
have to do. But you will have to be quick. Jorgensen will
not stop at anything once he knows about those metals."

Lovaas smiled. "You do not like direktör Jorgensen,
eh, herr Dahler?"

His emphasis on the direktör was like a goad to Dahler.
"Like him!" he almost screamed. "If I had——" He
stopped abruptly, smiling secretly to himself.

Lovaas laughed. Then he turned quickly to me. "Now,
Mr. Gansert—do we work together, or not? What is your
offer?"

"At the moment, there is no offer, Captain Lovaas," I
answered. "But if you can produce Schreuder—then we
might perhaps talk again."

Lovaas smiled. "I understand. That is what you
English call C.O.D." He rose to his feet. "Very well,
Mr. Gansert. When I have the man, we will talk again."
He paused in the doorway. "Don't forget the diver,
Mr. Gansert."

"He has gone to Bovaagen," I said.

"Ja, he was in Bovaagen. I had some speak with him."
He smiled. "That was very good Scotch. It has make
me warm in here." He slapped his huge belly. "Warm
and friendly, Mr. Gansert."

We watched him go in silence. His heavy footsteps
sounded on the deck. He bellowed an order in Norwegian.
Then all was quiet. The saloon seemed almost empty
without him.

"Did he really have a talk with Sunde, do you think?"
Dick asked.

I didn't answer. I was wondering whether I could use
Lovaas or not.

Dahler struggled to his feet. "I am going on deck,"
he said. "I must have some fresh air." He pushed past
me. His face was deathly pale. He staggered slightly as
he went through the door.

" Follow him up," I said to Curtis. " Don't let him see you. But just make certain he comes to no harm. He's so full of liquor he's just as likely to walk into the sea as on to the quay."

Jill sighed. " Poor Mr. Dahler," she said. " Life hasn't been very kind to him."

A moment later Curtis was back in the saloon. " Dahler all right ? " I asked.

" Bit unsteady. But sober enough to get on to the quay and go on board *Hval Ti*."

" *Hval Ti* ? " I cried.

He nodded and picked up his drink. " That's right. He went straight along to see Lovaas. What do you make of that, skipper ? "

I sat back trying to think it out. " He might have some sort of hold on Lovaas," Dick suggested. " It's clear Lovaas hasn't spent all his life catching whales."

" Jorgensen is more likely than Dahler to have a hold on him," I answered. " We'll have a little chat with our friend when he comes back."

It was over an hour before Dahler returned. And then we had to put him to bed. He was completely drunk. " *Aquavit* on top of whisky," Curtis said, smelling his breath. " We'll get nothing out of him for an hour or two."

Back in the saloon Curtis said, " Sunde is the man we want to see."

I nodded. " If any one knows where Schreuder is, he does."

" Would he have told Captain Lovaas, do you think ? " Jill asked.

" No," I replied. " I don't think so." I was thinking of the scene at the midday meal with Sunde nervously trying to avoid Lovaas's questions. " And if Lovaas had known then he would have adopted a different attitude when he came on board this evening. Lovaas knows something. But it isn't the whereabouts of Schreuder."

Curtis refilled his glass. " The way I see it," he said,
" Sunde could be made to talk."

" How do you mean ? " I asked.

" He wouldn't tell Lovaas anything at Bovaagen. He
was safe there in the village. But if he returns here——"
He looked at me significantly and raised his glass. " After
that little pep talk from Dahler, Lovaas will stop at
nothing. He'll get hold of Sunde and wring the truth
out of him somehow."

I had been thinking the same thing. I suddenly made
up my mind. It was a long time since I'd had to do
things this way. I helped myself to a cigarette and pushed
the tin across to the others. " It will be high tide in
about an hour," I said. " That means the current will
be slack in the cutting behind the whaling station. We
leave our berth here and make a show of putting on sail
as though we were off to Fjaerland. Once outside the
islands, we double back and drift up the cut behind the
factory. We wait for Sunde there."

Curtis nodded. " You're gambling on Sunde having
rowed to Bovaagen."

" I'm certain there should have been two boats in that
inlet we saw this afternoon," I said. " That length of rope
trailing in the water——"

" I quite agree," Curtis said. " But Lovaas may have
the same idea."

" Quite possibly."

He grinned.

" Right," I said. " Dick. Will you go and collect
Wilson and Carter from *Hval To* ? Shout to them. Tell
them we're sailing. I want Lovaas to know. Get the idea ?
Then have the engine started. Curtis. You go up to
the Kielland's place. See the steward or the secretary
of the company. Check that there should be two boats
in that inlet. Also, make certain that Sunde hasn't
returned."

As they hurried on to the deck, I turned to Jill. She
was sitting with her elbows on the table and her chin

resting on her hand. " As soon as we've got Sunde," I said, " we'll make for Fjaerland."

She looked up at me. " I shall be glad when all this is over," she said. She looked past me and stared unseeingly at the emergency lamp in its gimbals. I wondered what was in her mind. She sighed and took a sip at her drink. Then quite suddenly she said, " It amounts to kidnapping him, doesn't it ? "

" Sunde ? " I said. " Well, yes. Shall we say— protecting him from Lovaas. Don't let it worry you. I take full responsibility for it."

" I wasn't worried about that," she replied quietly. " I was just wondering what he would be able to tell us."

There were shouts from the wharf. I heard Dick's voice giving orders to the hands. Then footsteps moved on the deck over our heads. A moment later the engine started. I dived up the companionway. The sun had set. In the cold, dead light of approaching darkness the factory buildings loomed very black above the packing sheds. " Lovaas heard all right," Dick said. " He's up there on the bridge, watching us."

I looked up at the tall bow of *Hval Ti*. I could just see the outline of the bridge. Lovaas was standing with legs straddled on the catwalk. Dick tapped my arm. " Here's Curtis," he said.

I turned. " Well ? " I asked as he came aft to the cockpit.

" You're gambling on a pretty safe bet," he said. " I had a word with an electrician who lives in the steward's quarters. He says there are normally two boats in that inlet. They belong to the station. This afternoon, just after *middag*, he saw Sunde rowing one of them down the cut. He hasn't returned yet."

" Is he expected back ? " I asked.

" Yes. All his things are here. Besides, he's a stranger in Bovaagen. The electrician johnny says there'd be no reason for him to stay there the night."

" Good." I turned to Wilson. " Let go fore and aft,"

I ordered him. " Dick. You and Curtis clear the mains'l cover. Up on peak and throat as soon as you're ready." I picked up the speaking tube. " Half ahead," I told Carter as the last of the warps thudded on to the deck.

As we slid past *Hval Ti*, Lovaas leaned over the rail of the catwalk and hailed me. " Where do you go, Mr. Gansert ? " he asked.

" Fjaerland," I replied. " You'll find me there if you have anything to tell me."

" Okay. *På gjensyn !* " He raised his hand.

The mains'l cover was off now and they were at the halyards. As the grey shadow of the catcher merged into the darkness astern of us, the gaff rose through the topping lifts. A moment later the mains'l was a great splash of white, catching the navigation lights and fading into the blackness above us. Behind us, the lights of the two catchers shone like a village against the dark shape of the factory. As we went out through the islands, we set jib and mizzen. Then I put the wheel over and we swung away to starb'd. The lights of the catchers vanished behind the islands. By the time we reached the inlet leading to the cutting, all the sails were stowed again.

The tide was slackening as we glided slowly into the cut. At the first convenient spot I got a rope ashore and moored up, for I was scared of submerged rocks. *Diviner* swung slowly with the in-running tide until she lay snug against sheer rock, chafing gently at her fenders. We found a way ashore and explored a route along the edge of the cutting to the bridge. My plan was to catch Sunde at the bridge after he had moored his boat.

It was very dark and silent among the rocks. We reached the bridge and stood there, listening to the gurgle of the water as it ran through the cut to some basin further inland.

" Suppose he lands at the quay ? " Jill said.

" I don't think he'll do that," Curtis answered.

" No," I agreed. " He'll want to steer clear of Lovaas."

" For that reason he may stay in Bovaagen," Dick
suggested.

" It's possible," I replied. " But he's no reason to
suspect Lovaas would go to such lengths."

Curtis laughed. " It'd be funny if Lovaas had the same
idea as us."

" If so," I said, " he'd be more likely to pick him up on
the station."

" Maybe," Curtis acknowledged. " Still——" He
caught my arm. " What's that ? "

I listened. But I could hear nothing beyond the gurgle
of the water under the bridge.

" I thought I heard somebody call—up towards the
factory."

" Probably one of the staff," I said. " It's early yet."

We stood there for some time, listening to the sound of
the tide among the rocks. But we heard nothing more.
We returned to the ship then and had food whilst Wilson
and Carter kept watch.

Shortly after eleven, Dick, Curtis and I went ashore.
We were wearing rubber shoes and dark clothes. The
moon was beginning to rise and a faint light illumined
the sky. We settled ourselves behind a broken jumble of
rocks near the bridge. There was no sound from the
cutting now. The tide was at the high and the water
slack. It began to get cold. The light in the sky steadily
whitened. Soon we could see the bridge and the dark
shadow of the cut.

Suddenly, away to my left, I caught the creak of oars.
" Did you hear it ? " Dick whispered. " He's coming up
the cut."

I nodded.

A loose stone rattled down against the rocks away to
our right. I barely noticed it. I was listening to the
creak of the oars, peering through the opaque uncer-
tainty of the light to where I knew the inlet was. But I
could see nothing—only the vague shape of rock and
water. The creaking of the oars ceased. Silence for a

moment ; then the jar of a boat against rock. There was
the clatter of oars being shipped and then, after a pause,
the sound of boots coming towards us across the rock on
the other side of the cutting.

" There he is," Dick whispered in my ear. As he spoke I
caught sight of a human figure moving towards the bridge.
His boots slithered on the rock. The hard sound of his
footsteps became hollow as he stepped on to the plankings
of the bridge. It was Sunde all right. I could recognise
him now. " Soon as he's across the bridge," I whispered
to the other two. I tensed, ready to dart forward and
grab the man.

And in that instant, a sharp command was given in
Norwegian. Sunde stopped. He hesitated, as though
meditating flight. The voice spoke again. It was a strong,
commanding voice. Then two figures emerged from the
shadow of some rocks away to our right. In the pale
light of the still unrisen moon I recognised the squat bulk
of Lovaas. He held a gun in his hand. With him was his
mate, Halvorsen.

Sunde began to reason with him. Lovaas cut him short.
I heard a name that sounded like Max Baker mentioned,
and Lovaas laughed. The two men closed in on the diver.
And then, one on either side, they marched him away
towards the whaling station.

I waited till their shadowy forms had vanished over a
crest of rock. " Quick ! " I said. " We must get between
them and the ship."

" The factory," Curtis whispered. " It's the only place
where we can surprise them."

We struck away to the right then, making a wide
detour and running hard. As far as possible we kept to
gullies in the rock. Our rubber shoes made no sound.
We reached the wire surround that kept the starving
island sheep from getting into the factory and entered by
one of the gates. I paused in the shadow of the office
block and looked back. The sky was getting lighter. The
moon's tip was edging up over the black outline of the

hills. I could just make out three shadowy figures moving towards us across the bare rock.

We went down the cinder track towards the flensing deck. By the boiler house we stopped. The path was narrow here with buildings on either side. Dick and I slipped into the warm darkness of the boiler-room. Curtis stationed himself in a doorway opposite. We agreed a signal for action and waited.

We could hear the sound of their feet on the rock. But they didn't enter by the gate we had used. They kept outside the wire, moving along behind the factory. Curtis slipped out from his hiding-place. "There's another gate," he whispered. " I saw it this afternoon when Kielland was showing us round. It's at the back of the factory. And there's a door leading into the place where the oil vats are."

" Then we'll have to get them inside the factory," I said. " We must stop them getting to the catcher."

We ran down the cinder track and across the greasy surface of the flensing deck. The moonlight was quite bright now. By comparison the inside of the factory was very dark. One solitary light glowed at the far end. It showed the shadowy shapes of the oil vats rising to the roof. I moved cautiously forward and almost immediately stumbled into a thick, evil-smelling mass. It was a pile of waste from the vats, still warm like a dung hill. The place was silent, yet full of the sound of escaping steam. The steady hiss of it seemed as much a part of the building as the heavy warmth and the smell. The sound of the steam was all round us like a singing in the ears. And through it came a faint bubbling sound. It was boiling oil trickling down the gutterings between the vats.

Curtis gripped my arm. On the other side of the building a rectangle of pale moonlight showed the doorway that he had remembered. For a moment it was blocked by shadows. Then it was clear again. Something fell with a crash of iron and there was a muttered curse in Norwegian. Then a torch was shone on the floor. " You take Lovaas," I told Curtis. "Dick. You get the other fellow. I'll look after Sunde."

We closed in on them from behind. It would have been easy if Dick hadn't stumbled against something. There was a clatter. Then the torch swung on to us. I saw Curtis go forward in a diving tackle. The torch spun across the floor. There was the thud of bone on bone as Dick hit out. And then everything was a wild jumble of curses and blows. "Sunde," I called. "Quick. The yacht is down in the cutting." He must have heard me, for I saw his small figure dive for the doorway. Curtis and Dick called to each other. Then we were all through the door and running for all we were worth across the open rock. Sunde was ahead of us, clearly visible in the moonlight. His boots slithered on the smooth rock. We quickly overhauled him.

Behind us came a shout. I glanced over my shoulder. The corrugated iron of the factory was quite white in the moonlight. Lovaas was following us. A stab of orange flame was followed by the whine of a bullet. He was firing as he ran.

We topped a rise and saw *Diviner's* masts. I shouted for them to get the engine started. My breath was coming in great sobs. I was badly out of training. The engine burst into life as we scrambled down the rocks into the cutting. Jill waved to us from the cockpit. Wilson was holding the boat against the outgoing tide on the after warp. "Let go," I told him as we reached the deck. Instantly the tide dragged her clear of the rocks.

Jill caught my arm. "Thank God you're all right, Bill," she said. "Was there shooting?"

"Yes. Lovaas." I called to Carter for full speed and took the wheel. Sunde looked all in. His face was pale. "Get him below," I told Curtis. "And have Jill see to that hand of his." Sunde had a nasty cut across the knuckles. "You all right, Dick?"

"Fine," he replied.

I looked back. Two lines of ripples stretched diagonally across the inlet, marking our progress. A figure appeared on the rock under which we had moored. It was Lovaas. He stood watching us for a moment, quite still and silent. Then he turned and went back towards the factory.

"Take over, will you, Dick," I said. "I want to have a talk with Sunde."

"Where shall I head for, skipper?"

"Sognefjord," I answered. "We're going to Fjaerland."

CHAPTER 6

HERE LIES THE BODY

BEFORE going below to interview Sunde, I went into the chartroom and worked out our course. There was a good deal of cloud about and I wanted to avoid any islands until we opened the entrance to Sognefjord. " Is the log out ? " I called to Dick.

" No," he answered. " Shall I stream it ? "

" Please." I had little tidal information and it was difficult to work out any allowance for drift. But the course we were sailing was marked by two lights and we should have to work on these. I drew in the lines of our course and then went out into the cockpit. Dick had left the wheel and was fitting the log line to its bracket. I held the wheel as he dropped the heavy, finned spinner overboard. The thin line trailed aft in out wake and as he let the last loop drop overboard the log wheel began to turn. He came back and took the wheel. " What's the course ? " he asked.

" North thirty west," I answered.

The Nordhordland coast by Bovaagen was already no more than a low line of rock, shining white in the moonlight. It straggled out in a series of hummocks along our starb'd beam until it thinned to a narrow line and vanished. To the west lay open sea. Ahead of us a light winked steadily. " That's Hellesöy light," I said. " It's on the island of Fedje. Leave that to port, but keep as close to the island as possible. Utvaer light should then be on the starb'd bow. Hold your course for ten miles and then turn to bring Utvaer fine on the port bow. I've marked it out on the chart. Okay ? "

" Fine," he said. " What about watches ? "

" I'll see about that when I've had a talk with Sunde,"

I replied. His face looked pale and very young in the moonlight. A livid bruise was darkening round his eye.

" You got a nasty clip," I said.

" Oh, that," he said, feeling his eye. " It's nothing. It was his head did that."

" Feeling all right ? "

" Fine, thanks. Bit chilly, that's all. Could you pass me a duffle coat ? "

I opened the cockpit clothing locker and flung him one of the coats. " I'll send Wilson up to relieve you," I said and went for'ard to the main hatch.

As I descended the ladder I heard Sunde's voice through the open door of the saloon. " Oi tell yer, Oi don't know nuffink, miss," he was saying. He gave a quick gasp of pain.

" Sorry—am I hurting you." Jill's voice was soft and coaxing. " There, that's fine. I'll have that hand right in no time. Mr. Sunde. I want you to help me."

" Oi'll do anyfink I can, miss."

I stopped at the bottom of the companionway. They had not heard me coming down in my rubber shoes. Through the open doorway I could see Jill's face, very intense, very determined. She was sitting facing the diver across the saloon table and she held his bandaged hand in hers. " It means a lot to me," she said. Her voice was quiet. " A man called George Farnell was killed about a month ago on the Jostedal. He was——" She hesitated. " I was very fond of him, Mr. Sunde. Until the other day I thought it was an accident. I thought he had been alone. Then I discovered that someone had been with him. His name was Schreuder—an Austrian Jew who worked for the Nazis. Instead of going to the authorities and telling what he knew about Farnell's death, he came to Bovaagen Hval, shipped as a hand with Captain Lovaas and tried to escape to the Shetlands. That was the man who jumped overboard from *Hval Ti* yesterday morning—the man you picked up."

" Nah look 'ere, miss. Oi don't know nuffink aba't

it, see. Oi'm just a diver, Oi am. Oi don't want no trouble."

"You had trouble to-night, didn't you?" Jill said slowly. " Major Wright told me all about it. If it hadn't been for Mr. Gansert you might be dead now. You'd have told Captain Lovaas what you know and then he might have disposed of you. You owe your life to Mr. Gansert and the two others who were with him—Major Wright and Mr. Everard. Isn't that so ? "

" Oi 'xpects you're roight, miss," Sunde answered. His voice sounded hoarse and uncertain. " But Oi don't want no trouble, see. There's me partner, too. 'E an' Oi were in it tergever durin' the war an' Oi ain't never done any one dirt, see."

Jill sighed. " Listen, Mr. Sunde. Nobody will get into trouble. All we want to know is where Schreuder has been taken. We want to find him and talk to him. We want the truth about Farnell's death. That's all. We don't want to turn him over to the authorities. We just want to know what happened. Please—won't you help us ? " She took hold of his other hand. " Mr. Sunde," she said and her voice was hardly audible, " I loved George Farnell. I want to know how he died. I've a right to know. This man Schreuder could help. Now please— where is he ? "

The diver hesitated. His dark face was white with exhaustion. He passed his sound hand across his eyes. " Oi dunno. It's all like a ruddy dream, that's wot it is. But Oi ain't tellin' nobody nuffink, see. Not wiva't Oi talk ter me partner first. 'E's the brains of the outfit. Oi'm just a diver. The best ruddy diver in the 'ole of Norway. But it's 'im wot's got the brains. 'E manages the business side, see. I bin wiv 'im ever since 'forty. We was in Oslo when the Germans come in, doin' a bit of salvage work da'n in Pipervika. We went up inter the mountings and joined an army unit wot was forming. But we got smashed up by the Jerries and finds ourselves across the border in Sweden. Well, we starts the great trek—'cross Sweden and Finland, down inter Russia, 'cross Siberia inter China. The British Consul in Hong Kong sent us on ter Singapore and from there we went to India where they put us in a ship ba'nd fer Clydeside. Me partner—'e organises the 'ole ruddy trip." He shook his head and sighed. " We bin through a lot, Peer and Oi. And Oi don't do nuffink wiva't Oi consult 'im first. 'Es always tellin' me—Alf, 'e sez, you ain't got the brains of a louse. Only 'e sez it in Norwegian, see." He grinned. " Peer's a great thinker. Reads books like *Altid Amber*—wot 'e calls the classics."

Jill was leaning forward now and sudden excitement showed on her face. " Alf," she said. " What happened after you and your partner got to England ? "

" Oh, we didn't stay there long, miss. We does a bit o' training up in Scotland and then we're parachuted back inter Norway. Makes yer laugh, don't it—all that trouble ter get a't o' the country—all the way ra'nd the world we goes ter get ter England—an' then they goes an' drops us back inter Norway." He passed his hand across his face again. He was dead beat with weariness. But he couldn't stop talking. He'd reached the stage where he had to talk. " But we comes back wiv more than the rucksack we goes a't wiv. They drops a case o' bren guns an' nitro-glycerine an' grenades wiv us. Oh, we 'as a fine ol' time. We comes da'n ter Bergen an' starts sabotaging ships. To this ruddy day they thinks the ammoonition ship wot blows up by the ol' Walkendorff Tower is due to the carelessness o' German welders." He giggled. " Well, it weren't, see. It was me an' Peer. Blimey, Oi'm a ruddy good diver. Ask any one in the shippin' business in Bergen. They'll say Alf Sunde—his loaf's all wood, but 'e's the best diver in Norway."

" When you were dropped in Norway," Jill interrupted, trying to conceal her excitement " What unit were you with ? "

" Why, the Norwegian Army, miss."

" Yes—but what unit."

" Oh, I see—Kompani Linge."

Jill's eyes lit up. " Put it there," she said, holding out her hand. " We both worked for the same people."

" Wot you, miss—in the Kompani Linge ? " Sunde's whole face had lit up too, infected by her enthusiasm.

" Yes," she nodded. " I was one of their radio operators."

" Blimey," he said, seizing her hand. " Oi thought there was somefink familiar aba't your voice. You was one o' the girls wot used ter give us our instructions on the radio." Again she nodded. " Well, knock me fer a row o' little green apples ! An' I never met you. Ever meet my mate—Peer Storjohann ? Corporal, 'e was."

Jill shook her head. Then she leaned towards him. " Did you know most of the Kompani ? "

" We was trainin' wiv 'em fer nearly a year—that was 1941. We knew most 'o 'em who was in Scotland then."

" Did you know Korporal Bernt Olsen ? "

" Bernt Olsen ? " Sunde's face froze. " Yus—Oi knew Bernt Olsen. Why ? "

" Bernt Olsen's real name was George Farnell. It was Bernt Olsen who was killed on the Jostedal. And Schreuder was with him at the time. Now please—please tell me where you have taken Schreuder. You did pick him up this morning, didn't you ? "

I shrank back farther into the shadows by the companionway, praying that he would tell her all he knew.

" Well—yus, miss." His voice sounded puzzled and uncertain. " That is ter say——Look miss—we picks a man up this morning. All roight. But Oi dunno who 'e is or wot 'e is. If yer wants ter know more aba't 'im—well, you go an' talk ter Peer. 'E's the one ter tell yer. If Olsen's yer boy friend—well, you go an' talk ter me partner."

" Yes, but where will we find your partner ? "

" A-ah." He rubbed his dark chin. " Oi dunno as Oi roightly oughter tell yer that. 'Cos if I told yer that it'd be tellin' where—this man is, wouldn't it now ? "

" But you must," Jill whispered.

" Who must ? " Sunde banged his hand on the table.
" Nah look 'ere, miss. Oi ain't never told nobody nuffink,
see. I bin in the 'ands of the Gestapo once an' Oi never
said nuffink. An' Oi ain't goin' ter talk now, not when a
comrade's life may be at stake."

" Comrade ? How do you mean ? " Jill asked.

" Well, 'e's a comrade, ain't 'e. We was in it tergether."

" The man you picked up this morning ? " Jill seized
hold of Sunde's arm and shook it. " I've already told
you—he's an Austrian Jew who became a naturalised
Norwegian and then worked for the Germans."

Sunde passed his hand wearily over his face again.
" You're gettin' me all mixed up," he said. " Oi don't
know rightly wot Oi'm sayin'. Fair droppin' wiv tiredness,
Oi am. Why don't you let up, miss ? Proper third degree.
Let me get some sleep. Then Oi'll be able ter fink
clearer."

" All right," Jill said wearily.

I went in then. " Hallo, Sunde," I said. " How are
you feeling ? Hand all right ? "

" Not so bad," he answered. " Thanks fer wot you
done, Mr. Gansert. Proper bastard Lovaas is."

" You went to Nordhanger this afternoon ? " I said.
He hesitated. " *Ja*," he answered.

" Had Lovaas been there before you ? "

" Yep. I saw 'im at Bovaagen when 'e come back in
the *drosje*."

" And then you went out to Nordhanger yourself ? "

" That's roight."

" Did Lovaas get anything out of Einar Sandven ? "

" Einar wasn't there."

" Where was he ? "

" I ain't sayin' where 'e is."

" What about his wife ? "

" She won't say nuffink."

" Does she know where Schreuder is being taken ? "

" She might guess. But she wouldn't talk." He got up

and staggered as the table on which he had leaned his weight tilted.

I pushed him back again into his seat. " Sit down," I said. " There are still one or two things I want to ask you. What happened this morning—yesterday morning, rather ? You heard the catcher go by in the mist. You probably saw it. Then you heard shouts and a few minutes later a man was swimming towards your boats. Were you down below then ? "

" No. I'd come up fer a breaver an' a pipe. I'd still got me things on. I was just takin' a little rest."

" And what happened ? You pulled him on board. But what made you up anchor and clear out so quickly ? You must have known the catcher would be searching for the man."

" Well, we knew all aba't 'im, see. So as soon as 'e says——" And then he stopped.

" How do you mean, you knew all about him ? " I asked.

" 'Ere you'll be getting' me sayin' things." He got to his feet again. " Lumme, give a bloke a chance, can't yer ? Oi'm fagged a't an' that's the truth."

I said, " Sit down."

" But look 'ere, guvner—just let me——"

" Shut up," I said. " And listen to me. I want to know where this man Schreuder is. Miss Somers wants to know because she was a friend of Bernt Olsen, otherwise Farnell. She wants to know what happened up there on the Jostedal glacier. And I want to know—for other reasons. What's more, Sunde, I intend to find out."

" Well, yer won't find out from me," he answered sullenly.

" Look," I said angrily, " who got you away from Lovaas, eh ? "

" You did," he responded. " Oi already said 'ow grateful——"

" I don't want your thanks," I interrupted him. " I want information. Can't you see we're your friends ?

We're not going to hurt Schreuder. We just want to know what happened, that's all."

Curtis poked his head round the galley door and said, " Soup up."

" Okay," I said. " Let's have it. Maybe it'll help him to talk."

But it didn't. For two solid hours I sat there like an intelligence officer examining an enemy prisoner. I tried every approach I knew short of hitting him—and I almost did that once I got so exasperated. But it had no effect. Every time I came up against the blank wall of—" You ask my partner."

At last I said, " Well, where is your partner ? "

He gave a wan smile. " If I tol' yer that, yer'd know where the other fellow was nah, wouldn't yer ? "

" Then what's the use of telling me to ask your partner ? " I demanded irritably.

" Tell yer wot Oi'll do," he said suddenly. " Next place we touch at, you put me ashore an' Oi'll telephone a message ter Peer ter meet you some place. Where you makin' fer ? "

" Fjaerland," I said.

" In Sognefjord ? "

I nodded.

" That's easy then," he said. " You'll be off Leirvik in the morning. Put me ashore there an' Oi'll phone me partner an' 'e can meet yer at Fjaerland on 'is way back."

" Back from where ? " I asked.

But he smiled and shook his head. " Yer won't catch me like that, Mr. Gansert. Back from where 'e's been, that's where."

" He's taken Schreuder right up to Sognefjord, has he ? "

" Yes. No 'arm in yer knowing that. You put me ashore at Leirvik an' Oi'll phone Peer to meet yer at Fjaerland."

" And you'll come on to Fjaerland with us ? "

" Okay," he said. " Then me an' me outfit can come back together."

With that I had to be content. At least I had some idea where Schreuder had gone. I let him go to his bunk. He had all the obstinacy of the Cockney driven into a corner. Maybe we could have handled him better. Perhaps if I'd left it to Jill. " There can't be so many places right up the Sognefjord," I said to her. " If this damned partner of his doesn't turn up, we'll make inquiries at every quay in the fjord."

" That'll take us some time," she said.

" Anyway, they probably didn't touch at any of the landing stages," Curtis said. " They probably slipped him in at night on a deserted stretch of the shore."

" Probably," I said. " If only we could make the little diver fellow tell us what he knows."

Jill pressed my hand. " Don't worry about it," she said. " I'll have another session with him in the morning."

Curtis got to his feet and stretched. " By God, I'm sleepy," he said, rubbing his eyes. " Think I'll make some coffee."

At that moment Dick's voice hailed us. " There's a breeze springing up, skipper," he called down. " What about setting some sail ? "

I remembered then that I had forgotten all about relieving him. " Coming," I called back. " Curtis. Give Wilson a shout, will you. We'll be getting sail on her."

Jill caught my arm as I turned towards the companionway. " Thanks for what you did to-day," she said. She was smiling. Her lips were very red against the pallor of her skin. " It made me feel I wasn't alone any more—that I had good friends."

" I didn't do anything," I said and turned away from her quickly. But as I climbed the ladder to the deck I realised again how much more important this was to her than to me—how much more important emotion was than the hard financial gain of the thing.

I felt the breeze as soon as I poked my head out through the hatch. It was icy cold and refreshing. " Sorry,

Dick," I said. " Losing my grip. Completely forgot you hadn't been relieved."

" It's all right," he answered. The moon had disappeared behind cloud and he was just a dark bundle of duffle coat humped over the wheel and outlined against the slight phosphorescence of our wake. " I came to remind you once, but I could hear you grilling the poor devil, so I left you to it. What luck ? "

" He won't talk without his partner's there," I answered angrily. " He's phoning him in the morning."

The others came up then and we hoisted sail. Hellesöy light was already astern, the black bulk of Fedje Island standing in silhouette against the swinging beam. On the starb'd bow another light winked. " Utvaer Fyr ? " Jill asked.

" Yes," I said, looking up at the set of the sails as we leaned over to a fine reaching breeze. " Another eight by the log and we'll alter course. We'll be headed straight for the entrance to Sognefjord then." I called to Dick who was slacking off the weather topping lift. " You and Curtis better turn in and get some sleep. You too, Jill," I said.

" What about you ? " she asked.

" I'll sleep in the chartroom bunk."

I packed them off below—Carter, too. I wanted them to get as much sleep as possible. There would be work to do to-morrow if we were going to try and sail up the Sognefjord. Finally I was alone on deck with Wilson. I stood in the cockpit and leaned my arms on the chartroom roof, gazing up to the tall mainmast where canvas and rigging showed in a dim blur against the night. The whole ship was leaning gracefully, roaring through the water with the lee rail well under and the water seething along the scuppers. It was a fine night for sailing. But there was a frozen bite in the wind. I shivered and went down into the chartroom. " What's your course, Wilson ? " I asked.

" North thirty west," he answered.

I checked it on the chart. We were well clear of all the countless islands that dotted the coast to starb'd of us.

" Wake me when you turn on to your new course," I said and climbed into my bunk. The slight movement of the ship and the rhythmic creak of the rigging lulled me into instant sleep.

When we altered course, I took the wheel and sent Wilson below for some sleep. It was four o'clock and bitterly cold. The wind blew right through me, It seemed incredible that men ever sailed round the Horn. I felt numbed with the cold. The wind was on our port quarter now and the ship rode upright, main and mizzen booms pressed well out to starb'd. I watched Utvaer light come abeam and move across the quarter till it was lost behind a hump of land. The dawn came up out of the east, cold and grey and clear. The mountains emerged from the darkness of the night and gathered round. They were grey and heavy-looking. But except for one, shaped like an enormous sugar loaf, they were not exciting. I might have been in Ireland or sailing up a Scottish loch. There was little sign of snow. These were but the foothills of the giant snow-fields inland. As the light increased the mountains grew blacker. Clouds gathered all across the sky. Grey scuds rolled up and wrapped themselves round the tree-clad slopes. The sky reddened till it blazed in fiery red and then the sun rose like a flaming cannon ball over the mountain tops. The sea boiled red along our sides. Then the scuds gathered thick like fiends of misery to drench all warmth and the bright fire died out of the sky. Suddenly the sun was gone and all was grey again— grey and drab as the mist rolled over us.

And yet it was then that I felt the excitement of the place. I was alone at the wheel of my own ship. And I was entering the longest fjord in Norway. For 130 miles it stretched eastward into the very centre of the most mountainous section of Norway. It was two to five miles wide with towering mountains falling sheer to the water and it was as deep as the mountains were high. I had read all about it and here I was actually sailing into it. And not just sailing for pleasure, but sailing with a purpose. I was going to Fjaerland, which lay under the largest glacier in Europe—580 square miles of solid ice. And there, I hoped, I'd find the truth about Farnell. The reason for his death was as important to me now as the thought of what he might have discovered. I had seen the troubled look in Jill's grey eyes and something of the urgency in her had communicated itself to me.

The cold dampness of the mist should have destroyed my excitement. But it didn't. It increased it. Every now and then some change of the wind would draw aside for an instant the grey veil and I'd catch a glimpse of the mountains, their tops invisible, but their bulk suggestive of the greater bulk behind. This was the way to see new country, I thought. Like a woman, it should be revealed gradually. As I gripped the wet spokes of the wheel and felt the steady thrust of the wind driving *Diviner* deeper and deeper into the mountains, the mystery of the place held me in its spell and I remembered *Peer Gynt* again and the saeter huts high up in the hills.

Lost in my thoughts, the time, usually leaden-footed at the dawn, passed quickly. At eight o'clock the wind shifted abeam and I hauled in on main and mizzen sheets. Then I called Dick and went below to get some sleep. " Watch the wind," I said, pausing with my head just out of the hatch. " You can't see them, but the mountains are all round us."

I must have been dead beat, for I fell asleep at once and the next thing I remember is Curtis shaking me. I sat up at once, listening to the sounds of the ship. We were canted over and moving fast through the water, cutting through a light sea with a crash and a splash as the bows bit into each wave. " When do we reach Leirvik ? " I asked.

He grinned. " We left Leirvik an hour ago," he said.

I cursed him for not waking me. " What about Sunde ? " I asked.

" He made his call."

" Is he back on board ? "

" Yes. I saw to that. I went with him."

" You don't know what place it was he rang ? "

He shook his head. " No. He wouldn't let me come into the call box with him."

" Has Dahler come round ? "

" Yes, he's all right. Got a hangover, that's all."

I got up and went into the saloon. Dahler and Sunde were there facing each other over the remains of a rice pudding. And again I heard the name Max Bakke mentioned—this time by Sunde. His voice was nervous and pitched a shade high. He glanced round as I entered and I was aware of a sense of relief at my interruption.

" Who is Max Bakke ? " I asked as I settled myself at the table.

Dahler rose to his feet. " A business acquaintance of Mr. Sunde," he said quietly. And then to the diver : " We will talk of Max Bakke later." He turned to me. " Has the weather cleared yet, Mr. Gansert ? "

" I don't know," I said. " I haven't been up top."

He went out then and I was left alone with Sunde. " Who is Max Bakke ? " I asked again as I helped myself to bully beef.

" Just somebody Mr. Dahler and I know," he replied. Then with a muttered excuse he got up and hurried out of the saloon.

When I had finished my lunch, I went up on deck. It was raining. The ship was shrouded in a thick mist. The mountains on either side were a vague blur. The wind was abeam, coming in gusts as it struck down invisible gullies in the mountain sides. Dick was at the wheel, his black oilskins shining with water and little beads of moisture clinging to his eyebrows. Jill and Dahler were standing in the cockpit.

" Had a good sleep ? " Jill asked. Her face was fresh and pink and wisps of fair hair escaped from below the peak of her black Norwegian sou'wester. Her grey eyes smiled at me teasingly. She looked little more than a kid.

" Fine, thanks," I answered. " Has it been raining all the time ? "

" All the time," she said.

" It always rains in the entrance to the Sognefjord," Dahler said. " It is a very wet place." He glanced up at leaden sky. " Soon it will be fine. You will see."

He was quite right. By the time we were off Kvamsöy the sun was out. The wind changed and blew straight down the fjord. We took the sails in and started up the engine. The mountains had receded. They were higher and more massive. But they were not impressive. Deep snow capped their rounded tops, but the thickly wooded slopes dropped gently to the quiet waters of the fjord. They basked in the sun, a symphony of bright green and glittering snow, and somehow I felt cheated. They should have been towering and black with precipitous cliffs falling sheer 4,000 feet to the water with the white lacing of giant falls cascading down their granite cliffs. This smiling land seemed much too kindly.

The wind died away. The surface of the fjord flattened out to a mirror. The ship steamed in the noonday warmth and, sitting at the wheel, I found I was hot even with nothing on but a short-sleeved shirt. Dick had turned in and Dahler had also gone below. The rest of the crew lay stretched out on the deck, sleeping in the sun. Jill came aft and sat beside me in the cockpit. She didn't speak, but sat with her chin resting on one hand, gazing ahead towards a wide bend of the fjord. She was waiting for her first glimpse of the Jostedal.

I often think of that afternoon. It was the beginning of something new in my life. As I sat there at the wheel watching the bend of the fjord slowly opening up ahead of us, I was conscious for the first time of someone else's feelings. I knew what she was feeling, felt it as though it were myself. She was dressed in a deep scarlet jersey and green corduroy slacks and her fair hair stirred in the breeze, glinting in the sunlight like spun gold. Neither of us spoke. The only sound was the rhythmic beat of the engine and the gentle stirring of the water thrust aside by the bows.

Gradually the great headland on our port bow slid back, revealing more and more of the mountains to the north. And then suddenly we were clear of the enclosing mass and looking right up to Balestrand and Fjaerlands-fjord. It was a breath-takingly beautiful sight. The mountains rose in jagged peaks, tier on tier for miles inland, crag over-topping crag till they seemed tilted up into the blue bowl of the sky. The dark green of the pines covered the lower slopes and there was emerald in the valleys. But higher up, the vegetation vanished and sheer precipices of grey-brown rock piled up like bastions holding back the gleaming masses of the snow-fields.

" Isn't it lovely ? " Jill whispered. But I knew she wasn't thinking about the wild beauty of the place. She was gazing for'ard across the bows to where the snow-field of the Jostedal glittered like a fairy carpet in the sun and remembering Farnell.

She didn't speak for some time after that. She just sat there, thinking about him. I could feel her thoughts inside me and in some strange way they hurt. Her left hand was flung out along the edge of the cockpit. It was a slender, almost ivory hand, with slender wrist and little blue veins. It was very close to mine where it lay against the warm brown of the varnished mahogany. Without thinking—conscious only of the reflection of her emotion in me—I stretched out my hand to hers. The fingers were cool and smooth, and the instant I touched her I felt close to her—closer than I'd been to any one before. I started to withdraw my hand. But her fingers closed suddenly on mine. And then she looked at me. Her grey eyes were wide and misty. She clung to my hand as though it were something she feared to lose. " Thank you, Bill," she said softly. " You've been a dear."

" He meant so much to you ? " I asked, and my voice came strangely to my lips.

She nodded. " So much," she said. Then she looked

away to the mountains again. " So much—so long ago."
She was silent for a moment, her hand still holding mine.
" Six weeks," she whispered, as though to herself. " That's
all we had. Then he was gone."

" But you saw him later—after the war ? " I said.

" Yes. For a week. That was all." She turned to me.
" Bill. What makes a man throw love away for—for
something a woman can't understand ? You, for instance.
Have you never been in love ? "

" Many times," I answered.

" But not really. Not so that it was more important
than anything else ? "

" No," I said.

Her hand suddenly tightened on mine so that I could
feel her nails biting into my palm. " Why ? " she cried
softly. " Why ? Tell me why ? What was there more
important ? "

I didn't know how to answer her. " Excitement," I
said. " The excitement of living, of pitting one's wits
against every one else."

" Meaning a wife is an encumbrance ? "

I nodded. " For some men—yes."

" And George was one of them ? "

" Perhaps." I hesitated. How could I tell her what
made a man like George Farnell love metals more than
he loved himself. " Jill," I said, " Farnell was an artist.
He knew more about metals than any man I know. And
the driving force in his life was the belief that he could
open up these mountains here and let them pour out their
store of mineral treasure. To the average person he is a
cheat, a swindler, an escaped convict, a deserter. But in
his own mind that was all justified. It was the means to
the end. His art was everything. And he staked his whole
self on the belief that there was metal up here under the
ice that you see now. If he hurt you in the process—well,
that was no more than the hurt he had done himself."

She seemed to understand, for she nodded slowly.
" Everything had to be subordinated to that." She

sighed. "Yes. You're right. But if only I'd known. Then I——" She stopped. "No," she said. "Nothing would have made any difference. It was that singleness of purpose, that inward fire that attracted me." She sat for some time with her eyes closed. Her hand was relaxed and soft in mine. "What about you, Bill?" she asked at length. "You say you've been in love—many times. What was it drove you on?"

I hesitated. "I'm not sure," I said. "Excitement, I think. The excitement of running things, of always being faced with problems that were too big for me until I beat them. I'm a climber—in the industrial sense. I always had to get to the top of the next peak."

"And now?" she asked.

I shrugged my shoulders. "Now I have had my fill—for the moment," I answered. "During the war I reached the top. I exhausted myself, satiated my urge for power. Now I'm content to lie and bask in the sunshine—or was."

"Or was?" The slender line of her brows rose.

"I don't know," I said. "All the time we have been sailing towards these mountains, that old sense of excitement has been rising inside me. If I can find out what Farnell discovered——" I stopped then. It sounded ghoulish this search for a dead man's plunder.

"I see," she said and looked away to the mountains. And then suddenly with a violence I had not expected she said, "God! Why was I born a woman?"

She got up then and went below, and I sat on feeling suddenly alone. The mountains were not so bright and the sky seemed less blue. I knew then—and admitted it to myself for the first time—that I'd missed something in life. I had held its hand for a moment. That was all. It didn't belong to me. I had borrowed it from a dead man.

One of the motionless bodies laid out on the deck stirred. It was the diver. "Sunde," I called.

He sat up and rubbed his eyes. Then he got to his feet

and came aft. " Where are we meeting your partner ? "
I asked.

" Fjaerland," he answered.

" He'll be coming up to Fjaerland in Einar Sandven's
boat ? "

" *Ja*."

" When ? "

" Dunno. Yer see, Oi only left a message fer 'im."

" So he might be coming down the fjord right now ? "

" That's roight." He shaded his eyes and gazed up
the wide stretch of shimmering water. Then he picked
up the glasses. But he shook his head. " Don't see 'im,"
he said.

I took the glasses from him and examined the wide sweep
of the fjord. There were several boats in sight, but none
small enough. I swung the glasses towards the mountains
and the narrowing gap of Fjaerlandsfjord. Fir-clad slopes
dropped steeply to water that was curiously different in
colour—a cold green. On a tongue of land that was green
and fertile the white façade of a big hotel gleamed in the
sunlight. It was all very peaceful and serene. The tongue
of land was Balestrand and a steamer was moving in to
the quay. A white plume of steam showed for an instant
above its red funnel. A moment later the mountains
reverberated to the distant sound of the vessel's syren.

" It is beautiful, eh ? " I looked up. Dahler was
standing beside me.

" Balestrand, isn't it ? " I asked.

He nodded. " The sunniest place in all Sognefjord,"
he said. " The hotel you see is the Kviknes Hotel. It is
very big, and all built of wood. The best hotel in Norway.
I have many happy memories of that place. The Kaiser
used to anchor his yacht here." He turned and nodded
to a low headland over our starb'd quarter. " That is
Vangsnes. If you look there you will see a big bronze
statue. Once I have climbed to the top of him." Through
the glasses I could see it quite plainly, a colossal statue
of a man on a pedestal of rock. " It is the statue of the

legendary Frithjof placed there by the Kaiser. He wished so much to be remembered that man. He put another statue at Balholm. It is of King Bele, one of the Vikings. There is something Wagnerian about the Vikings. If Hitler had travelled more I think perhaps he also would have erected statues in this place."

"It all looks so peaceful," I said, gazing again at Balestrand and the white gables and balconies of the hotel.

"You expected it to be wild and terrible, eh?" He shook his head. "The Sogne is not wild and terrible. But the smaller fjords, yes."

"Wait till we get into Fjaerlandsfjord," Sunde said.

Dahler smiled. "Yes. Mr. Sunde is right. Wait till we are in Fjaerlandsfjord. The water is like ice and the mountains are dark and terrible and at the end the Boya and Suphelle glaciers fall into the fjord. I do not think you will be disappointed when you see Fjaerland."

He was right. Once past Balestrand the gloom of the mountains closed in around us, throwing back the sound of our engine. The sun still shone and the sky was blue. But the day ceased to be warm. In Fjaerlandsfjord the water was a translucent, ice-cold green. It took no colour from the sky. The fjord was nothing but a twenty mile crevice in the mountains. Sheer cliffs of rock hemmed us in. And where there was a slope, it was so steep that the pines that covered it seemed tumbling headlong towards the cold waters. Up frightening, boulder-strewn gullies deep snow pierced by grey, ice worn rock glittered in the sunlight. In places there was snow right down to the water's edge. The streams that cascaded like white lace down the gullies, burrowed under these patches of snow to form fragile bridges. Small black and white birds with long orange beaks flew from crevice to crevice along the rocks. The gloom of the place was something that only Milton could have described. It closed in on us like the chill of fear and silenced all conversation.

For an hour we ran up that narrow fjord. There was no

breath of wind. The ice-green water was flat like glass and in it was mirrored the gloom of sunless pines and sheer, dark rock. Then we rounded the last bend and saw the Jostedal. It stood high up at the end of the fjord, very white in contrast to the green of the water and the still brighter green of valley grass bathed in sunshine. It was a beautiful, terrifying sight. A giant steeple of rock rose like a bastion, black against the blue sky. That alone seemed to hold back the vast deeps of snow behind it. And on either side the glaciers tumbled down to the fjord. To the right was the Suphelle—a piled-up mass of blue-green ice like a frozen wave breaking over the lip of the snow-field into the valley below. And on the left the narrow Boya glacier ribboned down a gully as though to swamp the little settlement below.

The colour of the fjord changed. The green of the water became more livid until it looked like some chemically-coloured liquid. It was the coldest colour I have ever seen. The gloom of the mountains on either side of us contrasted oddly with that colour. And even more odd was the sudden basking warmth of Fjaerland and the cold ice-green and white of the frozen snows behind it.

As we ran into the quay, Dahler gripped my arm. " Look," he said. " They are building a boat. And they build him just the same as they build boats two thousand years ago."

Just beyond the quay lay the yellow skeleton of a boat. Five men were working on it. " They are using nothing but axes ? " Jill said.

" That is so," Dahler answered. " They use nothing but the axe. That is the way the Vikings build their boats. And up at Fjaerland they have always built their fishing boats that way. They make carpets from local wool and stockings and jerseys—all by the method and in the pattern that they have always used. Nothing is new here —except the hotel and the steamers."

We ran past a little wooden church, past the hotel, half-hidden in trees, and in to the wooden piles of the jetty. " Is that your partner's boat ? " I asked Sunde, pointing to a small tock-a-tock lying just beyond the quay. But he shook his head. His partner hadn't arrived and as though that were an omen, I suddenly had the feeling that things weren't going to go well.

I left the others and went up to the hotel alone. A waitress in national costume of black with embroidered bodice and frilled lace blouse stood in the entrance hall. " Is Mr. Ulvik in the hotel ? " I asked.

She shook her head and laughed. " *Et öyeblikk så skal jeg finne eieren.*"

I waited. There were tiers of postcards, all of ice and snow and violent, blasted crags. Behind the porter's desk hung hand-made rugs in brilliant colours, belts stamped out of leather and strangely-shaped walking sticks. On the desk were several pairs of slippers made by hand from what I later discovered to be reindeer. They had originally been made by the inhabitants for walking on frozen snow, but were now produced for the tourist trade on which the village lived. In a corner of the hall were piled rucksacks, rope, climbing boots, ice axes and a pair of skis. The atmosphere of the place was so different from the islands.

Footsteps sounded on the stairs. I looked up. A short, fat little man hurried towards me. He wore a black suit and white collar and looked as out of place as a clerk in a gymnasium. He held out a white, podgy hand. " You are Mr. Gansert, perhaps," he said. There was a gleam of gold fillings in his wide smile.

" Are you Mr. Ulvik ? " I asked.

" Yes. That is me." He spoke English with a slight American accent. " Come. We will go into the lounge. You have had tea ? "

" Not yet," I said.

" Then we have some tea." He took hold of my arm and led me into a room where walls and ceiling were delicately hand-painted. The place was empty. " It is early in the season," he said. " Fjaerland is too cold yet. The hotel is only just open." He ordered tea and then

said. " Now, Mr. Gansert, I must tell you that I have
not got what you want. Our application for the exhumation of this man, Bernt Olsen, is—how do you say it ?—
quashed."

" Quashed ! " I exclaimed. " Why ? "

He shrugged his shoulders. " I do not know." The
waitress came in with a tray laden with cakes and buttered
toast. When she had gone, he said, " First, everything
goes well, you understand. I see the doctor at Leikanger.
We go to the police. They say there will be no difficulty.
They take a telphone to Bergen. I am in Leikanger all
yesterday. The application is granted and I make the
necessary arrangements. And then, just as I am leaving
to catch the steamer, the police tell me the arrangements
must be cancelled. They have the telephone from Bergen
to say that it has been decided after all that there are
no reasons for the exhume."

" Look," I said angrily. " I told you I didn't care how
much it cost. Did you get on to lawyers at Bergen ? "

His white hand with its fat little fingers caressed my
arm as though he were a doctor soothing a fractious
patient. " Please believe me, Mr. Gansert. I do everything that is possible to do. I telephone our lawyers. I
telephone to a man very high in the police at Bergen. I
even telephone Oslo, to one of the members of the
Storting. But it is impossible. Something is blocking it.
It is against policy, I fear."

Against policy ! That could mean only one thing.
Jorgensen had used his influence to prevent the exhumation. Why ? That was what puzzled me. Why was he
scared to have Farnell's body exhumed ? Had the man
been murdered ? And had Jorgensen had something to
do with it ? I drank my tea in silence, trying to figure it
out. Jorgensen wouldn't directly involve himself in a
thing like that. But where big money was involved I
knew these things could happen—they could happen in
England and they could happen in Norway. " Who is
blocking the application ? " I asked Ulvik.

"I do not know," he answered. "I try to find out. But every one is very careful. I think somebody very important."

I looked at him. He fidgeted nervously under my gaze. Had he been bought? But I dismissed the thought. I didn't like him. But he was the company's agent. And the company was shrewd enough not to employ foreign representatives who could be bought. But still, the money might be bigger than was usually available for bribes.

"I do everything I can," he declared as though reading my thoughts. "Please believe that, Mr. Gansert. I have represented your company for fifteen years here in Norway. I work with the resistance. I build up contacts even while the Germans are here and Britain is losing the war. I do not often fail in anything. But this—this is something very strange. There is important business involved, I think."

I nodded. "It's not your fault," I said. I looked out of the window to the ice-green waters of the fjord. A man was fishing from a rowing boat. The sunlight, striking on the green of the opposite shore, had the brittle quality of evening. Why didn't they want Farnell's body examined? I was now more convinced than ever that the answer to the mystery lay in the little graveyard by the church we had passed. I pushed back my chair. "You've brought some money for me?" I asked.

"Yes—yes, of course," he answered, smiling with the relief of having been able to do something. "I have it here in my pocket all ready for you. One hundred thousand kroner. Will that be sufficient?"

"How much is that?"

"A kroner is a shilling." He brought out a thick pocket book. "There," he said, handing a pile of notes over to me. "That is five thousand pounds. Will you please sign this—for the accounts of my agency, you know."

I counted the notes and signed. Then I got to my feet. "It is enough, eh?" he asked. He was like a puppy wriggling for a pat on the head.

"It'll do for the moment," I answered.

" Now please, what will you wish me to do ? Sir Clinton Mann wrote me that I was to place myself unreservedly at your disposal. Anything I can be of service to you with, Mr. Gansert——"

" Go back to Bergen," I said, " and sit on the end of a telephone. What's your number ? "

" Bergen 155 102."

" Good. And find out for me just who blocked that exhumation order."

" Yes. I will do that. And I will wait for you to telephone me." He bustled after me as I went to the door. " I will leave to-night if you do not mind. There is a boat going to Balestrand to-night. It is much warmer at Balestrand. You have your boat here, eh ? Do you go to Balestrand ? "

" I don't know," I answered. An idea was forming in my mind. Thank God he was leaving to-night.

" Then I wait for you to telephone me, please. Anything I can do——"

" Yes, I'll telephone you," I said and went down the steps to the driveway.

At the road I hesitated. But instead of turning left towards the quay, I turned right and walked slowly towards the church.

It stood alone on a slight mound some distance beyond the hotel. Its white paint caught the slanting sunlight. It was a little fairy church, so bright and gay against the gloomy background of the fjord winding down to the Sogne. Above it, up a long, boulder-strewn valley, towered the mountains, cold and forbidding, their snows crystal white. Beyond the graveyard, a torrent went rushing down to the fjord. I opened the gate and went up the path towards the church, searching the graves as I passed. Some had stone monuments, but many were marked with small wooden crosses on which the names of the buried were painted in black. The shadow of the church lay right across the graveyard and out to the edge of the fjord. In the sunlight beyond, I found what I was looking for—a freshly painted cross with the name *Bernt Olsen* on it. It was just as it had been in that newspaper cutting—the small white cross and the church behind. What the cutting had not shown was the towering mountains beyond and the atmosphere of the place—so remote and chill. I remembered Farnell out in Rhodesia. I remembered him talking of places like this, talking endlessly of the snows and the glaciers up in the mountains and the narrow fjords as the lamp-smoke thickened in our hut and the whisky got lower in the bottle. It had all seemed so remote out there, for at that time of the year the land had been dry as dust under a blazing sun. But now I understood what he had been talking about. And I was glad to know he'd been buried here in the land he loved and for whose riches he had sacrificed everything.

As though I had spoken my thoughts aloud, a voice said softly—" This is where he would like to have been buried, isn't it ? "

I turned. It was Jill. Her face was very pale and her lips trembled. I think she had been crying, but I was not sure. " I was thinking just that," I said. I looked round at the fjord and the mountains. " This was what he lived for." And then I looked again at the little cross stuck in the heaped-up mound of earth that was so fresh that the sods had not yet bound together to form a solid covering of grass. Had he died a natural death—or had he been murdered ? Why had the application to exhume the body been blocked ? The answer lay right there. I had only to lift the sods and dig down to the coffin . . . I glanced at Jill. She had been prepared to face a legal exhumation. There was no difference really. And yet . . . " He'll be happy here," I said quickly, for fear she would divine my thoughts.

" Yes," she murmured. " Thank you for bringing me, Bill." Her lip was trembling again and she started off down the graveyard path to the gate. I followed her and as we reached the road she said, "When is the exhumation ? "

" There isn't going to be one," I answered. " The application has been refused."

She sighed. I think it was with relief. " I'm glad," she said. " There seems no point in disturbing him now."

I looked at her. " Don't you want to find out whether it was an accident or not ? "

" No," she answered. " Nothing that we do can bring him back to life."

I didn't say anything and we crossed the wooden planking of the quay. Dick and Curtis and Sunde were waiting for us as we came on board. " Well ? " asked Curtis.

" No good," I said. " The application has been blocked at the top. There's somebody doesn't want a post-mortem examination."

" Jorgensen ? "

" Maybe," I answered and ordered the boat to be cast off.

" Hold it," Dick said. " Dahler's up at the hotel, 'phoning."

" Who's he contacting ? " I asked.

But Dick didn't know. And when Dahler came on board he gave no explanation. " I am sorry if I delay you," he apologised.

" It's all right," I answered. " I'm only moving just down the fjord." I ordered Wilson to cast off and had the engine started.

The sun set as we left Fjaerland. For a moment the snows of the Jostedal high above the village were tinged with pink. Then the light faded and the fjord was a dark, cold gash in the mountains, its waters no longer green, but inky black. Night fell quickly and lights began to show in the huddle of wooden buildings round the quay.

Just beyond the headland, not a mile from the village, I steered the boat in to a wooden landing stage. Above it, perched precariously on a little plateau of green grass, stood a fisherman's solitary hut. We moored the boat to the rotting piles and I ordered the dinghy to be cleared.

" What's the idea ? " Curtis asked.

I glanced round. Jill was standing by the cockpit, watching us. " I didn't want to lie at Fjaerland with my representative staying up at the hotel," I said. " I had a bit of a row with him." Then I asked Jill to take Wilson and get some food prepared.

As soon as she had gone below, Curtis said, " Is your representative a short man in a black suit, with a round, chubby face ? "

" Yes," I said.

" Well, he boarded a fishing boat and went off down the fjord about ten minutes before you came back to the boat with Jill." He looked at me searchingly. " What are you up to, Bill ? " he asked. And then as I didn't answer immediately, he said, " You're planning to dig Farnell's body up, aren't you ? "

" Yes," I said. " The church is quite isolated. The moon rises just after midnight. We'll have four hours."

He caught hold of my arm. His eyes were suddenly angry. " You can't do it," he said.

" Can't do it ? " I laughed. " Don't be a fool. It's quite safe. There'll be nobody around. And even if we are interrupted, they won't know who we are. That's why I didn't want to moor up at Fjaerland."

" I'm not worried about your being discovered," he answered. " It's Jill I'm thinking about."

" Jill ? " I remembered how she had sighed and said she was glad there was to be no exhumation. " Jill mustn't know," I said.

" God almighty, man," he cried. " She's been standing there white as a sheet ever since you ordered the dinghy to be cleared. Do you think she doesn't realise why you've moored up here ? "

" I don't think so," I said. " Are you going to tell her ? "

" Of course not," he answered.

" Right," I said. " Now let's get on with clearing the dinghy."

But he caught hold of my arm and swung me round. I could feel his fingers like a vice on my flesh and the sudden thought crept into my mind that he was in love with Jill. "Are you going through with this?" he demanded angrily.

"Yes," I said. "Oh, for God's sake, Curtis—don't be childish. Jill needn't know anything about it. But I must know how Farnell died."

"Why?"

"Isn't it obvious? If he was murdered, then Schreuder knows the location of the mineral deposits. If the body bears no indication of a struggle, then perhaps the secret has died with him. I must know the answer to that."

"You must know the answer!" he sneered. "Can't you think of anything else but your bloody mineral grabbing? The girl wants the body left alone. She doesn't want the poor sod disturbed to satisfy your damned avarice."

"It's not my avarice," I replied hotly. "Work for a hundred thousand men could be built up out of those deposits—if they exist. And I mean to find out. Jill needn't know. And if she does discover it, then I think she'll understand. You needn't have anything to do with it if you're squeamish about corpses."

Curtis laughed. "I'm not squeamish," he said. "I'm thinking of the girl. If you're going on with this, then she must be told. She must give her permission."

"I'm not asking her," I answered shortly.

"But she's a right to be consulted."

"Right?" I said. "She's no rights in the matter at all."

"I tell you she has. She has the right——"

I caught hold of his arm. "Listen, Curtis," I said. I was tired of all this ridiculous argument. "Who's captain of this boat?"

He hesitated. "You," he answered.

"And who's in charge of this expedition?"

"You are," he answered reluctantly.

" Right," I said. " Now get that dinghy slung over the side. We meet up here on deck at eleven-thirty—the three of us ; you, Dick and I. Warm clothes and rubber shoes. I'll look after the girl."

For a moment I thought he was going to argue. But the long habit of obedience to command was stronger than his sudden outburst of conscience. He turned and began to haul the dinghy out over the rail.

At supper that night everybody seemed unnaturally quiet. Jill ate in silence, her eyes on her plate. Only Dahler was talkative. I wondered who he had telephoned from the hotel. " What is your next move, Mr. Gansert ? " he asked me quite suddenly.

" Wait for Sunde's partner," I answered.

" It is a pity Mr. Sunde will not talk without his partner." His eyes met mine. Some devil of laughter was there in the dark pupils. He glanced at Sunde.

The diver looked up quickly. Then his eyes fell to his plate again. He seemed nervous.

Dahler smiled. An unnatural excitement emanated from the man.

After the meal, I got every one off to bed. It had been a long day and they were tired. Moreover, the sudden transfer from coast to mountain air had made us all sleepy.

I went and lay on my bunk. Sunde, who was sharing my cabin, came in shortly afterwards. He lay tossing for a long time. I fought off the desire to sleep and lay staring into the darkness. The ship was silent. There was no movement, no sound of water lapping against the hull. The utter stillness seemed unreal. Sunde began to snore. I thought of the grave in the churchyard under the mountains. There was something frightening about the thought of opening it up. Perhaps Curtis had been right. Perhaps we shouldn't do it. Body-snatching was something revolting. But we weren't body-snatching. We were trying to get at the truth of a man's death. The desire for sleep left me then and I lay in the dark, wondering how the hell I was to tell whether Farnell had died a natural death without a doctor to examine the body.

But I had made up my mind to see Farnell's body and at eleven-thirty I rose quietly and slipped on my rubber shoes. Dick was waiting for me up on deck. A faint light showed behind the mountains. The moon was rising. We only had one pick and one shovel. I got these from the lazaret and lowered them into the dinghy which Dick had pulled alongside. Curtis came up and joined us. I got my torch from the chartroom. "In you get," I said to Dick. He lowered himself quietly over the side. Curtis followed. Then a hand gripped my arm. I swung round. Dahler was standing beside me. "I have been waiting for you," he whispered. "I also wish to see the body."

"How did you know what we were going to do?" I asked him.

He smiled. I could see the line of his teeth in the dark. "You are a man of determination, Mr. Gansert," he replied. "You do not come all the way to Fjaerland for nothing."

I nodded to the boat. "Get in," I said.

I followed him down. Dick and Curtis had the oars out. I pushed the boat clear. The outline of the yacht's hull vanished in the darkness as the rowlocks creaked to the thrust of the oars. The jagged rim of the mountains sharpened to a black line against the moonlit sky as we rowed towards Fjaerland. We rounded the headland and hugged the line of the shore. There were no lights showing at Fjaerland now. There was a deathly stillness in the air. The only sound was the creak of the oars and the gurgle of water coming down from the mountains.

As the sky brightened and our eyes became accustomed to the darkness, we were able to make out the dark line of the shore and the huddled mass of buildings round the quay at Fjaerland. The sound of water grew louder as we approached the torrent that ran into the fjord below the church. And then we saw the church itself, standing black and silent on its mound. I directed the boat towards the shore. We spoke in whispers. The bows suddenly jarred against a stone and then grated on pebbles. We clambered out and slipped the painter round a rock. Then we started up the slope to the graveyard.

That graveyard—it is difficult to describe how it felt in the half darkness with the mountains towering over it. It was just like any other graveyard really, and yet . . . The trouble was we came as thieves in the night. And a guilty conscience isn't the best companion in a graveyard. We located the newly painted cross and fresh sods of Farnell's resting place without difficulty. I seized hold of the shovel and cleared the turves and pulled up the cross. Then we began to dig. The ground below the surface was hard as iron. We sweated and grunted as we swung the pick head into the frozen soil. Slowly, very slowly, the narrow pit opened up. It was hard, back-breaking work. We stripped to our vests and sweated in the chill air, our breath steaming.

Then the moon rose over the lip of the mountains. The snow shone white and cold. The piled-up ice of the Suphelle glacier glistened a cold green. The waters of the fjord looked blacker than ever. As I stood back and handed my pick to Curtis, I glanced past the church to the village. All was quiet as the grave. Yet I had the awful feeling that we were being watched, that at any moment irate villagers might rush to protect their little graveyard from this sacrilege. " See anybody ? " Dick asked in a whisper.

" No," I answered. My voice was harsh.

He leaned on his shovel and watched the village.

" Give me that," I said and took the shovel from him and began lifting out the earth loosened by the pick Curtis wielded.

Every time I paused I was conscious of the moonlight and the silence. The little torrent hissed and gurgled over the boulders to the fjord. The stillness of the mountains stood over us, cold and remote. We must be visible for miles.

The earth became softer, less frozen. The grave pit deepened until suddenly the pick struck wood. In a few minutes we had cleared the soil from the rough pine coffin. Then we bent down and lifted it out of its shallow grave.

And at that moment Dahler stiffened beside me. " Somebody is coming," he hissed.

" Where ? " I whispered.

His head was turned towards the stream. " Something moved down there."

" You're getting jumpy," Dick whispered.

I turned back to the coffin. Curtis had the pick again. " Come on," I said. " Open it up."

But he didn't move. He, too, was staring down towards the stream where it ran into the fjord. " There is some-body there," he said. " Look ! " He seized my arm and pointed.

In the moonlight I saw a figure moving across the bed of the stream. It was white in the moonlight—a human figure dressed in white. It stopped and looked up towards us. Then it began to move again. It crossed the torrent and started up the slope.

" Who can it be ? " Dick whispered.

I caught a glimpse then of a scarlet jumper and I knew who it was. " Open up that coffin," I snapped at Curtis.

But he didn't move. A moment later Jill stopped, facing us. Her breath came in great sobs of exertion and her eyes were wide in her white face. She was wearing a light-coloured raincoat. It was torn and muddied. Her slacks were wet to the knee.

I stepped forward. " You shouldn't have come," I said.

But she was staring at the coffin, lying aslant on the pile of loose earth. " How could you ? " she breathed. And she began to sob uncontrollably.

I looked at her torn clothing and realised how she must

have hurried through the darkness and the moonlight along the rough foreshore. " I had to," I answered roughly. Then I turned to Curtis. " Open it up," I said.

" No," he answered. " You shouldn't have done this without her permission."

" If you won't do it, I will," I said, and seized the pick from him. I heard Jill cry out as I brought the point down into the crack between the top and sides. With a splintering of wood, I prised up the top. It came away in one piece. Few nails had been used. I ripped it up with my hands and flung it back. Curtis had pulled Jill away. Her face was buried against his chest and she was sobbing. Very gently I pulled the white shroud away from the body.

Then I shuddered. The body was a mangled mass of frozen blood and flesh. The head was smashed in, the neck broken and the left arm and hand crushed to a pulp. I straightened up. How was I to tell whether Farnell had had died by accident or design ? The body was so broken and destroyed that I couldn't even recognise it as Farnell. It wasn't decomposed at all. The frozen ground had seen to that. It was just that there was nothing left by which to recognise him. The face was pulp and the hand . . . I suddenly bent down. Why had that hand been so badly battered ? Of course it could have happened naturally. He'd fallen a great height. Boulders might have crashed down on top of him. But I'd seen a lot of accidents— accidents in mines where men had been crushed by fallen rock. Hardly ever had I seen a man as badly smashed up as this. It was almost as though the body had been deliber- ately smashed in such a way that it wouldn't be recog- nisable. That left hand. I picked up the broken, lacerated member. The torn flesh and congealed blood were stiff and frozen. In the light of my torch I saw that the bones of the fingers were all crushed and the splinters stuck out like sharp teeth from the flesh. I examined the little finger. The top two joints were missing, just as Farnell's had been missing. But a long sinew stuck out from a torn joint.

A sudden surge of excitement swept through me. What other identification marks had Farnell got? I couldn't think of any, but surely there must be something, some mark on his body. I turned to Jill. "Jill," I said. "Is there anything by which you would know George Farnell, other than by his face and the little finger of his left hand?"

Something in my voice must have communicated itself to her, for she stopped sobbing and turned her head towards me. "Why do you want to know?" she asked.

"Because I want to know if this is, in fact, the body of George Farnell." I had spoken slowly, and as I finished she straightened up and came towards the coffin.

I pulled the shroud over the corpse. "No," I said. "It's not a—a very pretty sight. Just tell me—will you? Anything by which I can identify him?"

"Yes," she said. Her voice was quite clear now. "He had marks on the soles of his feet. The Nazis caught him once here in Norway. They beat the soles of his feet. But he wouldn't talk and they released him."

I looked down at the coffin. Both feet were intact— one was twisted round where the ankle had been broken, that was all. I forced the stiffened right leg out of the coffin and shone my torch on to the sole of the foot. It was unmarked. So was the other. I looked up at Jill. Her eyes were bright with excitement. "Are you certain about that?" I asked.

"Yes. Yes, of course, I'm certain. They were like white scars. Are they there?"

"No," I said.

"And there was the mark of a bullet under the right armpit."

I forced up the right arm. There was no mark under the armpit.

I stood up then and crossed over to her. "Jill," I said. "You're quite certain about those identification marks?"

"Yes," she answered. She clutched at my arm. "That's not George then—is it? That can't be George if those marks aren't there."

"No," I said. "That is not the body of George Farnell. It's somebody else's body."

"But—but how did it get there?" Curtis asked.

I looked at him. Life had been such a very straight-forward business for him. "That man has been murdered," I said.

"But Farnell's—papers were found on the body."

"Exactly," I said and glanced at Jill. Her eyes met mine and I saw that she had understood the point. I turned to Curtis. "The body has been mutilated in such a way that it would be identified as Farnell's if the necessary papers were found on it."

"But why?" he asked.

"What's it matter why?" Jill said. "He's alive. That's all that matters."

I looked at her and felt a deep pity. That was all that mattered, was it? For the moment, perhaps. But later . . .

"Where do you think he'll have gone?" she asked.

"That we must find out from Sunde," I said.

"Sunde?" Her face looked blank for a moment and then she stared. "You mean the man that jumped over-board from the catcher——"

"Yes," I said. "That was Farnell." I nodded to the body at my feet. "This is Schreuder."

"Then Farnell——" Curtis checked himself.

I nodded. "Looks like it," I said. "Now let's put the body back and then we'll go and talk to Sunde."

CHAPTER 7

THE SAETER HUT

THE SHOCK of discovering that the body was Schreuder's and that Farnell was alive seemed to leave Jill completely stunned. She stood quite still, with a dazed expression on her face, as we put the coffin back and filled in the grave. The frozen slabs of earth rattled on the thin pine lid with a hollow sound. We replaced the sods and the little wooden cross with Bernt Olsen's name on it and then went down to the boat. Nobody spoke as we rowed back to the ship. Occasionally I glanced at Jill seated on the thwart opposite me. Her face was set and expressionless. I wondered what was going on in her mind. That it had been a shock was understandable. But there was something in her eyes and in the set expression of her face that puzzled me. There should have been excitement and happiness. But there wasn't. Only that dazed look that stirred something deep inside me. It hurt me to see her like that.

That I think was the first intimation I had that I was in love with her. I didn't consciously realise it at the time. That came later. But I felt disturbed and unhappy. She was so tense and strained. She ought to have been happy —happy at the thought that he was alive. But she wasn't happy. I remembered the urgency in her when she had first met me in that Thames-side pub. She had wanted so much to get to Norway and see his grave. And now . . . I didn't know what to make of it. Schreuder had been murdered—and by Farnell. Was that what hurt her so ? Or was it the knowledge that he would do anything—lie, cheat, desert, even murder, for the thing that had driven him all his life ? I suddenly realised how little she could have meant to him. She was just a side show—a pleasur-

172

able moment in a man's hard struggle to achieve what he had set his heart on. There was that conversation we had had coming up the Sognefjord. What was it she had asked me ? *What makes a man throw away love for something a woman can't understand ?*

I looked at her again. She was gazing out across the bows to where *Diviner's* spars showed white against the black background of the pines shadowed by the mountain-side. There was a stony, withdrawn look in her face. It was no longer the face of a girl. It was the face of a woman, tired and somehow forlorn. And I realised then that perhaps Farnell dead was more attractive to her than Farnell alive.

Jill wasn't the only one who was affected curiously by the discovery that Farnell was alive. Dahler sat in the stern, his sound hand gripping the gunn'l so that the knuckles showed white. He was excited. I could see it in his eyes, which glinted strangely in the moonlight. His face was taut, his whole body tense. He sat in the boat as though he were riding a horse in the Grand National. The lines at the corners of his mouth were etched deep and his lips were drawn back so that his teeth showed. His face looked cruel—cruel and excited.

As soon as we were on board I had the engine started and cast off. I got Wilson and Carter on deck and, leaving them to run the boat down the fjord, I went below to the saloon. The others were already there. Dick was pouring whisky into tumblers. Jill was seated on one of the settees, very still and silent, her face quite white against the dark red of the mahogany panelling. Dahler was standing in the doorway of his cabin, his hand plucking at his jacket and his eyes bright. " Get Sunde," I said to Curtis. " I want to talk to him."

" There is no need." Dahler's voice was tense.

Curtis stopped and turned. We all looked at Dahler.

" I can tell you all you wish to know," Dahler said. He sat down with a quick movement and leaned his weight on his withered arm. " Sit down, please," he said. " Mr.

Sunde will not talk to you. He will do nothing without his partner. But to-day I have spoken with him. I used some persuasion—a little smuggling he has been engaged in with a man I know."

" Was that why you telephoned from the hotel at Fjaerland ? " I asked.

" Max Bakke ? No."

" Who did you telephone then ? "

He smiled. " That is my business, you know. Come, sit down—all of you, please." He was leaning forward and there was that same strange glint in his eyes that I'd noticed in the boat. It was a savage, triumphant expression. I felt a shiver run down my spine. This cripple was suddenly in charge of the situation, dominating us all.

I sat down. " You know where Farnell is ? " I asked.

" That is better," he said. " Yes. I know where Farnell is."

" Where ? "

" He will be up in the mountains by now," he replied. " He is trying to escape. There is a warrant issued for his arrest."

I looked at Jill. She was sitting motionless, staring at Dahler. " How do you know ? " I asked.

" What did you expect Jorgensen to do ? " he demanded. " He must find Farnell. So, he uses the police."

" But what is he to be arrested for ? " Curtis asked.

" For murder," Dahler answered.

" But nobody but ourselves knows that the body in that grave isn't Farnell's," I pointed out.

He laughed. It was a quick, sharp sound and it grated in the expectant silence. " You do not quite understand. Farnell is Schreuder now. It is Schreuder who is being arrested—he is to be arrested for the murder of Farnell."

" But——" I hesitated. The irony of it ! " Does Jorgensen know that it is Farnell who is alive ? "

" But, of course. As soon as Kaptein Lovaas describe the man who escapes from his ship, Jorgensen knows it is

Farnell. The little finger, you remember? No man can hide that. You did not know it was Farnell, eh?" He smiled as though it amused him.

" No," I said. " And nor did you."

" Oh, but I did," he answered. " I knew as soon as Mr. Sunde admitted that his partner and Einar Sandven had helped the man."

" But how?" I asked.

" How?" His voice became suddenly harsh. " Because Schreuder was an Austrian Jew and had worked for the Germans. You forget that Sunde and Storjohann were of the Kompani Linge. Old Einar Sandven was also in the resistance. It had to be Farnell—Bernt Olsen, as they knew him. Listen. You wish to know how that message was placed in the whale meat. Well, I will tell you. Farnell came by boat from Fjaerland to Bovaagen after he had killed Schreuder. He came to Bovaagen because he had friends there who had hidden him during the war. He stayed at Nordhanger with Einar Sandven and his wife. It was Sandven who placed the package in the whale meat. It was Sandven who approached Kaptein Lovaas and got Farnell shipped as a hand on *Hval Ti*."

I stared at him. I had no doubts about the truth of what he said. It all fitted in so easily with what I knew. It couldn't have happened any other way. Farnell had probably met Sunde or Storjohann at the whaling station when he was reporting for duty on board the catcher. Then, when his plan to get to the Shetlands failed, he had remembered the divers. He had probably known where they would be working and had planned his desperate escape from the catcher with that fact in his mind. Yes, it all fitted in. And I cursed under my breath to think that I had been talking to Lovaas on board his catcher and the man, locked up in the cabin below decks, had been Farnell himself. If I'd made Lovaas a high enough offer. . . . But I hadn't. And now Farnell was up in the mountains, on the run with the police after him for murder—for murdering himself. It was a ridiculous situation. " Where is he now ? " I asked.

" I tell you—in the mountains."

" Yes, but where ? "

Again that crooked smile of his. " First we go to Aurland."

" And then ? "

" Then we will see."

I watched him, wondering what he was after. His eyes were black in the glare of the lights. His withered hand was crooked like a claw. In some peculiar way he was enjoying the situation. " Get Sunde," I told Dick.

When the diver came in, rubbing the sleep from his eyes, I said, " Where's Farnell—Bernt Olsen ? Is he at Aurland ? "

Sunde's eyes opened wide with surprise. " 'Ere, who's bin tellin' yer——" Then he broke off, staring at Dahler. " Oi told yer not ter tell 'em nuffink," he muttered angrily.

" Then he is at Aurland ? "

The diver's expression became obstinate.

I caught Dick's arm. " Fetch the chart, will you ? " I said.

When he returned I spread the sheet on the table. Aurland was farther up the Sogne—the next fjord to the south. I looked up at Sunde. " Have you any relations at Aurland ? " I asked.

" No." His voice was sullen.

" Has Sandven or Storjohann ? "

He didn't answer.

" All right," I said. " We go to Aurland." I looked at the chart again. Dahler had said Farnell would be up in the mountains. From Aurlandsvangen a valley ran up to Vassbygden and from there he could go on up the Stenbergdal to . . . My eyes followed the possible route with sudden excitement, for the Stenberg valley led up into the mountains towards Finse and the Jökulen. I looked across at Dahler. " Farnell would know people up at Finse, wouldn't he ? "

He smiled, but said nothing. He was like a cat—a cat that has been presented with a dish of cream. I could almost hear him purring. Damn the man ! What infernal pleasure did he get out of the situation ? I looked down at the map again. The railway running through Finse was marked quite plainly. That would be the Bergen-Oslo railway. I looked up at Dahler again. It would be quite easy to reach Finse from Bergen. And Jorgensen was at Bergen. " Who did you telephone from Fjaerland ? " I demanded.

He smiled. But he made no reply.

A sudden anger seized me. I wanted to take him by the shoulders and shake him till he answered. " Was it Jorgensen ? " I asked, gripping the edge of the table.

" Why should I telephone Jorgensen ? "

I straightened up. Why should he telephone Jorgensen ? He hated the man. What had made me think he'd telephone him ? I was being a fool. I looked round at the others. They were all tense, all watching Dahler. Jill's face was white, like the little church at Fjaerland in the moonlight. " We'd better all get some sleep," I said. " We only need two on watch at a time."

Dick handed me a tumbler of whisky. I drank it off and went up on deck. The moon stood like a silver ball above the white snows of the Jostedal. It struck down the fjord, turning the water to a bright blade of light between the sombre mountains. " Call me at six," I told Wilson. Then I went below again.

The saloon was empty. The tumblers rattled on the table to the shaking of the engine. Sunde was already back in bed when I slid open the door of my cabin. I sat down on his bunk and explained just why I wanted to contact Farnell. But all I got out of him was a promise to let me talk it over with his partner.

I undressed and got into my bunk. I was tired, but my mind was too full of problems for sleep to come easily.

I lay in the dark, listening to the juddering of the engines and thinking of Farnell climbing up through the valley to the snow-capped mountains. Thank God I could ski. Then I was asleep and the next thing I remember was Dick shaking me. "Come up on deck—quick," he said. His voice was excited.

I jumped into some clothes and hurried after him up the companion. It was just past six and the sun was rising behind the mountains over our stern. Wilson was still at the wheel. Dahler was leaning against the chartroom, his small, crippled figure bundled up in a duffle coat that reached almost to his ankles. We were off Balestrand. The white façade of the Kviknes Hotel showed bright in the growing light.

"Look!" said Dick, clutching my arm and pointing for'ard.

Ahead of us lay the wide sweep of the Sognefjord. And fine on our port bow the grey shadow of a whale catcher showed against the darker background of the mountains. It was tearing up the fjord at full speed like a corvette, a high bow wave showing white against its grey paint.

I dived for the chartroom and got the glasses. The twin lenses brought the catcher close and on the side of the bridge I was able to pick out the name—*Hval 10*. I put the glasses down and looked at Dahler. He was watching me. "So that's who you telephoned," I said.

He turned his head and stared down the fjord towards the catcher. I took a step towards him and then stopped. I wanted to hit him. I wanted to get hold of his scrawny little neck and shake him till he was senseless. But it wouldn't do any good. "Dick," I said. "Take Dahler below and have him fix some breakfast. Send Sunde up to me." I went aft then and relieved Wilson at the wheel.

When Sunde came up, I pointed to the catcher. "That's your friend Dahler's doing," I said.

"No friend of mine," he answered.

"He telephoned Lovaas—yesterday, from the hotel."

I seized his shoulder and swung him round. " Listen ! "
I said. " We've got to get Farnell before Lovaas does. Do
you understand ? "

He nodded.

" We'll pick your partner up either on the way or at
Aurland. If we don't will you guide me to Farnell ? "

" Yes," he said. Then he looked at the slim lines of
the catcher ploughing up the water as it raced down the
fjord. " Lovaas is a proper bastard." He turned to me
again. " Mr. Gansert," he said, " I'll do anyfink you
say, 'cos Oi reckon you're the only bloke wot can get
Bernt Olsen safe a't o' Norway. Pity we didn't know you
was a friend o' his. We could 'ave smuggled 'im aboard
your boat instead of runnin' 'im up inter the mountings."
He struck his fist violently against the chartroom roof.
" Ter fink 'o Bernt Olsen on the run again. As if 'e 'adn't
'ad enough of it during the bleedin' war. Peer and Oi
worked wiv 'im up 'ere in the mountings. We was busy
derailing trains on the Bergen-Oslo line at one time. Olsen
was a brave man. The Jerries caught 'im, but they couldn't
make 'im talk. Me an' me partner owe our lives to him.
An' a'terwards, 'e still went on working wiv us, till we was
sent down to Bergen to sabotage shipping." He seized
my arm. " Oi don't care wevver 'e did kill Schreuder.
It was no more than wot the little swine deserved.
Schreuder was up at Finse working for the Jerries. Oi
don't care wot Olsen done. If Oi can 'elp 'im ter escape,
Oi will."

The violence in his voice surprised me. " Why did
you tell Dahler where Farnell had been taken ? " I
asked.

" 'Cos 'e threatened me," he answered. Then he looked
at me quickly. " Oi wouldn't 'ave told 'im then only I
knew wot Olsen done fer 'im up at Finse an' Oi thought
he were a't to 'elp 'im. Mr. Gansert," he added. " I
reck'n Dahler must be mad."

" Why ? " I asked.

" I dunno. 'E says 'e wants ter get ter Olsen so's 'e

can disprove the charges wot've bin made against 'im. But
Olsen can't disprove them charges. They're true."

"But I thought Olsen got him and five others away in
areo engine cases."

"That's roight. So 'e did. But 'ow did Dahler fix fer
the guard to be relaxed? Oi dunno. But it looks sort o'
fishy ter me." His gaze wandered again to the catcher,
now disappearing round the headland which I was
cutting fine. "As fer Lovaas," he murmured. "If the
war were still on an' Oi 'ad a tommy-gun——" He made a
motion of mowing an enemy down.

"Did Lovaas work for the Germans?" I asked.

"'Course 'e did," he replied. "Lovaas goes where the
money is. Why d'yer s'pose 'e's a'ter Olsen now?"

The catcher had disappeared. "I suppose he is bound
for Aurland," I said.

"Why else would 'e be racin' up the Sognefjord?"
Sunde answered. "Ain't no whales in the Sogne. An'
every minute 'e's away from the whalin' gra'nds, is
money lost. That means there's bigger money up 'ere—
an' from wot Oi've gathered, that means 'e's a'ter Bernt
Olsen. 'Course 'e's makin' for Aurland."

As we rounded the headland, the catcher came in
sight again. But she was stern on and fast disappearing
into a light haze. The best *Diviner* could do was eight
knots. *Hval 10* was doing a good twelve.

I stayed on at the wheel, wondering why Dahler had
'phoned Lovaas. What did he hope to gain? What was
going on in that warped mind of his? I'd have stopped
and dumped him ashore at Leikanger or Hermansvaerk
if I could have spared the time. But I felt that every
moment was vital. The hours passed slowly. Jill came
up on deck as we reached Solsnes and turned south into
Aurlandsfjord. Her face was a white mask. She didn't
say anything. She just stood gripping the rail for a long
time and then went below again. Clouds had gathered.
The sun had vanished and the day was cold. The
mountains in Aurlandsfjord were different. There were

no tree-clad slopes and deep gullies full of water roaring down from the melting snows. The mountains were a wall of rock, rising sheer for 5,000 feet on either side of us. Their tops were bald and rounded, the ice-worn rock smooth and grey. And behind, the snow piled up like sugar icing.

Aurland was kinder than Fjaerland. It wasn't so wild. No vast ice fields stood over the little wooden town and it was set at the bottom of a fertile valley. But all round it were the mountains, a gloomy background of black rock and cold, grey-looking snow. It was raining and the clouds swept down like a curtain across the fjord. It was just short of midday as I picked up the glasses and focused them on the town. A steamer was moving into the quay. A plume of steam showed at the funnel-top and the sound of her siren echoed and re-echoed through the mountains till it died away in the stillness of distance. For a moment I thought Lovaas wasn't there. Then I saw the grey lines of the catcher, barely visible in the mist, emerge from behind the steamer.

I left Dick to run *Diviner* in to the quay farthest away from *Hval 10*. Sunde was with me in the bows and as we slid into the wooden piles, I jumped. He followed me. "Which way?" I asked. I knew we were too late. But I was still in a hurry to get there.

"Up here," he said and led me through a cutting between wooden warehouses.

We reached the main street and turned right into a small square with an old stone church. We crossed it and reached a bridge spanning a wide river, that sucked and eddied round the wooden piles of the bridge. The water was a cold green and very clear. The bed of the river was all boulders torn down from the mountains and the water curled in a thousand little white-caps as it bubbled over the rocks. Our feet made a hollow, wooden sound as we hurried across the bridge plankings. Sunde turned in at the gate of the second house on the right past the bridge. Two kittens, one white and one ginger, stopped their play and watched us out of wide, interested eyes. They ran mewing towards us as we knocked on the door.

" Who lives here ? " I asked.

" Peer's sister," Sunde replied. " She's married to an Aurland man." He pushed the kittens away with his boot and knocked again. The iron knocker made an empty sound on the wooden door. He looked down at the kittens who were sitting, mewing at him. " They're hungry," he said and beat violently on the door.

" *Hva vil De ?* " called a voice. A fat woman with a white apron had come out of the neighbouring house. " *Men det er jo hr. Sunde,*" she said.

" *Hvar er ?* " he asked.

There followed a quick conversation in Norwegian. Finally Sunde broke a pane of glass and climbed in through the window, taking the two kittens with him. I followed. " Where are they ? " I asked.

" They left early this morning," he answered. " Gerda, her husband, Peer and a stranger."

" Farnell ? "

He nodded, and led the way through to the kitchen. The kittens followed him, mewing plaintively. He poured some milk into a saucer and placed it on the wooden floor. " They all had heavy packs and skis." He opened the door of the food store and put a plate of fish on the floor for the kittens, together with the remains of the milk in a bowl. " Gerda would never have left the kittens with nothing to eat unless she was upset."

" But why did she go with them ? " I asked.

" Why ? " He laughed. " You ain't got much idea of wot the mountings is like, eh ? Olsen goes inter 'idin', see. Maybe 'e's makin' fer one of the *turisthytten*, maybe fer one o' the old saeters—that's our summer farms. Well, there ain't nobody up there this time of the year. It's all snow. So every bit o' food's got ter be taken up. That's 'ow we lived durin' the war. We lived in the mountings an' people like the Gundersens next door an'

Gerda—yes, women as well as men—brought food up to
us." He went over to the kitchen range and put his hand
up the chimney.

" What are you looking for ? " I asked.

" War souvenirs," he answered.   " Gerda's husband
kep' 'em up the chimney. But they're gone now."

" What sort of war souvenirs ? "

" Pistols. Two Lugers we took off some Jerries."

" So Farnell is armed ? "

" That's roight. An' lucky 'e is, too—'cos they only
got ab'at four hours' start."

" How do you mean ? "

" Lovaas was 'ere only an 'our an' a 'alf back. 'E'll
be on 'is way up inter the mountings by now." He went to
the window and peered out. The rain was little more
than a light mist. " If it's snowin' up in the valley they'll
be orl roight. But if it ain't snowin'." He shrugged his
shoulders. " Listen, Mr. Gansert. Oi'm goin' after Peer.
Can you ski ? "

I nodded. " I'm pretty fair," I said.

" Okay. I'll be at the ship in half an hour. I'll 'ave
rucksacks, skis, food—everyfink. What size boots do you
take ? "

I told him. His air of command had taken me by
surprise. Before the next few hours were out Alf Sunde
was to give me several surprises. " We gotter move fast,"
he said as we went through the front door and turned back
towards the bridge. " Yer'll want light oilskins an' warm
clo'ves," he said. " Got a gun ? "

" Yes," I replied. " I've got two Smith and Wesson
three-eights."

" Bring 'em bo'f."

" Good God ! " I said. " Lovaas wouldn't risk a
shooting."

" Wouldn't 'e ? " He laughed. " Not normally 'e
wouldn't. But this is different. From wot I've gavvered
o' this business it's big enough fer 'im ter go a'tside
the law an' get away wiv it. Wot's the deaf of a few

men when a new industry's at stake, you just tell me that ? "

I remembered the scene that night in the whaling factory. Sunde was right. Lovaas, knowing what the prize was, would stick at nothing. " I'll bring the guns," I said.

We parted in the square and I hurried back to the ship. Jill was leaning against the rail with Curtis as I stepped on board. " Where is he ? " she asked. " Captain Lovaas left over an hour ago with Halvorsen, his mate, and one of his men—a man named Gaarder. They had rucksacks and skis. What's happened, Bill ? "

" Farnell's gone up into the mountains," I said. I glanced round the deck. " Where's Dahler ? " I asked.

" He's gone," Curtis answered. " He caught the steamer."

" Back to Bergen ? " I asked.

" No. It went on up the fjord towards Flaam."

" Flaam ? " The name meant something to me. I dived into the chartroom and looked at the map. Jill and Curtis crowded round me. Flaam was at the head of Aurlandsfjord. And from Flaam there was a mountain railway which joined the main Bergen-Oslo line at Myrdal. From Myrdal he was within an hour's run of Finse. I swung round. " Can you two ski ? "

" Yes," said Jill.

" A bit," Curtis replied.

" Right. As soon as I've got my things together, Dick will run you up to Flaam. You may catch up with Dahler there. If so, don't let him see you. If he's gone, take the next train to Myrdal and from there catch the Oslo train to Finse. If my guess is right, you'll pick up Dahler's trail there—or if not Dahler's, Jorgensen's. Wait at Finse for them. Understand ? "

Curtis nodded. But I saw an obstinate look come into Jill's face. " Where are you going ? "

" Sunde and I are going up into the mountains."

" I'm coming with you," she said.

" No." She began to argue, but I stopped her. " You'll only slow us up. We've got to move fast. We've got to catch Lovaas up before he gets to Farnell. Oh, for God's sake ! " I cried as she started to argue again. " Do as I say. Follow Dahler. I know what Lovaas is up to. But I don't understand Dahler's game. For all I know he may be the more dangerous of the two." I went down to my cabin then, calling for Dick. " Dick," I said. " You'll stay with the boat. Run Jill and Curtis up to Flaam and then return here. Lie off in the fjord and keep watches. Wilson and Carter will remain with you. Don't move from here for any message whatever."

I reached down into the bottom drawer of a locker and brought out the two service revolvers. I saw his eyebrows lift. " Okay," he said. " You'll find me lying off wherever the water's shallow enough to take my hook. If you want to come aboard at night flick me G-E-O-R-G-E on a torch."

" Right," I said. I opened my wallet. " Here's fifty thousand kroner. Give Curtis twenty and Jill ten. Keep the rest yourself. If you want Ulvik, his number is Bergen 156 102."

I was running through drawers, taking out the things I needed—socks, sweaters, gloves, oilskins. " Get me some cigarettes, matches, chocolate and a half-bottle of whisky," I told Dick. " And a couple of candles. They're in the galley. There's a small torch there, too."

In five minutes I was ready with everything jumbled into an old kitbag. I dumped it over the side on to the quay. " Let go for'ard," Dick ordered. Wilson ran to the warps. Jill came towards me. " Good luck ! " she said. Her grey eyes were clouded as though with pain. " Please God you reach him in time," she whispered. Then suddenly she leaned forward and kissed me on the mouth. " Thank you," she said softly and turned quickly away.

" Let go aft," Dick called to Wilson. The engine came to life with a roar. I turned to Curtis. " I'm relying on you to catch up with Dahler," I said. " Don't follow him if he goes to Bergen. Go on to Finse. I want you there, between us and Jorgensen."

" Okay," he said.

" I'll get in touch with you at the hotel at Finse just as soon as I can."

He nodded and I jumped down on to the quay as the ship went slowly astern. In the thin drizzle I stood and watched *Diviner* swing gracefully on the flat surface of the water. The propellers frothed at her stern and she glided away up the fjord, her slender spars devoid of sail, but her brasswork gleaming proudly even in that dull light. I watched her until she was no more than a ghostly shape in the thickening curtain of mist.

An open tourer swung on to the quay, hooting furiously. Sunde jumped out from the seat beside the driver as the *drosje* came to a standstill. The back seat was littered with rucksacks and skis. " You jump in the back," he said, grabbing the kitbag. " You can get yer rucksack packed then." He opened the door and threw the kitbag on top of the rucksacks. I climbed in and the car started off before he was back in his seat. " We can go as far as Vassbygden by car," he said, as we tore up into the square and turned left along the bank of the river.

That was one of the wildest drives I have ever had. The driver was one of Sunde's resistance friends and evidently he knew something of the urgency of the matter, for he drove as though the devil were behind us. The road was little more than a stone track. We bumped and swayed up the valley. The mountains ahead were a grey-white world of snow half obscured by mist. On either side they closed in on us till we were winding along under beetling cliffs that looked as though they would rain boulders down on us at any minute, so cracked was the rock by the ice of countless winters.

Sunde turned in his seat as I was struggling to pack my rucksack and still prevent myself from being jolted out of the car. " Lovaas is exactly an hour ahead of us," he said. " Harald here "—he nodded towards the driver —" had only just returned from driving him up to Vassbygden when I sent for him."

An hour ! If we went really fast we could still catch up with him. I thought of Lovaas's big girth. Then I remembered how quick he had been on his feet. An hour was quite a lot to make up. But we had one advantage. We knew he was ahead of us. He did not know that we were behind him. " Who was with him ? " I asked.

" His mate and another man," was the reply.

The cliffs above us flattened back to pine-clad slopes. A long sheet of water filled the valley. " Vasbygdi," Sunde shouted. Houses huddled at the farther end, their reflections clearcut in the soft green water.

We skirted the lake and went on for another mile up the valley to the village of Vassbygden. There the *drosje* stopped. It was the end of the road. We piled out and got our rucksacks on to our shoulders. They were incredibly heavy. Apart from clothing, we were carrying food—cheese and chocolate mainly. The skis we tied across the top. Harald and the *drosje* disappeared down the track and we turned our faces to the mountains. The air was cold and damp. The rucksack dragged at my unaccustomed shoulders. My borrowed ski boots were too big. I cursed Farnell and began to sweat.

For all that he was a skinny little man about half my size, it was Sunde who set the pace. And when I asked him whether he thought to catch Lovaas up that afternoon, he said, " We gotter get to Osterbo *turisthytte* by nightfall. That is unless yer want ter sleep in one of the old disused saeters."

" There's a moon," I panted in reply. " We'll push on by moonlight."

" Per'aps," he said. " But wait an' see 'ow yer feelin' by then. Osterbo's quite a way—over two Norwegian miles ; an' there's seven English miles to each Norwegian."

We climbed in silence after that. We were moving up

into the mist, climbing along the side of a valley. Below us the river thundered by narrow gorges down to Vasbygdi. Every now and then the track flattened out and the river rose to meet us. We trudged through a narrow gorge where the water ran deep and swift. Damp-blackened rock rose sheer on either side, its summit lost in a cloud so that it seemed as though it might go up and up into infinity. Ahead of us was the thunder of water. It grew louder and louder until the white froth of a fall emerged like a broad grey ribbon out of the mist. Speech was impossible as we climbed beside the live, swirling water. The river was full of the early melting of the snows and the water curved over the rock ledges in thick green waves. The whole rock-walled valley seemed to shake to the weight of the water thrusting down it to the fjord.

At the top of the fall the rock fell back a little and slopes of lush spring grass ran up to black buttresses that had no summit. Lone rocks as big as houses lay scattered up this valley. In the shelter of an up-ended slab stood the broken remains of a wooden hut. " Almen saeter," Sunde shouted in my ear. " It's over two hundred years old, this saeter. A long time ago an old fellow used ter live 'ere winter and summer. An' 'e killed every soul wot come along this valley. Proper myffylogical, 'e was."

The hut was old and broken. Its walls were made of great beams axe-cut to dove-tail into each other, the ends protruding at the corners like a pile of sticks. The roof was turf on a layer of birch bark. The huge, up-ended slab of rock protected the building from rock falling from the cliff buttresses high above us. I paused to get my breath and ease the suffocating beating of my heart. " Come on nah, Mr. Gansert," Sunde called. " You ain't started yet." He turned and continued up the defile. His small body seemed dominated by the heavy pack. He was like a snail with his house on his back. And he didn't seem to hurry any more than a snail. Yet there was a rhythm about the steady movement of his legs. Unhurriedly, steadily he covered the ground. His bare legs above the white ankle socks were hard with muscle at each forward thrust. Those muscles were the legacy of a youth spent in the mountains on foot and on ski.

I started after him again, trying not to hurry, trying to catch the swing of his easy movement. But my legs ached and my heart pounded. The sweat was pouring down my face, oozing from every pore, soaking my clothes. I thought of Farnell, out ahead, not knowing that he was being followed, and I pressed on. I had to reach him before Lovaas. I had that to drive me. If I was out of condition for this sort of thing then my will-power would have to see me through.

The valley widened and split in two. We took the left fork, crossed a flimsy wooden bridge and worked our way over the shoulder of a hill to the other fork of the valley. Here we saw our first snow—a long, white streak lying in a gully across the river. This and the fact that we were on one of the brief descents raised my spirits. I increased my pace and caught up with Sunde. I pointed to the snow. " We'll be on ski soon," I panted. I was thinking of the relief to my aching limbs of gliding across snow.

He looked at me. His face was fresh and barely sweating. " The less ski work we 'ave ter do the better. Nah, just you try an' go steady. Keep the same pace all the time. 'Um a toon—Tipperary or somefink. Get a swing into it. We're going too slow."

" You mean Lovaas will be going faster than this ? " I asked.

He nodded. " Orl roight," he said. " Oi know it ain't your fault. We're used ter this sort o' walkin'. You ain't. Just shut yer ma'f, get yer 'ead da'n an' keep goin'. An' remember, Oi'm settin' the pace. Nah yer loosened up a bit, we'll get goin'."

He went on then. I watched his feet. They began to twinkle, moving with a supple, effortless ease—a long, lithe movement, the stride never varying in length or pace whether going up or down. For a while we were close to the river, the spray of several small falls whipping across our faces. I kept pace with him here, imitating the supple movement of his limbs regardless of the ache of my knees. Then we began to climb, a steady, relentless climb. Try as I might, he began to draw ahead. I put my head forward and my hands on my thrusting knee-caps. I must get to Farnell in time. I gritted my teeth and thought of Farnell. I must reach him in time. I began to hum a tune, hissing it through my teeth with each gasp of breath. It fitted the beat of my feet. And the beat of my feet fitted the words—I must reach Farnell in time. *I must reach Farnell in time.* My feet were hot and tired through to the very bone. My legs ached—ached so that my boots were a leaden weight. My body poured out sweat, blinding my eyes, suffocating my lungs. And over all, the heavy rucksack dragged at my shoulders, cutting into the light flesh over the collar bone, tearing at my neck muscles. Determinedly, doggedly, I clung to the beat of those words—*I must reach Farnell in time.* But gradually my mind became too numb and too dazed even to breathe through my teeth the beat of my feet. Soon the words were wiped away. My mind was a blank. I forgot Farnell. I forgot everything. My world became bound by a stony path winding up, ever up, and the little figure of Sunde with the enormous rucksack bobbing ahead.

We were swinging away from the river now, climbing the side of the valley. At the top the mist was thicker. There were little patches of snow. There was little sign of a path. We were in a wild place, a jungle of huge, lichen-covered stones topped with snow. Every now and then we came upon a large red T painted on the rock— the tourist association, blazing the trail. Then suddenly among some desolate, gnarled-rooted trees— BJORNSTIGEN in large black letters on a flat slab with an arrow pointing to the left. Sunde was waiting for me here. "The Bear's Ladder," he said. "It's a short-cut. If Lovaas takes the easier route we may catch up wiv 'im. It's a bit of a climb, this."

My heart sank. I had no illusions about what Sunde meant when he talked of " a bit of a climb." He started off to the left up an easy slope. " We'll pause for a bite at the top," he said over his shoulder by way of encouragement.

" Why the Bear's Ladder ? " I asked. I was following so close my face was almost touching the battered canvas of his rucksack.

" An ol' bear used the route, I expect that's why."

" Were there bears up in these mountains ? "

" 'Course there were. Me fa'ver used ter 'unt them. There's still a few fa'nd. But they don't 'unt them nah."

We fell silent as the slope became steeper. Soon we were struggling up under a sheer, buttressed wall of rock. The blood pounded in my ears. The sweat trickled down the small of my back. Mist and sweat gathered in beads on my eyebrows. We went through a drift of snow. The marks of nailed boots showed deep in the drift. Sunde pointed to them. " All goin' up. None comin' da'n. We may meet Peer yet."

" Has Lovaas been this way ? " I panted.

" Can't tell," he answered.

The world was very still in the mist. The river was no more distant than a rumble of water. A small grey bird chattered on a rock, dipping his body as he talked. Another drift and then loose rock covered by snow rising right up into the mist. Beyond the mist, there was probably mile on ghastly mile of piled-up, snow-capped peaks. But I could see nothing through the sweat but that treacherous, snow-covered trail winding up under the blank wall of the mountains we were climbing. Sliding and cursing, gripping with my hands as well as my feet, thrown off balance by the weight of my pack, sweating and panting, I worked my way up. I thought of the old bear whose ladder this was. He'd had four legs and had not been encumbered by pack and skis. There were patches bare of snow and there Sunde's feet dislodged

rocks that rolled down against my legs. I, in turn, dislodged others that clattered below us, some losing themselves in the snow in sudden silence, others rattling down
till the sound of them was lost in the distance.

More and more often Sunde paused to give me a hand.
But at last we reached the top and in a wild spot of giant
boulders loosened from the mountains by the frozen
wedges of winter ice, we paused and slipped off our packs.
I flung myself against a rock, tired, exhausted, throbbing
with heat and weariness. Sunde produced what he called
heimebakt flatbrod—wafer-thin home-made bread and
brown goat's cheese. " Better eat quick," he said. " We
can't stop more than a minute or two. An' don't eat no
snow."

Whilst I lay back, trying to eat, he cast about in the
snow patches, examining the footprints. But in the end
he shook his head. " Impossible ter tell 'ow many people
bin past 'ere."

I closed my eyes. I didn't care. I didn't care if Farnell
were killed. I wouldn't have cared if Lovaas had materialised out of the mist and pointed a gun at me. To be shot
would be a merciful relief. I was dead beat. The mist
wrapped round me like a clammy blanket. It seeped
through my sweat-damp clothing and right into my bones.
From being hot I was in an instant shivering with cold.
" Okay," Sunde said. " We'll move on now."

I opened my eyes. He was looking at me with a kindly
smile. " Yer'll soon get used to it," he said.

I struggled to my feet, every muscle in my body crying
out with pain. In that brief rest I seemed to have stiffened
up so that every joint seemed rusted, immovable. Sunde
helped me on with the rucksack. We struggled on through
deepening snow across a shoulder of the mountain. Soon
we had to put on skis. Sunde waxed them first. The
Norwegians use different waxes, not skins, for climbing
through snow. The skis felt heavy and clumsy on my
tired feet. It was as though I had strapped a pair of
canoes to them. New muscles began to cry out in agony

as we side stepped up the shoulder. Then for a brief
spell we were running downhill, following the tracks of
other skis. There were seven ski tracks in all. The snow
ended in rock. I stemmed. The heavy rucksack swung
and I fell. Sunde helped me to my feet. "Lovaas is
ahead of us," he said.

I nodded. I had already realised that.

More climbing. Then another run on skis, in and out
amongst huge, snow-capped rocks. At one point Sunde
swung backwards and forwards across the mountain side,
quartering it as though in search of something. At last
he stopped by a large rock. I saw the pistol I had given
him in his hand. He moved forward quietly on his skis.
I ran up carefully towards him. He disappeared as I
approached. A moment later I stemmed and came up
facing the back of a small saeter hut almost buried in
snow.

Sunde emerged from the side, shaking his head. "Holmen Saeter," he said. "No one there. The ski tracks pass
above it. But Oi thort Oi'd just make sure." He pulled a
map out of his pocket. "Just wonderin' if we can make
anuvver short cut 'ere." But after a moment he shook his
head. "No. We follow the others."

We began to climb then. The ache of my shoulders
was less now the rucksack was freed from the skis. But my
legs felt like the legs of a sawdust doll from which the sawdust is gradually seeping. The bones seemed to be no
longer solid, but liquid sticks that bent and folded. I had
difficulty in keeping my skis straight. If only we could get
a nice long run down. But I had a vivid picture in my
mind of the route. It was steadily up-hill all the way
from Aurland to Finse—a good fifty miles the way we
were having to come.

From Holmen Saeter we climbed in a steep zigzag,
sometimes on foot. At the top there was a chill breeze.
The mist was being blown to the head of the valley. It
was like a white fog, one moment drawn aside to show the
silver line of the river far below us and the black cliffs

opposite, the next sweeping down, thick, impenetrable, choking. The snow was crisper here. But after only a short, downhill run boulders began to show like white molehills and we had to tramp forward on foot. Soon we were at the river again on a broad path where ski-ing was possible. The valley widened and the river became a series of lakes. Beside the largest of these was a well-cared-for saeter. But again the marks of the skis ahead of us ran on past it. Doors and windows were bolted. An out-house was similarly locked.

Sunde stopped and pointed to the ski tracks. Three ski tracks ran off at an angle, crossing the tracks we were following. " Peer has gone back," he said. " See their marks ? "

" Why didn't we meet them ? " I gasped. I didn't really care. I was past caring. My mind was a haze in which the ability to keep going was all that mattered.

" Probably they went the long way round for the ski-ing," he answered. "Besides, the *Bjornstigen* would be difficult going down."

He went on. I stumbled after him, trying to hold the killing pace. I wanted to pick up snow and cram it into my mouth. I wanted to lie down in the white softness of it that packed so easily with a crunching sound under our skis. But above all those desires was the thought of Far-nell, alone now, sitting by a log fire in some lonely saeter farther up in the hills. The ski tracks would be plain— plain as though his route had been marked off on a map. And whilst he sat there, tired and lonely, Lovaas and his two companions would be approaching him. It was that thought that spurred me on. We had to catch up with Lovaas. We had to warn Farnell. If we got there too late . . . I wasn't afraid that Farnell would talk. He wouldn't tell Lovaas where the thorite deposits lay. Nothing would induce him to do that. But if they killed him . . . I remembered the hot temper that had blazed in Lovaas's grey eyes. I remembered what Dahler had said of him. Frustrated, he might well kill Farnell.

And if they killed him, then all he had worked for would
be lost for ever.

Near the end of the lake the path hugged a sheer cliff.
Wooden boards on iron supports took us across a gap
below overhanging rock. Beneath us the lake lay black
and cold. It was then I think that I first noticed that the
light was beginning to fade. I looked at my watch. It
was nearly seven. We climbed again for a few minutes.
Then we were out on a hillside and looking up a widening
valley. The mountains fell back as we advanced, opening
out till they were no more than grey shapes, slashed with
cold, dirty white. The mist swept down again, as though
in sudden alliance with night. The grey of the valley
deepened to a sombre half-dark in which rocks and river
had a remote, unreal quality.

Soon it was dark. It came slowly and our eyes were
given a chance to accustom themselves to it. But
even so, it was pretty dark. Only the snow at our
feet glimmered faintly to prove that we had not been
struck with blindness. Sunde went slowly now, picking
his way with care, his head thrust forward as though
he were smelling out the route. He had a compass
and he worked on that. Sometimes we were close to the
water's edge, going forward by the sound of it rippling
over the stones, at other times we were clambering over
some shoulder of land. The rocks were thick and dangerous on these shoulders. But at last we were out in the open,
clear of rocks and river, with the vague, white glimmering
of snow all around us. Our skis slid crisply over the even
surface. And then he found the ski tracks of the others
and followed them through the black and glimmering
white that was night in the mountains. There was not a
sound in all the world. It was as though time stood still.
This might be that world of shadow between life and
death ; it was chill, remote and utterly silent. The only
sound was the slither and hiss of our skis. I wasn't panting
now. The blood no longer throbbed in my ears. I felt
numb and cold. The loneliness of the place ate into me.

Sunde slithered up beside me. "Listen!" he said.

We stopped. A distant murmur could be heard through the sound of the stillness. It was water running over rocks. "That's Osterbo," he said. "Wiv any luck we'll find 'im there."

"What about Lovaas?" I asked.

"Dunno," he replied. "He ain't come this way. See —there's four ski tracks here. So that's Farnell's party. Maybe Lovaas stayed back at Nasbo, that saeter by the lake. He could rest up there and go on to Osterbo by moonlight."

"But it was all locked up," I said.

"Maybe he turned back when it began to get dark."

"But we'd have heard him if he passed us," I pointed out.

"Not if he passed us da'n by the river." He gripped my arm. "Look! Stars showin' nah. Goin' ter be a fine night."

We went on then, following the four dim ski tracks. The sound of water grew louder. We reached a stone wall, followed it and came to a bridge across a torrent. The snow on the wooden cross-planks had been churned up by many skis. It was impossible to tell how many people had crossed. Across the bridge we swung to the right. And there, straight ahead of us, was a faint glimmer of light—red and soft, like the flicker of a camp fire.

Stars were patterning the sky ahead of us as we glided across the snow towards that light. The drawn veil of the mist gave shape to things—stone wall, a graveyard with two solitary crosses, the dull steel of a lake beyond. I drew my pistol from my rucksack. Soon we could see the sprawling shape of the *Turisthytten*. Nearest the lake was the old, original saeter, stone-built with turf roof. Behind it ran a new, wooden building. It was from this that the light shone. And as we got nearer we could see that it was the flicker of a fire. The snow ran smooth and white to the edge of the building. No shadow moved. Complete silence save for the murmur of the stream. The ski tracks ran to the door of the hut. And coming in from the left, other tracks ran to the window and thence to the door.

The click of a lock sounded through the starlit darkness. The click of a lock or was it the cocking of a gun? We froze in our tracks. There it was again. It came from the house. Sunde suddenly gripped my arm. "The door," he said.

The door swung to with a click. A moment later there was a dark gap. Then it swung to again. Someone had left the door to the hut open and it was swinging in the chill breeze. Somehow it made me think of the heels of a hanging man. "You take the winder," Sunde said. "Oi'll take the door."

I nodded. It was only later that I realised to what extent my weariness had allowed him to assume direction of the situation. I skied up to the dark wall of the hut and then worked my way along. What should we find? That open door—surely Farnell wouldn't have left the door open? Or was he standing there, watching and waiting for visitors?

Sunde's shadow slid up to the door. I saw him remove his skis and creep in through the entrance, pistol in hand. I glided along to the window and peered quickly in. At first glance the room looked empty. But as I drew back out of sight I realised that there had been a bundle of something in the far corner. I looked again. There in the far corner were three rucksacks. Around them lay a litter of clothes and food. There was more food on the table. And an axe and a pile of logs lay beside the fire. I nearly cut my nose on a broken pane trying to peer more closely into the room. I touched the framework of the window. It moved. I pulled it open and felt the warmth of the fire. The door was flung wide and Sunde stood there, his pistol in his hand. He looked at the three rucksacks. Then at me, peering in through the open window.

"So, he's gorn, 'as 'e?"

My numbed mind didn't think as fast as that. All I saw
was the warmth of the fire. Farnell could wait. There was
no hurry now. There were his rucksacks. He had a
warm fire blazing. I thought of a cup of tea. I took off my
skis and hurried round to the door. I dragged myself
along a dark corridor with little cubicles leading off.
Then I was in the room with the fire. I staggered
toward it and slipped my rucksack to the ground.

God, it was wonderful, that fire ! My numbed body
received its warmth with unbelievable gratitude. If I
could have purred, my life would have been complete in
that moment.

" Can't 'ave left long," Sunde said, scratching his head
and spreading his hands to the blaze. He still had his
rucksack on his back. He carried it as though it were
part of him.

" What do you mean ? " I asked.

Sunde stared at me. " Gawd ! " he said. " This ain't
like you, Mr. Gansert. 'Ow many rucksacks d'you see ? "

" Three," I answered sleepily. But some little thought
was nagging at my mind, burrowing up into consciousness.
Then I got to my feet. " My God ! " I said. " Three.
There should be four."

He nodded. " That's roight. They bin ahead o' us."

" Lovaas ? " I asked.

" That's roight. Come in by the winder. Opened it
by that broken pane." He looked at me sharply. Then
he dropped his pack to the floor and burrowed deep
into one of the pockets. " 'Ere, you 'ave a nip o' that,
guv'ner," he said, handing me a flask. " Oi'm gonna 'ave
a look ra'nd."

I unscrewed the cap and took a swig at the fiery
liquor. It was brandy. The fire of it warmed me deep
inside. Sunde was back in a few minutes. " Place is
empty," he said. " No sign of a struggle. Everyfink in
order. There weren't no trouble." He scratched his head
and took a swig at the flask. " The way I see it, Olsen went
part of the way down with Peer an' the others an' then

coming back 'e saw Lovaas an' party before they saw 'im. Probably 'e 'ad glasses." He looked across at me. " 'Ow yer feelin', eh ? "

"Better," I said. "Much better." What he said seemed to make sense. And it cheered me. For it meant that there was still hope of our getting to Farnell before Lovaas. Farnell warned was a very different matter to Farnell lying in a saeter, unsuspecting. I looked into the embers. "He can't have left long," I said. "The fire is too bright."

" 'Ere, take annuvver swig o' this." He passed the flask across to me and, putting his gun down on the table, got out a knife and began cutting bread and butter and cheese from the food on the table. "We'll 'ave a bite to eat. Then we'll get movin'."

Get moving ! My limbs cried out in one great ache at the thought. But he was right. Our only hope of catching up with Lovaas was to get moving and keep moving. "All right," I said and got stiffly to my feet.

And at that moment a voice said, " *Stå stille !* "

I saw Sunde freeze in the act of cutting the square slab of brown cheese. He dropped the knife and started for his gun which lay at the other end of the table. " *Stå stille ellers så skyter jeg.* " He stopped and stared at the window. I followed the direction of his gaze. Framed in the opening were the head and shoulders of a man—and the muzzle of a gun. The flickering firelight shone on him with a ruddy glow. His face was dark and bearded. His eyes were like two coals. He wore a fur-skin cap with ear flaps. " *Hva er det De vil ?* " Sunde asked.

The man's voice was harsh as he replied in Norwegian. And when he finished his teeth showed white in his beard as he grinned.

"What's he say ? " I asked.

" 'E says 'e won't do us no 'arm, s'long as we don't cause no trouble. 'E's the third of Lovaas's party— Lovaas an' 'is mate 'ave gone on a'ter Farnell. Seems they spotted us just as it were gettin' dark. 'E's bin 'angin' ara'nd, waitin' fer us ever since. Gor blimey ! Couple o' mugs we are."

I looked at my revolver. It lay more than a yard away from me. And suddenly a deep sense of drowsiness crept over me. This meant that I couldn't go on. I could just stay here and rest. But something in Sunde's eyes caused my lethargy to vanish in a flash. His small body was tense, his hands crooked like claws under the edge of the table. " *Kom inn*," he said, quietly.

CHAPTER 8

ON THE SANKT PAAL GLACIER

THE MAN at the window hesitated, considering how best to lever himself through the narrow gap. The room was very still. The only sound was the hiss and crackle of the logs blazing in the stone grate. The flames threw flickering shadows on the walls of the hut. Sunde's motionless figure was a shadowy giant sprawled from floor to ceiling. I felt my limbs relaxing. God, how tired I was ! The luxury of knowing that it was impossible to do anything further, that the matter had been taken out of my hands, stole over me in a comforting wave of lethargy. My whole body sighed luxuriously as the muscles relaxed.

But I could sense Sunde's alertness. He glanced at the fire and then back to the window.

The man put both his hands on the window sill. " *Stå stille !* " he ordered, and his eyes gleamed in the firelight.

Sunde took a step back as though he were scared, tripped over nothing and sprawled flat beside me, his head almost in the grate. The man at the window tensed, the gun gripped in his hand. My stomach turned over inside me. For a moment I thought he was going to fire. " *Hva er det De gjör ?* " he snarled. Sunde moaned. His right hand was almost in the fire. He pressed his left hand over it and squirmed as though in pain. At first I thought he had burned himself. But as he explained what had happened in Norwegian, I saw his supposedly injured hand move out towards one of the blazing logs.

I turned back to the window. The man was still watching us tensely. The muzzle of his Luger seemed pointed straight at my belly. The dark metal circle of it gleamed dully in the light of the flames. Then he relaxed.

He held the revolver over the sill and, with a quick jerk, lifted his body on his two hands and got his knee on the sill.

In that instant, Sunde half rose from the floor. His right hand came up and a blazing log flew like a flaming torch across the room. It crashed against the dark shadow in the window with a burst of sparks and then fell flaming to the floor. There was a cry of pain, a curse, and then the flash and crash of a gun. I heard the thud of the bullet hitting something soft as I rolled over towards my own pistol. Sunde was twisting round by the table. There was another shot from the window. I seized hold of my gun. The rough grip of the butt was comforting to my hand. I pushed up the safety catch. And just as I raised it to fire, there was a stab of flame from beside the table and in the sound of the explosion, there was a ghastly, choking scream and the figure in the gap of the window sagged like a rag doll and then slowly toppled backwards.

The next instant Sunde and I were alone in the smoke-filled room. Everything was silent as before. The only sound was the hiss and crackle of the flames in the grate. And the only indication of what had happened was the single log blazing on the floor below the window. The window itself was an open rectangle, showing the glimmer of white snow beyond. I picked up the log and threw it back on to the fire. Sunde leaned heavily on the table. His face was white and strained. " Anybody'd fink we was at war again," he said uncertainly. Then he straightened up and went to the door. A moment later his head appeared at the window. " Give us a torch, will yer, Mr. Gansert," he said.

I got the torch from my rucksack and took it across to him. He shone the beam on the body huddled in a heap in the snow below the window. He turned it over. The skin of the man's face was very pale below his beard. His mouth was open and his eyes were beginning to glaze. A trickle of blood ran from the corner of his mouth. It had marked the snow in a blotch of livid crimson. A neat hole showed in his forehead.

I felt a shiver run down my spine. To Sunde this was just one more man killed up in these mountains. This was the sort of thing he'd been doing all through the war. But to me—well, I couldn't help thinking of the repercussions. Killing men during a war is legalised. But this was a peacetime killing. And Norway was a law-abiding country.

" We'll take 'im da'n ter the lake," Sunde said.

I went out into the cold night air and helped tie the body to a pair of skis. Then we dragged it across the snow to the lake, near where the stream flowed down. We tied stones to the man's feet and tossed him in. I can still remember the cold, sickening splash with which he hit the dark water. For a moment ripples showed. Then all was still under the stars again. If it had been the carcase of a dog it couldn't have been disposed of with less ceremony. And I remember wondering then—as I have wondered before and since—whether man was as important in the scheme of things as he would like to believe.

Back at the hut again, Sunde began to get his rucksack on to his shoulders. He had some trouble with it and I had to help him. Then he helped me on with mine. " Where now ? " I asked as we went outside and fixed on our skis.

" Steinbergdalen and then Gjeiteryggen—both *turis-thytten*," he replied. " After that we'll see. Maybe Finse via the Sankt Paal glacier. Or maybe he'll turn off to the west, to Hallingdal and Myrdal an' pick up the railway there."

" How far is Gjeiteryggen ? " I asked.

" 'Ba't twenty miles."

" Twenty miles ! My heart sank. I glanced back at the flickering glow from the saeter window. My feet felt like lead as I followed the track of Sunde's skis through the snow. Twenty miles ! He might as well have said two hundred. The pack tore at my shoulders. My feet felt blistered and raw. Every muscle in my body cried out against further movement. I put my head down and trudged on, automatically, trying to think of something other than the utter weariness that engulfed me.

At the top of a long incline Sunde paused. I stood beside him and looked back. The stars were a myriad pinpoints of light in the frosted darkness of the sky. Below us stretched a wide plain of virgin snow. And in the centre of it lay Osterbo saeter, a dark huddle of huts with the firelight still shining in a dull, warm glow through the window. I thought—*a man has been killed down there to-night. We have killed a man and thrown his carcase in the lake.* But it meant nothing. It was as though it had never happened. Like a dream, it seemed unreal. Only my feeling of exhaustion was real. Nothing else mattered.

We turned and trudged on up the path, winding steadily until we were climbing below cliffs that reached their dark shadows to the stars. A curtain of silvery water, like flowing lace, rippled down from above. We climbed and climbed until I thought we should never reach the top. But at last there was nothing above us but the stars. And ahead of us was the distant murmur of a waterfall.

We went on, down to the water, and then turned away along the side of a racing torrent till we reached a bridge. The moon came up, throwing the seried edges of the mountains into black outline before it topped their summits. Then suddenly the circle of its light was shining on the silver tracery of countless lakes running up a long valley. And beyond, were the mountains, hard and crystal-white with snow and ice.

We descended by sudden rushes to the lakes, our skis sizzling pleasantly on the frost-glistening snow. The joy of moving without effort ! And always we followed in the track of other skis. Farnell and Lovaas had been this way before us. Along by the lakes the going was better. Our skis slid forward with little effort. Only my pack seemed heavy. But soon we were climbing again. Whether it was the cold freshness of the night or the fact that my muscles were becoming resigned to the unaccustomed work I was giving them, I couldn't tell. But I found I was now able to keep pace with Sunde. Of course I was bigger than he was. And plenty of pully-hauly work on the boat had kept me fit. Diving wasn't a particularly healthy occupation, sweating underwater in a rubber suit.

He was pausing quite often now. And whenever I caught glimpses of his face in the moonlight, it looked white and strained. Once I suggested he took a rest. But he replied sharply : " Lovaas won't be restin', will 'e now ? "

And the mention of Lovaas turned my mind to the chase that was going on ahead of us. Farnell had had a longer rest than Lovaas. He was slight and wiry and his muscles were probably hardened to this sort of work. But Lovaas was bigger, more powerful. He was probably a good skier —he had all the winter in which to ski. Soon perhaps we'd catch sight of them. There would be Farnell out in front, a lone, small figure, in the waste of moonlit snow. And behind him two other figures, seemingly connected to him by the slender twin threads of his ski tracks. And Lovaas would stop at nothing. That was obvious from what had happened to us down at Osterbo. He knew now what he was after—knew that the prize was big enough for him to get away with anything so long as he had the information Farnell possessed.

The thought made me press on faster. And now I found myself held back by Sunde. Several times I moved out ahead of him and had to wait for him to come up. New strength seemed flowing into my muscles, whilst he flagged more and more. I began to chafe at his slowness. His face looked white and drained in the moonlight. The sweat glistened on his forehead, whilst I was no longer sweating. Twice, when he paused, he peered at the map. His breath was coming in short, haggard gasps.

We came to a waterfall, tumbling down to the lake we were leaving. I waited for him and let him pass to lead the way. As I followed, my eyes bent on the ground as we climbed through a jungle of giant boulders, I suddenly noticed a red spot on the snow. A few yards on was another, and another. I glanced up at Sunde. He was bent forward under the weight of his pack and his left arm hung slack in front of him. Good God! I suddenly had an awful sense of shame at my feeling of impatience. At the top he paused. I came up to him and glanced at his left hand. Blood was dripping slowly on to the snow. It had congealed on his fingers, but down the back of his hand a crimson line glistened wet in the moonlight. "You're hurt," I said.

"It's nuffink," he answered. "The bastard got me in the shoulder."

I thought of the weight of the pack he was carrying and squirmed inside. God, how that pack must hurt him! "Let's have a look at it," I said.

But he shook his head. I saw his lips were bleeding where he had bitten through them with the pain. "We're not far from Steinbergdalen. I'll stop there. You'll have to go on alone."

I shook my head. "I can't leave you alone up here."

"I'll be all right," he said angrily. "It ain't nuffink serious." And he turned and went on, trudging steadily forward on his skis.

I followed, my head bent, seeing nothing but the crimson spots on the snow that became more and more frequent. And I had thought I was tougher than him, that diving had softened him up! I thought of all the times he had paused for me on the way up to Osterbo. And I hadn't been wounded. I'd just been tired.

The rocks gradually became less frequent. Then suddenly we topped a ridge and there in the valley ahead of us was the hut. It was a square building, constructed of logs. At the back were outhouses. The little colony of huts, looking like models in the moonlight, was set on a big outcrop of rock, that showed black through powdery, wind-driven snow.

Ski tracks ran straight up to the door of the hut. I told Sunde to wait and skirted round the back, coming down on the far side. There, clear in the white light of moon on snow, were the ski tracks going on and on until lost in the infinity of cold whiteness—three separate and clearly defined tracks.

I whistled to Sunde. " They've gone on," I told him as we approached the door of the hut. I lifted the latch. The door opened. Inside it was warm. The ashes of a log fire smouldered in the grate. With the door shut the warmth of the place stole over us like a soporific. I realised once more how tired I was. It was two o'clock. I had done some twenty-six miles of stiff climbing on foot and on ski in twelve hours. I dropped my pack on the floor and kicked the embers into a blaze. I got Sunde's pack off and then went out into the kitchen and found more logs. With a blazing pine fire to warm us I hacked at the blood-hard clothing of the little diver's shoulder. At last I had cut it free. The bullet had torn through the muscle on the outside of the upper arm, just by the shoulder joint. I heated some snow to water on the fire, bathed the wound and then bandaged it with strips from a torn shirt.

When I had helped him into a jersey, he pulled a wooden settle to the fire and sat down. " Nah, Mr. Gansert, yer'd best get movin' if yer goin' ter catch up wiv the others," he said. " We lost time on the last leg."

Lost time ! What sort of a pace did he expect us to keep up ? I sat down on a bench and removed my boots and stockings. My feet were red and swollen. The flesh was tender and the bones ached as though they had been bruised. I looked across at Sunde. His face was white in the long moonbeams that slanted in through the windows. The firelight threw a grotesque shadow of him on the great logs that formed walls and ceiling. I cursed myself for not having realised that he'd been wounded. He'd lost a lot of blood. There was no question of his going on.

But to go on alone ! With him for company the mountains had seemed remote, but friendly. But now I thought of those white, jagged monsters waiting for me outside—and they suddenly seemed cold and wild and cruel. We were still climbing. Soon, if I kept on going, those ski tracks would lead me up to the ice-capped summits, on to the glaciers. Sunde knew this country. He was at home here. I had not had to trouble about direction. I had relied on him. But to go on alone—that was different. Suppose a mist came down ? Then I should still be able to follow the other's ski tracks. But what about a snowstorm ? With the ski tracks obliterated, how should I find my way then ? I shivered. Every bone in my body cried out to stay here by the fire. I opened my mouth to tell him that I wouldn't go on alone. Then I remembered Farnell, and instead I said, " I'll just change my socks, then I'll get moving."

He nodded as though there had never been any doubt. And whilst I got myself ready, he produced map and compass from his rucksack. " The next leg ain't so bad," he said. " Keep followin' the line of the river till yer come ter a lot o' lakes. Yer'll find Gjeiteryggen there. Yer can't miss it."

" I seem to have heard that before," I muttered as I pulled on my boots.

He grinned. " Well, just you remember ter keep along the course o' the valley. There's a bit o' a climb at first up ter the Driftaskar—that's a pass up above the valley here where the farmers used ter ca'nt their cattle as they passed through. After that a good deal of the route's da'n 'ill."

" How far to Gjeiteryggen ? " I asked.

" Aba't fifteen kilometres," was his reply.

Another eleven miles ! I got wearily to my feet and began to eat *flatbrod* and goat's cheese. " What's at Gjeiteryggen ? " I asked. " Another tourist hut ? "

" That's right. Ain't as nice as Osterbo or Steinberg-dalen. A bit wild like. But you'll get shelter there."

" And after Gjeiteryggen ? "

He hesitated. " My guess is he'll make for Finse an' the railway. He'll be gettin' tired by the time he gets to Gjeiteryggen."

" And how far is Gjeiteryggen from Finse ? "

" Aba't another fifteen kilometres. An' it's tough going. Yer turn sa'f at Gjeiteryggen an' climb from aba't thirteen 'undred metres, right up ter seventeen 'undred. Let's see nah." He screwed his leathery little face up till it looked like a monkey's. " That'll be a climb of near on fifteen 'undred feet—right up ter the Sankt Paal Glacier. Yer go right across the top of the glacier. Yer'll find a hut up there if yer need a bit of a rest. An' there's posts markin' the route—or should be. Take my tip an' if mist or snow comes da'n, don't lose sight o' one post before you located the next. You're right up in the Halling-skarvet an' if yer lose yer way, well——" He shrugged his shoulders. " 'Ere's compass an' a map. The map ain't much good. It's one the Germans made an' it ain't accurate. If mist or snow comes da'n, see you got a bearing before it closes in on you."

I took the map and slipped it into the side pocket of my rucksack. The compass was an elementary little thing, the sort I was given to play with as a kid. I put it in my pocket. " You stay here until I organise a relief party," I said as I humped the rucksack on my aching shoulders.

He shook his head. " You don't need to bother aba't me. I'll make me way back by easy stages. I don't aim ter get cut off up 'ere. It's still early enough in the year for a bit of a blizzard to blow up. Only sorry I can't come wiv yer. But it wouldn't be no good. I'd only 'old yer up." He got to his feet and stood, rather weakly, holding on to the settle. " Well, good luck ! "

I grasped his hand. " An' remember wot I says," he added. " If yer crossin' Sankt Paal, don't get a't o' sight o' one marking post before you've located the next. An' there's a 'ut right at the top. Built by the 'otel association for the convenience o' skiers. It can save yer life. It saved mine once." His friendly, wizened face puckered into a grin. " An' if anybody asks yer, we didn't meet no bloke off of *Hval Ti*, see. We ain't met nobody. Well, good luck—an' Oi'll be seein' yer da'n at Aurland."

" Fine," I said. " If you can't make it, don't worry. I'll send a party up from Aurland, if you're not with *Diviner* by the time I get back."

" Okay," he said.

He came with me to the door and stood, sniffing at the moonlight and the chill glitter of the mountains, whilst I put my skis on. A thin powder of snow blew in my face. " Wind's goin' ter get up," he said. " Looks like the weather's goin' ter break." He caught my arm as I straightened up and put on my gloves. " Mr. Gansert," he said earnestly, " if you aim ter 'elp Olsen, yer've gotter move fast. They bin gainin' on us all evening."

" I'll go just as fast as I can," I said.

He nodded and grinned. I bent forward and thrust with my sticks. My skis slid forward across the fine snow and a moment later I was whistling down the slope in the tracks of the others' skis, the wind cold on my face. Faint behind me came Sunde's shouted, " Good luck ! "

Then I was alone and the only sound was the hiss of my skis and the quiet whisper of the wind brushing the snow like sand across the valley.

In places the ski tracks I was following were already half obliterated. In other places they ran deep and clean as though Farnell and Lovaas had only just passed. The down stretch to the valley floor was all too short. Soon I was climbing steadily. The path became steeper, winding in giant zigzags up the shoulder of a mountain. That climb seemed endless. I climbed until my limbs ached and became like liquid. The path went up and up through a litter of boulders till all the mountain tops for miles were visible, their smooth ice caps glinting in the moonlight—so cold and remote, like pictures of the south pole. But at last I reached what Sunde had called the

Driftaskar. I paused at the top of the pass. The moon was high overhead now. The wind had risen and all about me the powdery top layer of snow was on the move, sifting across the rocks like the sand before a desert storm. The place was as desolate and white as the moon itself viewed through a telescope. I put on a windbreaker and then began to descend. There was no clear run, for the ground was strewn with rocks. But it was easier going. And after the sweaty heat of climbing, the cold night air chilled me to the bone.

Shortly after this I crossed a stream and began to climb again. After that I don't remember very much about the journey to Gjeiteryggen. I only know that the country I passed through was wild and desolate, that as dawn grew nearer it got unbearably cold, and that I was stiff and dead with tiredness. I kept on repeating Sunde's words over and over again as I trudged on through the snow—" *You gotter move fast. They bin gaining on us all evening.*"

Often I thought I'd lost the way. The ski tracks vanished, obliterated by the snow. Then in panic I'd have recourse to map and compass. But always, sooner or later, in some spot sheltered from the wind I came upon them again. The moon sank towards the west and soon its light began to fade as a cold, grey luminosity spread over the mountains. Dawn came creeping like death across a snow-clad world. And I barely noticed it. I was beyond caring. With head bent I somehow kept going. But it was will-power, not the strength of my limbs that drove me. And all the time I kept on thinking—the others can't be going on like this, without pause, unendingly. But always the tracks of their skis ran ahead of me to prove that they had.

The moon sank at last behind the mountains. The snow on the mountain tops no longer glinted like sugar icing at Christmas time. It was grey and cold and the first light of day stripped the place of all beauty, leaving it bleak and empty. I was conscious then of the utter loneliness of these mountains. In summer a constant stream of walkers would tread this path. But now, with the mountains still in the last grip of the winter snow, there was nobody. I remembered Sunde's wizened, friendly face and wished he were with me. Only the half-obliterated ski tracks that showed where the route was sheltered from the biting wind linked me with any other human.

I was descending now to a long, frozen lake. In the valley below me the water was not frozen. It ran swift and black, like a jagged crack in the white carpet of the snow. At the bottom I stopped behind a tall rock and rested. I set my pack down on the snow and had an early breakfast of more *flatbrod* and brown cheese. I felt dazed and numb. Nothing was real. And when I went on, my movements were automatic as though I were ski-ing in my sleep.

Thin clouds streaked the paling sky and as I worked my way along the lake they became suffused with a pink glow. The glow grew until the whole sky flamed a violent red. It was a beautiful, terrifying sunrise. The sun came up, a red, angry disk, bloodying the snowy summits and casting an orange glow over everything. The sky reddened till it blazed with crimson. Then slowly it faded until all that was left was a cold, watery sunlight that had no warmth nor any promise of warmth. The last tinge of pink clung to high-piled cumulus lying to windward along the Norwegian coast.

At last I stood on the shoulder of a hill, leaning wearily on my sticks and looked down on Gjeiteryggen. The hut was without beauty. It was painted a dirty red and it stood there like a barracks in one of the most hideous stretches of country that I have ever seen. A broken series of lakes, frozen and piled with snow, lay about it in a semi-circle. Between the lakes were the black marks of moving, unfrozen water. The hills in which the lakes huddled were smooth. The boulders that littered the place were smooth. Only here and there a rock showed a jagged edge, as though smashed by a giant sledge hammer.

The place was marked and scored and hammered out by ice. It was an awful, unhappy place.

But there was the hut. And I thanked God for that. I wasn't thinking then about Farnell, or about Lovaas and his mate. I was thinking that I could light a fire and sink down in a chair and rest. God, I was tired—tired and cold and wretched ! Nothing mattered. Nothing at all. In that moment I could have been offered the mines of Solomon, the treasure of the Incas, all the wealth of the Indies, and I wouldn't have cared a damn. What are the world's minerals worth when you're sick with exhaustion—weary right through to your bones and to the very marrow of your bones ?

I started down to the hut. And then I stopped. Something had caught my eye—something that moved. I screwed up my eyes, trying to clear their vision which was half blinded by the whiteness of the snow. It was away to the right of the hut on the further shore of the largest of the frozen lakes. It was moving towards the valley that led up to the sombre mass of Sankt Paal. Was it reindeer ? A bear, perhaps ? But I think I knew what it must be even whilst I considered all the possible alternatives. I felt the excitement of the chase send the strength pumping back into my tired limbs. Lovaas—or was it Farnell ? Had he given them the slip ? No. The object had separated—there were two of them. It was Lovaas.

I searched farther on up the white slopes of the valley. And there, high up on the valley side another tiny black speck moved steadily through the snow.

I didn't stop to think. I thrust my sticks hard into the snow and went hurtling down the slope to the flat ice of the lake. At least I could cut a corner here. Farnell—and Lovaas behind him—had gone down to the Gjeiteryg-gen hut. There they had had to turn sharp right. By cutting across the lake I might save a mile, maybe two.

The chase was on now. Before, the quarry had been mythical, something that was there ahead, but only visible through the lines of the ski tracks. But now I could see them. They were real. No thought of what I should do if I came up with them crossed my mind. All my efforts were now bent on one thing—making the best possible speed and lessening the distance between myself and Lovaas.

I tumbled down a steep drift of snow and my skis scrunched as they bit the harder snow on the frozen lake. The ice held and I went forward easily across the flat surface. As I started to climb the long valley leading to Sankt Paal I wasn't more than a mile behind Lovaas and his mate. Every now and then, on a shoulder of the valley, I caught a glimpse of their two figures, black against the snow. I could even pick out Lovaas—he was so much shorter and stouter than the other. Once I caught sight of Farnell, a lone dot high up on the mountainside.

The tilt of the valley became steeper. Soon it was sheer will-power and nothing else that drove me forward. Every effort was concentrated on pushing forward. Twice I saw Lovaas turn and glance over his shoulder. He couldn't fail to see me. And yet I still gave no thought to what I was going to do, how I was going to get past them to Farnell. It was enough that they were in sight. And I could spare no thought for anything other than the task of holding the pace.

The tracks of the skis ahead were deep and clear now. There was no question of looking for the route. I had only to follow. But God how my legs ached ! My breath came through my teeth in rasping gasps. Soon I was side-stepping up. I had not the energy to stride forward, my skis wide like crows' feet. Nor could the others apparently. And it was some comfort to know that I was not the only one who was feeling exhausted.

Once, on a particularly steep stretch, I paused. The sweat was like ice on my forehead where the wind touched it. The sun had vanished now. The day had a bleak, wintry look. And away to my right the clouds were rolling in from the sea, covering the mountain tops. It was a bad outlook for crossing the glacier. If it were mist it might enable me to get past Lovaas to Farnell. But if it were snow . . . The thought sent a chill through me. A snowstorm at just on five thousand feet wasn't a good prospect. It would obliterate the ski tracks. It might even hide the posts marking the route.

I turned and pressed on. The fear of those clouds piling up from the west was what drove me forward now. I felt I had to get across the glacier before they reached me. But I hadn't a hope. In five minutes visibility was diminishing and the air was becoming much colder. I stopped and took a quick bearing on the direction that I knew the peak of Sankt Paal to be. Then I trudged on —climbing, climbing all the time. The clouds had no form now. They were a grey veil obliterating the valley behind me, swirling chill fingers round black outcrops of rock until nothing remained. Then my world became reduced to a small compass of snow that looked dirty and bleak in the half-light. The rest was a grey void. My only link with the world beyond that void was the sharp-cut lines of the ski tracks. They disappeared ahead in the curtain of mist, yet they always continued as I advanced.

The wind was very cold now. There was a damp chill in the driving force of it. I might have been in Canada, up in the mining camps of the Rockies. But then I would have been properly equipped with moccasins and fur cap and plenty of woollen clothes. Here the wind blew right through me, eating into bones that were already numb with exhaustion.

A tall slender pole emerged from the mist. It was thrust deep into the snow by a black granite outcrop. The first of the markers. I was at the top of a ridge. The ski tracks ran level ahead of me into the impenetrable murk. Before I had lost sight of the marker behind me, the next was in sight. The ski tracks ran close by it. Another and another followed. Then I was climbing steeply again, side-stepping steadily so that my limbs ached. The rarefied atmosphere and the cold began to tell. I felt I should never make the top of that ridge.

Surely this must be the top of Sankt Paal? But after that ridge there was another and another.

And then suddenly, at the top of that third ridge, close by one of the markers, the ski tracks turned away to the left and ran downhill. I followed them automatically. for two hundred feet or more I ran smoothly and easily down. The wind whipped through my windbreaker, turning the sweat of my body to an icy dampness. It was as though I had no clothes on at all. A flurry of torn-up snow leapt to meet me out of the mist. Fortunately I was not going fast. I did a half Christi and followed on the line of the ski tracks. Below me, to the left, the snow fell away in a sheer drop. My heart leapt in my mouth as I saw the white tendrils of the mist swirling in an up-draught of air. I was ski-ing along the edge of a precipice. The drop might be a hundred feet. It might be a thousand. I couldn't tell. And I realised that I had passed no markers in the last five hundred yards or so. I stemmed and came to a standstill. As I stood there, looking down into the nothingness of moving vapour, I realised suddenly the game that Farnell was playing. He knew these mountains. He had deliberately led his pursuers off the marked track and was playing a game of hide-and-seek on skis, with the mist and all the perils of the mountains in his favour.

I hesitated. And as I hesitated the mist darkened. A myriad black specks began driving past me. It was starting to snow. I glanced ahead. There were the ski tracks, clear and deep. But even as I looked the edges became blurred and their sharpness was lost in the falling snow.

I turned then and in the fear of sudden loneliness hurried back along my tracks. The snow thickened. The wind was driving straight into my face, blinding me. In an instant my windbreaker was white and I was brushing the cold, clammy particles from my face.

God, how fear leant strength to my limbs! By the time I had reached the spot where I had had to Christi, the marks of the turn were barely visible. I started to climb the long slope down which I had run so easily. But before I was half-way up, the tracks made coming down were gone, as though rubbed out by a giant rubber. I stopped and got out my compass. No good going by the direction of the wind. It was eddying all over the place.

I reached the top at last and began to descend. I turned back then, certain I had crossed the line of the markers. I searched back and forth across a wide area. But there was nothing. Just snow and an occasional jagged outcrop of rock. I followed the compass bearing, casting back and forth across the direction it took me. No friendly posts came out of the mist to greet me. Perhaps the slope I had descended had curved. I cursed myself for not being able to remember. I had just followed the line of the ski tracks, blindly, unthinkingly. In a sudden panic I struck away to the right, climbing again. Soon I was on a ridge, the wind whistling past my face, driving the snow in a thick black cloud. Back and forth I cast, my heart hammering and a horrible emptiness in my belly. I began to descend, and then in panic turned back. I struck away to the left and in a few minutes was crossing a half-obliterated ski track that had been made by my own skis only a few minutes before. I climbed to the top of another ridge. And then I stopped. I was lost. Completely and utterly lost.

I had known men who had been lost in the bush in Africa. I had always thought it must be a ghastly experience. But it couldn't be as bad as this. At least there had been trees and warmth and sunshine. Here there was nothing. Just this empty, desolate waste of snow.

I was almost sobbing with fear. I'm not easily frightened. I've never been frightened of anything I could see. But I was cold and exhausted and alone. What was that story of Jack London's? Something about a wolf. Had London experienced the utter emptiness of exhaustion and lostness before he wrote that story? What had been the end of it ? What had happened to that man ? He had gone forward on all fours at the end. Had he killed the the wolf that was as exhausted as he ? Or had the wolf killed him ? I couldn't remember. And it was frightfully important. I was certain it was important. I knew my mind was wandering. But I couldn't help it. The story hammered at my tired brain. I couldn't think of anything else. I could see it so clearly. The man on all fours and the wolf—each waiting for the other to die, neither having the strength to kill the other. I was feeling drowsy. I wanted to sink down into the snow. That way lay death. But I didn't care. A merciful oblivion. What did it matter ? But I mustn't give up. There was Farnell. And there was Jill. Why did I think of Jill ? Farnell and Jill. What was that to me ? But I must go on. I must.

I can't remember much about what followed. Cold and exhaustion made everything seem unreal. I was dazed and numbed. All I know is that I began to move forward. I was climbing. And I kept on climbing. I had some crazy notion that if I went on climbing I'd get above the snow, out into the sunshine. And then suddenly I was standing in front of a long, slender pole stuck deep into the snow. I looked at it curiously, almost without interest. Then my brain seemed to function again and hope suddenly coursed along my frozen nerves. I cast about from the pole until I found the next and after that I kept moving from marker to marker, my teeth gritted and only some hidden force inside me driving my unwilling body forward.

And at last, on a ridge that sloped away on either side, something square and solid emerged out of the snowstorm. It stood on a platform of half-exposed rock. It wasn't until I had almost reached it that my brain recognised it for what it was. The hut. It was the hut Sunde had mentioned. The hut on the very summit of Sankt Paal.

I struggled to leeward of it and found the door. My frozen fingers fumbled with the bindings of my skis. But at last I had them off. Then I lifted the latch. It opened. I stumbled in and closed it behind me.

The sudden stillness was like oblivion. Outside the wind roared and I could hear the silent falling of the snow. But inside all was quiet. I was in a little passage. It was very dark after the glare of the snow. It wasn't warm. But the wind no longer cut through my clothing. There was an inner door. A pair of skis clattered to the floor as I opened it. Inside was a big room with a long deal table and benches. There was a rucksack on the table and an opened packet of sandwiches. A dull glow of warmth met me as I staggered towards a seat. That warmth—it seemed to rise up and lap me round. I felt suddenly dizzy. The table began to move. Then the whole room started spinning. I felt my legs buckle under me. I heard somebody cry out. Then everything was blank and I was sinking down, down, into a soft, warm darkness.

Was the hut all a dream? Was this how it felt to die in the snow? I struggled back to half-consciousness. I mustn't lie here in the snow. That way lay death. I knew that and I fought it. A man mustn't cease to fight because he's dead beat. To die in the snow! That was no way to end one's life. I fought back. I got my eyes open. A face swam in my vision, blurred and convulsed like something in a tank of water. It was a girl's face. I thought of Jill. If only I could get to Jill. Somebody spoke my name. It was far away. I was hearing things. It wasn't real. I relaxed. Everything slowly faded into oblivion.

CHAPTER 9

GEORGE FARNELL

I EMERGED into consciousness reluctantly, like a sleeper clinging to each separate minute of his bed. I felt numb and drowsy. I could hear the wind. But I could not feel it. It was as though I had lost the power to feel. I was shivering uncontrollably and I felt damp and chill. What was it I had dreamed about? A hut and a woman's voice. I opened my eyes quickly and found the vague outline of a boarded ceiling above me. I was lying on a wooden floor. I could feel it with my hands. And my head was pillowed on something soft, yet firm and warm. There was a warmth to the right of me. I turned my head. An old-fashioned, cast-iron stove showed the flicker of flames through a crack. On the top of it a tin kettle poured out a stream of steam. " Feeling better ? " It was a woman's voice, soft and gentle, and vaguely familiar. It sounded very far away. I sighed and relaxed. I felt so tired. I never wanted to stir again.

" Drink some of this." My head was raised and the rim of a glass tipped against my lips. The smell of hot brandy brought me back to full consciousness. I drank and warmth spread comfortingly through my body.

I mumbled my thanks and struggled into a sitting position. Then I turned and found myself looking into Jill's level, grey eyes. " How in the world did you get up here ? " I asked.

She smiled. " On ski." Then suddenly serious : " What happened, Bill ? Where's George ? I couldn't stay down at that hotel, waiting, whilst they all gathered for the kill. I left early this morning, when it was barely light. I thought I might go as far as Gjeiteryggen. Then the

snow came and I only just made this hut. Have you seen
George ? "
    " In the distance," I answered. " That was as we were
climbing up to Sankt Paal, before the snow came down."
I took the glass of hot brandy from her and drained it.
" Lovaas and his mate were about five hundred yards
behind him."
    " But where is he now ? "
    " Soon as the snow came down he swung away from
the marked route. He's leading them a dance all round
the precipices and crevasses of Sankt Paal. He'll get the
pair of them lost and then they'll die out there in the
snow."
    " Die ? But——" She stopped then and her eyes
looked troubled. Then she said, " You've had a long trek,
Bill. Vassbygden to Sankt Paal is quite a way. You can't
have stopped anywhere."
    " At Österbo and Steinbergdalen," I answered. " But
they were only brief halts."
    " Where's Alf Sunde ? "
    " At Steinbergdalen." I passed my hand over my face.
My eyes felt tired and I was still dizzy despite the warmth
of the brandy.
    " But why did you leave him at Steinbergdalen ? " she
asked.
    " He was wounded," I answered. " Bullet through the
shoulder." Why must she keep on asking me questions ?
Couldn't she see I didn't want to talk ? But there was
something I must ask her—something she'd said. Oh,
yes—— " What did you mean when you said you couldn't
bear waiting whilst they all gathered for the kill ? "
    Her eyes were wide. " A bullet through the shoulder ?
How did he get that ? What happened ? "
    I struggled to my feet. I felt light-headed and my legs
were weak. I stood close to the stove trying to absorb
the warmth of it into me. " Is there any more brandy ? "
I asked. My voice sounded strange.
    " Yes," she said and produced a flask. I poured some of

it into the tumbler and added hot water from the kettle. Then I stood, warming my hands round the glass and drinking in the smell of it. " Don't worry about Sunde," I said. " He'll be all right. Just a flesh wound. I want to know what happened down at Finse. Who was at the hotel ? " I took a pull at the drink. God ! How wonderful hot brandy is when you're all in ! " Was Dahler there ? " I asked.

" Yes. He came up in the train with us." She hesitated. " Then Jorgensen arrived. He came in the train from Oslo."

" Jorgensen ! " I swung round on her. " What brought Jorgensen there ? "

" I don't know."

Jorgensen at Finse ! Somebody must have tipped him off. Or perhaps it was just one of those strokes of luck ? " Was he intending to stop off at Finse ? " I asked. " Or was he on his way from Oslo to Bergen and suddenly saw Dahler and decided to stay the night ? "

But she shook her head. " No. I think he intended to stay. Dahler was in the bar, so Jorgensen couldn't have seen him from the train. He came straight in with a suitcase and asked for a room."

" Just for the night ? "

" No. He told the receptionist that he couldn't say how long he'd be staying."

" Did he bring skis with him ? "

" No—nor any ski clothes. But I heard him arranging with the manager for the loan of everything he wanted."

" And how did he react when he found Dahler in the hotel ? " I thought of Dahler telephoning from Fjaerland. Somebody must have got in touch with Jorgensen.

" I wasn't there when they first met," Jill answered. " But when I came into the bar later in the evening they were both there. Bill—what's the matter with those two men ? Jorgensen isn't exactly a nervous type. But he's scared of Dahler. And Dahler—I don't know— it's as though he were enjoying something. The atmosphere between them was noticeable even in a crowded hotel bar. Jorgensen positively started when he saw me. Then he glanced across at Dahler. Dahler gave me a little bow. But all the time he was looking at Jorgensen with that crooked smile of his and a queer glint in his eyes. It—it sent a cold shiver down my spine."

I went over to the table and dragged one of the benches to the fire. " Where's Curtis ? " I asked as I sat down.

" Still at the hotel." She brushed back the fair hair that had tumbled over her face. Her skin looked very pale in the cold light that filtered through the snow-spattered windows. " I started out before he was up. It was such a lovely morning and I wanted to warn George."

" Warn him ? What about ? "

" The police. I forgot. They arrived at Finse late last night on one of those railway trollies. An officer and six men. The officer reported immediately to Jorgensen." She leaned forward and touched my arm. " You're shivering. Have some more brandy and I'll get you some blankets. There are some in the cupboard here." She got to her feet. " The hotel association keeps this place stocked for skiers that get caught in mist or snow." In a moment she was back with two heavy blankets which she wrapped round me. I didn't have the strength to protest. I felt cold right through despite the brandy. I took another drink and tried to think. Dahler —Jorgensen—the police ; all down at Finse ! What did it mean ? And where would Farnell make for ? He'd give Lovaas the slip in the snow. No question of that. Then where would he make for ? I looked at the windows. They were almost blocked with snow. Through the half-obliterated panes I could see the dark flakes driving under the weight of the wind. He might come here. Or he might press on. And if he went on, where would he make for—Finse ?

As though she divined my thoughts, Jill said, " George will get away from Lovaas all right, won't he ? "

"Yes," I said.

"Then where will he go? If he goes down to Finse——"
She stopped there. And again I wondered how much
Farnell meant to her now. She looked cold and remote
and delicately lovely in her navy blue ski suit and red
socks and scarf. Red woollen gloves lay on the floor at
her feet. She was the sort of girl that never let up once
she had decided on something. "Are you still in love
with Farnell?" I asked suddenly, and my voice sounded
harsh in the immense silence of that hut.

She looked at me. "You shouldn't have asked me
that," she said softly. "Not now."

"I suppose not," I said dully. I hadn't the strength to
argue or even press the point. And it wasn't until later
that I realised that she had avoided a direct answer.

After that we didn't talk. I sat huddled against the
fire. I felt I wanted to press the warmth right into my
stomach. Gradually my shivering ceased. I took my
boots off and changed into a clean pair of socks. The
warmth on my face made me drowsy. Inside, the hut
was silent as though waiting for the tick of a clock.
Outside, the wind howled, rattling at the windows and
and shaking the massive timber of the walls. The blanketed
sound of the snow was audible even above the wind.
My eyes began to close. I felt myself dropping off to
sleep.

Then suddenly Jill said. "What's that?"

I started awake. "What?" I asked.

"I thought I heard somebody."

I listened. I could hear nothing but the wind and the
snow. "It's nothing," I said drowsily. "What did you
think it was?"

"I thought I heard a voice." She got to her feet and
went towards one of the windows.

"Nobody will be coming here," I said. "Lovaas and
his mate are out there somewhere in the snow. They'll
never find this place. And Farnell's probably miles away
by now."

" I expect you're right," she said. But she crossed over to the other window. Then she stopped. " There. Did you hear it ? "

I sat up, wide awake now. The sound was unmistakable —the clatter of wood against wood. There it was again and a voice speaking.

Next moment the outer door was flung open. Boots stamped in the narrow passage. A man's voice, deep and solid, spoke in Norwegian. Then the inner door opened and a draught of bitter cold air blew into the hut. With it came a flurry of snow. Then the outer door was closed.

Jill, her face alight with excitement, started across the floor. Then she stopped as though frozen. A man had entered. He wore a fur cap with earflaps. His face and body were thick with a white covering of snow. But the girth of the man, enhanced by the amount of clothing he was wearing, was unmistakable. It was Lovaas. He wiped the snow from his face. His skin was almost blue with cold. " So," he said. " It is Miss Somers and "—he glanced across at me—" and Mr. Gansert. *Kom inn, Halvorsen,*" he said over his shoulder. He came over to the stove. " Move please, Mr. Gansert. We need some warmth." His voice was thick and tired. His feet stumbled. " Your friend, Farnell, nearly finished us. It was only for luck that we find the hut."

His mate, a tall, hatchet-faced man, came in and closed the door after him. I moved over towards Jill, whilst they gathered round the fire. The snow steamed on their clothing as they huddled close to the red top of the stove. " What happened to my man, Gaarder, eh ? " Lovaas asked me.

" Who is Gaarder ? " I asked.

" One of my men. I leave him to look after you. What happens ? And where is your companion ? It was Sunde, wasn't it ? "

" Yes," I said. " Sunde was with me. But he turned his ankle. I had to come on without him."

"And I suppose Gaarder turns his ankle also?" His heavy brows were drawn together. His eyes, red-rimmed and narrowed, watched me closely. "What happens, Mr. Gansert?" And when I didn't reply, he suddenly shouted—"Answer, man! What happens to him?"

"How should I know?" I answered. "Perhaps he's lost his way."

I saw anger welling up into violence inside him. But he was tired. He only sighed and pressed his great belly closer to the cast-iron casing of the stove. "We will talk about that later," he said.

There was a momentary silence. I could see the blood flowing back into his face. It was no longer blue. His features began to take on a ruddy glow. The man was incredibly tough. He had done the same trek as I had and had been ski-ing steadily in the biting snowstorm all the time I had been here, huddled against the fire. Yet already he was recovering. I remembered how easily Sunde's little legs had covered the ground. And this man was accustomed to the cold. He had been on Antarctic whaling expeditions. I glanced across at Jill. He'd work on her. He was a dangerous man and he was playing for high stakes. He was going outside the law. And he would go further outside it to achieve his end. Only by discovering what Farnell knew would he be safe. I moved slowly towards my rucksack.

"Stay where you are please, Mr. Gansert." Lovaas's voice was sharp. "*Halvorsen. Gå gjennom tingene deres. Se om der er noen skyteråpen.*"

His mate crossed the room to my rucksack and took out my pistol. Then he searched Jill's pack. Finally he came behind each of us and ran his hands over our clothing. Then he took the gun across to Lovaas. He broke it open. "So," he said. "You have not fired any shot. But perhaps your friend, Sunde, fired a shot, eh?"

I ignored the question and gazed at the window. Then suddenly my nerves stiffened the tired muscles of my body. The snow was being pushed away from the window.

A hand was rubbing the glass clear from the outside. Then a face looked in through the cleared patch. Farnell? I couldn't be certain. I just made out the shape of nose and mouth and two eyes looked for a second into mine.

"Well? What happened to Gaarder?" Lovaas demanded.

I turned away from the window. If it was Farnell, then I must warn him. He couldn't have seen Lovaas from where he was looking in. But if I kept on talking he'd know someone else was in the hut. "Was this fellow, Gaarder, with you when you started out?" I asked.

"Of course," Lovaas answered. "There were three of us left Aurland. You knew that, Mr. Gansert. What happened at Osterbo?"

"What should have happened?" I asked.

"I am asking you what did happen?"

"And I am asking you what you expected to happen, Captain Lovaas," I countered. "You left him behind, I suppose. Was he meant to kill us?"

"I am not a fool. It would do no good to kill you. I have not yet discovered how much you know."

I sensed the draught of the outer door opening. I must keep him talking. "Then why did you leave him behind, Captain Lovaas?"

"How do you know I leave him behind?"

"I am only going on what you have told me, Captain Lovaas," I answered in a strong voice.

"I tell you nothing," he answered sharply. Then his brows dragged down again over his eyes. "Why do you talk so loud, eh? And why is it Kaptein Lovaas this and Kaptein Lovaas that? What are you up to, Mr. Gansert?"

"Ah—so it is you, Mr. Gansert?"

The voice came from behind me. But it was not the voice I had expected. I swung round. Dahler was standing in the doorway. His small figure was covered in snow. His features were grey, the lines about the mouth deeply etched. And he was smiling that crooked enigmatic smile of his. "Jorgensen has not arrived, eh?"

"Jorgensen?"

"Yes. He has not arrived?"

"No," I said.

"Good. I am glad. I followed him up from the hotel. Then I lose him in the snowstorm. He will arrive soon, I think." He lowered his rucksack on to the table and went over to the fire, rubbing his withered hand. "So, you have arrived, eh?" was his greeting to Lovaas.

"*Ja.* I have arrived and I have lost one of my men."

"How did you lose him? There has been trouble, eh?" He glanced quickly from Lovaas to me. "Who has been hurt?"

I did not reply.

"Where is Sunde?" he asked. "Did he not go with you, Mr. Gansert?"

"He's at Steinbergdalen," I replied.

"So." He looked up at Lovaas, cocking his head on one side like a curious raven. "Where's Farnell?"

"I do not know," Lovaas replied in a surly voice. It was clear he did not like Dahler. But faced by the cripple his bluster left him. It was as though he were afraid of the man.

"I do not know!" Dahler mimicked. "Well, you should discover what has happened. Jorgensen will be here soon. Then there will be trouble. He is not a forgiving man, Kaptein Lovaas. You have got in his way. And the police are with him."

"The police?" Lovaas growled. "Coming up here?"

"No. They are down at the hotel. But Mr. Jorgensen has told them to stand by to make other arrests than the man known at the moment as Schreuder."

Lovaas hesitated. Then abruptly he moved away from the fire. "*Kom, Halvorsen. Vi må gå.*"

Dahler caught at his arm with his sound hand. The

withered claw remained held over the red-hot top of the stove. " A moment, Kaptein Lovaas," he said. " You go too fast. Jorgensen has said nothing to the police—not yet." Dahler's small, black eyes were watching the whaler's face.

" What are you suggesting ? " Lovaas asked. His voice sounded nervous—ill-at-ease.

" I am suggesting nothing," Dahler replied slowly. " If you had caught Farnell—then it would be different. Then you would be safe. You were always too hasty, you know, Kaptein. You must always rush things. You should have kept within the law. Or if you wished to go outside it—then you should do so with success, eh ? If you had obtained what Mr. Jorgensen, and Mr. Gansert here, want from Farnell—then you would be justified. Without that——" he hesitated. Then he said quietly, " But it is a long way from here to the hotel, where the police are. And there is a snowstorm." He paused significantly, watching Lovaas like a cat.

Was he trying to get Lovaas to kill Jorgensen ? What was it that drove the man so ? Hatred of Jorgensen ? Desire to prove his innocence ? What made him follow Farnell, planning his destruction, yet seeking his help as he had sought it during the war up here in the mountains ? I remembered what Sunde had said : " *Dahler—I reckon he's mad.*" That was the only explanation. What he had suffered during the war had affected the balance of his mind. Maybe he had sold secrets to the enemy. But he didn't believe he had. He had thought himself into the desperate certainty that his innocence could be proved and that Farnell could do it. And he, like Farnell, was prepared to do anything to gain his own ends. Jorgensen was to him a symbol of something he hated and wished to fight—Jorgensen, who had been successful, who had taken the long view. He had tried to kill Jorgensen out there in the North Sea during the storm. Of that I was certain now. And now he was playing Lovaas off against Jorgensen, hoping against hope that

Jorgensen would get hurt in the clash. Yes, he was mad.

He suddenly turned towards me. "So you did not catch up with your friend Farnell, eh? And where is he now, I wonder?"

"Half-way to Finse, I should think," I answered.

He nodded. "Perhaps." He glanced at his watch. "It is just after eleven. The train for Oslo comes through Finse at twelve-thirty. Allow that it is half an hour late—our State Railways are always late. He has two hours. I think perhaps he will make it." He glanced up at Lovaas who had started to move towards his rucksack. "And the police will be on that train, Kaptein Lovaas."

Lovaas halted. Then he came slowly back towards Dahler. I could see by his face that he wanted to strangle the cripple. And yet something stopped him. There was something about Dahler's eyes that was cold and dead, and yet strangely excited. "The net is drawing round him, you see," he said with a little laugh. "And around you, eh?"

There was the sound of skis being placed against the side of the hut. Then the outer door opened. Dahler glanced at Lovaas, smiling. The outer door closed, there was the stamp of nailed boots and then the inner door opened and Jorgensen came in. His tall figure looked lithe and active in a white ski suit. His leathery features seemed darker than usual against the white of the snow that clung to him. He stopped and looked round the room—first at Jill and myself, then at Lovaas and his mate, finally at Dahler. "Where is he?" he asked. Then he turned to me. "You followed him, Mr. Gansert. Did you catch up with him?"

"You mean Farnell?" I asked.

"Of course."

"How did you know I followed him?"

"Norway is a small country for all its size, Mr. Gansert. I can keep track of anybody if I wish to. I see from your expression you were not successful." He turned to Lovaas. "So you did not obey my instructions, eh? I told you to await orders at Bovaagen Hval. But you decide to play your own hand. Well, Kaptein Lovaas, play it. But be careful." His voice was suddenly harsh. " I am not a person to disregard—unless you are successful. And I don't think you have been successful." He turned to me again, ignoring Dahler entirely. " Where is Farnell now ? "

" Somewhere out there," I said, indicating the snow-lined windows.

He nodded. " Aurland, Osterbo, Gjeiteryggen, Sankt Paal." He spoke the names softly as though to himself. " Then he will make for the railway. Good." He nodded as though satisfied with his arrangements. Then he turned to Dahler. " I should advise you to leave the country. Leave with Mr. Gansert."

" Are you having me thrown out ? " I asked.

He shrugged his shoulders. " Good heavens, no," he answered with pained surprise. " But now that your mission has failed you will naturally wish to go back to England—to start on your Mediterranean trip. I do not imagine Sir Clinton Mann will finance you indefinitely in Norway. Had you been successful in your mission——" He shrugged his shoulders. " Then it would have been different. Then we might have been business associates. As it is——" He left the rest of the sentence unfinished.

" But you will still need finance," I said.

" Perhaps."

" Sir Clinton Mann would be willing to discuss business on my recommendation," I added. " The only thing that held us up before was the feeling that you were insufficiently informed about the nature and location of these thorite deposits."

And then suddenly Jill spoke. " But, Mr. Jorgensen, you still do not know where the deposits are."

He frowned. " The police will pick Farnell up on the train, Miss Somers."

" Possibly," she replied. " But how will you make him talk ? "

"Oh, he will talk." He took a step towards her. "Listen, Miss Somers. George Farnell is wanted for murder. He may be tried as Schreuder for the murder of George Farnell. Or perhaps he will be tried as George Farnell for the murder of Schreuder. It is immaterial. He will be offered a free pardon if he is willing to assist Norway."

"Does your conscience never worry you, Knut?" Dahler asked with that crooked smile of his.

"What I do, I do for Norway," Jorgensen barked. "In everything I have done—both during the war and since— it has been of Norway that I have been thinking. Norway needs these mineral resources. Instead of a poor country, dependent on fish and timber, she might then become rich. What is one man's life against the livelihood of three million people, eh? And who killed Schreuder, if Farnell did not?"

"You still will not get the information you want," Jill said.

Jorgensen gave an abrupt laugh. "My dear Miss Somers. No man faces a life sentence if he can help it. Farnell will talk."

But Jill walked towards him. "I tell you, he will not talk. George has no interest in anything but these metals. He has sacrificed everything to that end—everything, I tell you. I know," she added softly. "The threat of imprisonment will not make him talk unless he wants to. He has never thought——"

The door burst open behind me and she stopped speaking. Her mouth fell open and then in a whisper she breathed, "George!"

"Get back against the table, all of you." The voice was hard, desperate.

I turned. Standing in the doorway, a Luger in his hand was George Farnell. If Jill had not spoken his name, I don't think I should have known him. His face was white and covered with several days' growth of beard. Snow was plastered over him. His voice was cold and metallic. " Go on. Get back. All of you. You too, Jill." That was all to her. He'd recognised her. But that was all his greeting.

" Farnell ! " I said. " Thank God you're here. Don't go down to the Oslo train. The police will be on it."

" I know. I heard. I've been listening outside the door ever since Jorgensen arrived. Go on, get back—you too, Gansert. I'm trusting nobody."

I backed away until I felt the hard edge of the table against my body.

" Jill. Go behind the table and get their pistols from them. Throw them over to me here."

But she didn't move. " George. You've got to listen to me. Mr. Gansert has his yacht at Aurland. We can get you away to England. You can't stay here. They're going to arrest you for the murder of a man called Schreuder." Her voice choked. " I saw his body at Fjaerland. You didn't—kill him—did you ? "

" Do as I say," he answered without a trace of emotion. " Get their guns off them."

Jill hesitated. " You didn't kill him, did you ? " she asked again.

" Of course, I killed him," Farnell replied harshly. " What else was I to do—have a swine of a Nazi collaborator steal all that I'd worked for ? For two years I worked up at Finse on forced labour, crawling to the Germans, ingratiating myself, earning the freedom to find out what I wanted to find out. And then after the war, always in hiding. Never able to return to England. What did you expect me to do with the bastard when I found he'd followed me and seen me at work ? Go on, Jill—now get those guns."

I glanced at her face. It was set and hard. She turned away and went along behind the table. In all, she collected three guns and threw them on to the floor at Farnell's feet. " That's better," he said. He kicked them into a corner and went over to the stove. " So you've got the police on the Oslo train, Jorgensen ? " His eyes peered at us through his glasses. " I wonder how the devil so many of you managed to converge here ? Somebody's been talking." He searched our faces. Then his eyes fell on the flask of brandy. He picked it up and took a long swig, " A-ah. That's better. So you came all the way from England in your own boat, Gansert—just to find me ? "

I nodded.

He smiled. " When you finally achieve what you've been fighting for all your life, then people will help you." He swung round viciously towards me. " And that's just when you don't need their help. When you need them, they're not there. When you don't, they come rushing half across the world in their fine yachts searching for you. God ! If only I'd been interested in archæology instead of mineralogy—how much pleasanter my life would have been ! There's no money in archæology. But minerals ! Remember how they wanted to get rid of us without even paying us the salary they owed us out in Southern Rhodesia. Then I located the copper. They couldn't have done more for us after that—the bastards." His face was drawn and bitter. He hadn't had an easy road. He seemed lost in thought for a moment. Nobody spoke. Slowly he looked up and stared straight at Jorgensen. " Jill was quite right, you know," he said quietly. " Your threat of prison wouldn't have made me tell you anything."

Jill took a step towards him. Then she stopped. " Why don't you tell Bill where the thorite is ? " she said. " He'll play fair with you—and he's got B.M. & I. behind him."

" So it's Bill, is it ? Big Bill Gansert." He laughed unpleasantly. " And you'll vouch for him, will you, Jill ? My girl calls him Bill and says she'll vouch for him, and I'm supposed to make him a present of my life's work. I'll see you in hell first," he shouted at me. He turned on Jill. " As for you——" And then he stopped and rubbed

his hand over his face. " No," he said. No. I guess it's
not your fault. It's my fault. If only I could make you
understand, Jill."

" But I do understand," she said softly.

He looked at her long and searchingly. " Maybe you
do," he said with a sigh. " But it's too late now." He
straightened up and looked us over, the muzzle of his
Luger following the direction of his gaze. " I'll get away
from you all—do you hear ? "

" There are police down at Finse," Jill said.

He nodded. " Yes. I expected that. I expected that as
soon as I saw Jorgensen here." He crashed the butt of his
pistol against the wooden wall. " I am hounded out of my
own country. Now I'm being hounded out of Norway.
Why? Why?" His voice was high-pitched, hysterical. "I
did what I had to do. These metals were my life work. I
needed money for research. Would any institute in
Britain give it me ? Would any of the big industrial
concerns ? No." He looked angrily at me. " Certainly
not B.M. & I. So I stole the money. I stole it from my
partner. He was a dull, unimaginative little man anyway. But now—now I've done the spadework and got
something they want—now they'd be prepared to condone
murder—if you can call killing a rat like Schreuder—a
traitor—murder. Well, you won't get it—any of you.
I'll get away. Right away. Somewhere where I'm not
known. Then I'll make my own terms."

" You can make your own terms right here and now,"
I said.

He looked at me. " How do you mean ? "

" I have full authority to act for B.M. & I," I pointed
out.

He laughed. " What will you offer ? "

I hesitated. What offer could I honestly make him?
" Do you want an outright figure or a percentage of the
ore lifted ? " I asked.

" What's your outright figure ? " He was watching me
with a sneer.

"A hundred thousand pounds," I said. "Payable over five years provided the deposits hold out that long."

He threw back his head and laughed. "A hundred thousand! If you offered me a million, it wouldn't repay me for what I've been through—or Jill—or that poor little wretch, Clegg. It wouldn't bring Schreuder back to life or stop my father from committing suicide. You didn't know about that, did you? He committed suicide. A million! Those deposits are worth tens of millions to the company that gets hold of them."

"What about a directorship in Det Norske Staalselskab and a part share in the business?" Jorgensen said.

He sighed. "You don't seem to realise what I've got here. It's bigger than D.N.S. Bigger than B.M. & I. It could be the world's biggest industrial plant. And anyway I don't trust you," he shouted. "I don't trust any of you."

"Well, who will you trust?" I asked. "What about the person you sent those samples to—in the whale meat. Will you trust them? Who was it?"

He stared. "You mean to say you don't know who it was? But I thought"—he looked across at Jill—"I thought that's why you were here. Didn't you tip Gansert off?"

Jill stared. "I don't understand?"

"Those samples—didn't you give them to Gansert?"

"I never received any samples. Mr. Gansert got some, but that was from Sir Clinton Mann."

"They were delivered to us as the result of an advertisement," I explained. "The address on the package had been obliterated by blood."

"Oh. So that's what happened." He looked across at Jill again. "I'm sorry. I thought——"

He rubbed his hand across his face. He was dead with tiredness.

"Why don't you trust Mr. Gansert?" Jill said again. "Please, George."

She moved towards him. But he waved her back.

" Keep there against the table, Jill. And throw me a sandwich from that packet."

She tossed him the packet. He took another swig at the flask of brandy and then began to eat. " He could get you out of Norway," Jill went on, pleadingly. " He's got his yacht here. Everything could be arranged. We could start again. Please, George—trust him."

" I'll trust nobody," he snarled, his mouth full.

I was watching Jill and I saw her lower lip tremble. Her eyes were dull and lifeless. Dahler began to agitate his withered arm. His right hand plucked at his ski suit. " Mr. Farnell," he said. " I wish to speak to you. I want to ask something of you. Once you saved my life, you know. Now I wish for your help again. I want you to tell them how I escaped. Tell them that I didn't sell any secrets to the Germans. Tell them——"

" Shut up ! " Farnell shouted violently. " I'm trying to think."

" But—please—they must be told. They will not let me into Norway. They say I am a traitor. I am not. I gave no secrets away. Tell them that, please. Tell them how you helped me to escape from Finse."

" Shut up—damn you ! " Farnell almost screamed.

I looked across at Dahler. His face was no longer cunning and there was no sardonic smile on his lips. He looked just like a child that has been refused a sweet. And in that moment I saw Lovaas's heavy body tense. Jill must have seen it too, for she cried, " George ! Look out ! " And then Lovaas plucked Dahler up in his hands and, using him as a shield, flung himself at Farnell.

Farnell didn't hesitate. His Luger came up and he fired from the hip. The noise was shattering in that confined space. Lovaas dropped Dahler with a cry and spun round, clutching at his left shoulder. Farnell crammed the rest of the sandwich into his mouth. " Next time I shoot to kill," he said. Blood was oozing between Lovaas's fingers. His face looked white and his teeth were bared with pain. " Gansert," Farnell said. " Come over here. I want a word with you."

I crossed the room towards him. He watched me. The gun still smoking, followed me. " Where did you say your boat was ? "

" Aurland," I answered.

He came close to me. Then he leaned forward and whispered in my ear. " Take it round to Bjorne Fjord, south of Bergen. Contact Olaf Steer. Wait for me there. I may come or I may not."

" Why not accept my offer ? " I suggested. " Or at least give B.M. & I. a chance to negotiate."

" Do as I say," he answered. " We'll talk about that later. Now get back over there." He turned to Dahler who was getting up off the floor where Lovaas had dropped him. " Go outside and slide all the skis except mine down the slope. Go on, move."

Dahler hesitated. But the violence in Farnell's eyes sent him out. " My skis are by themselves to the left of the door." Farnell picked up his rucksack and thrust his arms through the straps.

" You're being a fool," Jorgensen said angrily. " I can save you from all this trouble. We could have a development company, half English, half Norwegian if you like."

" And you dictating your own terms—blackmailing me for Schreuder and this." He nodded at Lovaas. " By God, you must take me for a fool, Jorgensen," he suddenly cried. " Do you think I don't know who Schreuder was working for ? No, I'll handle this my own way. And nothing you can do now will stop me."

" George ! " Jill took a step forward. " You haven't a chance. The police——"

" To hell with the police." He glanced at his watch. " Have you got rid of those skis, Dahler ? " he called.

" Yes," came the faint answer, brought in by the cold wind that entered from the open door. Drifts of light snow were whitening the boards near the entrance.

Farnell backed away, easing the weight of the pack

on to his shoulders. He stood for a moment in the doorway his teeth bared in a smile in his stubble beard. " I'll be on the Oslo train, Jorgensen, if you want me. But your policemen won't find me."

Then suddenly he was gone and we were staring at the closed door. And I became conscious again of the weight of the wind against the hut and the snow piling up against the windows.

CHAPTER 10

THE *BLAAISEN*

It was a moment, after Farnell had left, before any one in the hut moved. It wasn't so much that we were stunned by the suddenness of his exit as the fact that none of us had any plan. Lovaas was half bent over the table, holding his shoulder. Halvorsen was cutting his jacket away with a large jack knife. Jorgensen, usually so quick, stood motionless, staring at the closed door. I met Jill's eyes. She looked away as though it hurt her to look at me. Her face looked pinched and cold. Her jaw was set firmly like a man's. " Come on, Bill," she said suddenly. " We must do something. If the police get him——" She didn't finish the sentence, but started for the door.

I followed her, sliding up the zip of my windbreaker. As she opened the outer door, a swirl of fine, powdery snow swept up into my face. Outside, the force of the wind was driving the snow almost parallel with the top of the the ridge on which the hut stood. The whole world seemed moving, the myriad snowflakes showing as dark specks against the dismal grey light. Dahler looked up as we came out of the hut. He was fixing his last ski. I called to him. " Where are our skis ? " But he made no reply. He was working feverishly at the binding of his ski. Then he straightened up, pulling his sticks out of the snow and, with one last glance at us, turned and thrust himself forward into the driving snow.

" Mr. Dahler ! " Jill called. " You'd better wait for us."

He glanced back over his shoulder. Perhaps it was the light, but it seemed to me that his face was contorted in a frenzy of haste. Then he pressed forward. An instant

later he was no more than a vague shadow. Then he was
gone, swallowed up in the storm.

Jill caught my arm. " Quick ! " she said. " Our skis
are down there." She caught hold of the sticks still
leaning against the side of the hut, thrust a pair into my
hands and then started off down the slope, ski-ing forward
like a skater on her feet. I followed. Below the loose
surface the snow was a hard, frozen crust. The wind
whipped blindingly into my face as I descended. The
exertion and the cold brought my circulation back. By
the time I caught up with Jill she had already fixed one
of her skis. Fortunately all the skis had come to rest in
a pile on a drift. I found mine and fitted them to my
boots. As I straightened up, Jorgensen joined us. " Be
careful, Miss Somers," he said. " It is dangerous now.
You may get lost."

" I'll risk that," she answered and started off up the
slope towards the hut.

I followed her. My limbs had stiffened so that they
felt like boards with rusted joints. But by the time I
reached the top of the slope, they had loosened up a bit
and I was feeling warm with the exertion. There was no
no sign of the hut. The marks of our descent were already
obliterated. Jill had a compass in her hand. " We shall
never find the posts in this snow," she said. " We must
go by compass. Finse is just west of due south. Ready ? "

I nodded.

She thrust her sticks into the snow and glided off along
the ridge. " Keep close to me," she called. " And go
slowly. It may be dangerous."

So began one of the craziest trips I have ever done.
The snow was so thick that visibility was reduced to a few
yards. The wind cut like a knife. There were no markers
now. Jill was leading us by compass and intuition. And
I'll say this, she led well. She had a feel for the lie of the
country which was instinctive rather than reasoned. We
kept to ridges where possible. But every now and then
we dropped steeply only to have to climb again on the

far side. But as we went on the proportion of downhill to uphill work increased and in consequence the going became easier. Several times we found ourselves faced with drops into nothingness. Probably they were only a matter of twenty or thirty feet. But in the snow it was impossible to tell. Once we climbed a long, sloping snowfield only to find ourselves stopped by a sheer cliff of black rock splodged with patches of snow. We worked round this and then had a good run down a long cutting in the mountain.

On this run Jill disappeared completely. She was somewhere just ahead of me, for despite the snow, her ski tracks were still quite clear as I followed. But apart from the tracks, I might have been alone in the wilderness of falling and fallen snow. Then suddenly her figure loomed up at me out of the storm. She screamed something to me and waved her stick. I did a jump turn and fell with my face buried in the snow. A hand caught me under the arm and helped me to my feet. " What's the trouble ? " I asked, looking down into her face which was almost obliterated by snow.

She turned me round and pointed. I shivered. It was one of the most terryfying sights I have ever seen. Just beyond the point where she had churned up the snow in a quick Christi, the ground fell away and the colour changed from white to ice-cold green. We were on the glacier itself, and this was a crevasse. It was a big one— about fifteen feet across ; a great gap that disappeared deep down beyond our sight. I went as close as I dared, but I could not see the bottom. I was looking at a million years of ice packed hard and solid like green crystal. I looked at Jill and could see she was thinking the same thing. She had only just saved herself. Just a fraction faster and instead of looking down into the green depths of that giant crack, we should be down there looking our last at the narrow slit that marked the world above.

" Come on," she said. " We must go back and cross it

higher up." Her voice, though she endeavoured to control it, sounded shaky.

We turned then and began to trudge back, climbing parallel to the crevasse. Gradually it narrowed until at last it was bridged by snow. We climbed a little higher and then struck across the glacier. We found no more crevasses and were soon climbing a ridge on the far side studded with huge rocks, some of which outcropped from the snow. Beyond, was a long, sloping run. We turned south again and began to glide down. But this time Jill kept the pace down.

We found no more crevasses. And shortly afterwards the snow slackened and the dismal grey light seemed lessened by a strange iridescence. This iridescence strengthened gradually until it hurt the eyes to look at it. The snow suddenly ceased to fall. The iridescence was mist. A moment later it was agitated as though by some giant hand and then, in a flash, the obscuring veil was whisked away and the sun shone. The white of the snow was blinding. To the west the sky was blue. The snow-capped peaks smiled at us benignly. The driving snow-storm up at the hut seemed as unreal now as a nightmare. We were in a pleasant world of warmth and white snow and brown outcrops of rock. Jill turned and waved. She was smiling. The next moment I was crouched low on my skis and going like the wind. The ski points sizzled in the powdery, ice-crystal snow and the cold air whipped at my cheeks.

We were running down a long valley. Jill, leading, set the pace, and it was a fast one. As we went down and down that everlasting slope I felt my knee joints tiring. The exhilaration of going after Farnell, the concentration required to get safely through the snow, the fear that had gripped me at the sight of the open jaws of that crevasse—all these had combined to give me strength. But now, now that it was a simple, straightforward run, the strength ebbed away and I began to feel the effects again of the overlong, all night trek across the mountains.

At the bottom of the valley we made a wide sweep round the foot of a shoulder of the mountains. It was here that I had my first fall. I don't know quite what happened. The snow was deeper, I suppose, and I just hadn't the strength to force my skis round. The joints of my knees seemed to melt away under my weight and the next thing I knew I was slithering across the snow in a jumble of skis and sticks.

I had great difficulty in struggling to my feet. The snow was soft and my limbs just refused to supply the extra effort needed. Jill waited for me. And when I came up with her, all plastered in snow, she said, " Tired ? "

" I'm all right," I said.

She gave me a quick glance. " I'll take it a bit easier," she said. And we started off again.

I suppose the pace she set was slower, but it didn't seem so to my trembling and aching limbs. I fell again and again, wherever there was a difficult turn. Each time she waited for me. Twice she came back and helped me up where the snow was soft. Then at last the slope was gentle and we were running easier, side by side.

It was whilst we were crossing this gently tilted table-land of snow that we came across two ski tracks freshly made. Jill, who was slightly in the lead, swung into line with them. " George and Dahler," she flung over her shoulder.

" Must be," I called back.

We reached a jagged outcrop of rock and she stopped. There, spread out before us in the sunlight, was the pass with the slender, black line of the Bergen railway snaking through the white waste of snow. Directly below us was the white, flat expanse of the frozen Finsevatn. And on the nearer bank the tiny, box-like shapes of the Finse Hotel and the railway sheds and cottages stood out black against the dazzling landscape. And beyond Finse, standing over it on the other side of the valley like a huge crystal dome, was the white expanse of the Hardanger-jökulen. The sweep of the snow over the summit of the Jökulen itself was unbroken, but to the left the snow seemed to fall away, leaving glacial ice of a vivid blue exposed to view, veined with the black lines of the shadows in the crevasses.

Jill glanced at her watch. " It's half-past twelve," she said. " The Oslo train will be in shortly. See—they've got the snow-ploughs out."

I followed the curves of the railway beyond Finse. Whole sections of the track were invisible, running through great timber snowsheds completely covered by drifts. They were like tunnels through the snow. Here and there, between the sheds, the line showed as a dark cleft cut through the snow, the sides as vertical as if they'd been sliced with a knife. Only on the bends were the lines visible—two slender black threads gleaming dully in the sun. Farther still to the left, a great plume of white vapour moved steadily along the track. At first I thought it was a locomotive. I could see the black shape of it just showing above the sides of the snow cutting. Then I realised that it was a snow-plough. The plume of vapour was snow being flung out from above the spinning rotary snow-cutters.

Jill suddenly gripped my arm as faintly echoing through the mountains came the mournful note of a siren. She was pointing away to the right where the track curved round a shoulder of the mountains towards Bergen. Just below the tip of the shoulder a plume of smoke showed for an instant. " It's the Oslo train," she said. " See it ? " A moment later the plume of smoke was visible again and I could see the dark line of the train coming out of the tunnel-like entrance of one of the snowsheds. For perhaps half a minute it crawled along in the sunshine. Then it was gradually swallowed up under the snow as it entered another snowshed. Little puffs of smoke came from the side of the shed which was not covered with snow. I couldn't see the train, but I could measure its progress as it burrowed along under the snow by those little whisps of smoke that appeared and then hung motionless in the frosty air.

" Do you think George really meant it when he said he was going to catch that train ? " Jill asked.

" I don't know," I answered. " But it certainly looks like it. These must be his and Dahler's tracks. Surely nobody else would have been out in that snow ? And if they are his tracks, then he's certainly making for the railway."

" But look," she said, " they're not going down to Finse. They're curving away to the left. The next station down the line is Ustaoset. That's more than twenty miles away. He'd never make it in time. And he can't jump the train."

" Well, there's only one way to find out," I said.

She nodded and we started off again. The ski tracks led farther and farther away to the left until Finse lay over my right shoulder. The Oslo train was drawing into Finse station now. I could see the black snake-line of the carriages slowing to a standstill. A white plume of steam burst from the engine as though it were blown with the long climb up from sea level to over four thousand feet. I began to wonder whether in fact we were following the right ski tracks.

Then round a small nut of rock we came upon the figure of a man struggling up towards us. He looked up as we bore down on him. And then suddenly he shouted, "Is that you, Jill?" It was Curtis. I recognised him as soon as I heard his voice.

" Yes," Jill called back.

" Thank God ! " he said. " I wondered what had happened to you. I've been trying to look for you, but I'm not very used to these things yet." He pointed to his skis. Then he saw me. " Hallo, skipper ! So you made it all right."

" Has Farnell passed you ? " I asked as I ran up towards him.

" Dunno," he answered. " Two men went by a little

time back. One a long way behind the other. The second looked rather like Dahler. Couldn't have been, could it? But neither he nor Jorgensen were at the hotel when I got down to breakfast. And police all over the place. Where have you been?" he asked, turning to Jill.

"Up on Sankt Paal," she replied.

Down in the valley the train whistled. The siren note was thrown back by the mountains, growing fainter and fainter as it slipped away into the infinity of snow-capped peaks.

"That was Dahler all right," I said. "The man ahead of him was Farnell."

"Good God!" I heard him mutter. But I was already past him, thrusting with my sticks to gain impetus. Jill came up beside me. Now that I was within sight of the quarry, I felt the excitement of the chase bringing the strength back into my legs. If only I could get Farnell alone—away from people like Lovaas and Jorgensen. He was bitter, tired of being pursued. He needed to be handled carefully. If I could talk to him quietly.

We topped another slight rise and there ahead of us, connected to us by the double lines of their ski tracks, two figures showed black against the snow. They were close above the railway now. The whistle of the train at Finse sounded again, the wail of it coming up to us from the valley and being thrown back by the hills. I glanced over my right shoulder. Great puffs of smoke were belching from the engine, condensing white in the thin air. The smoke turned black. I could hear the thick panting of the heavy locomotive. The long line of carriages began to move.

Jill came up alongside me. "We must stop him getting on to that train," she panted. Then she raised her stick and pointed to the sharp-cut line of the snow-ploughed railway below us. Little figures were moving along above the cutting. "Police," she said.

I nodded and plunged my sticks into the soft snow. All thought of my tiredness had vanished. If Farnell were captured by the Norwegian police, there was little chance of my getting the information I wanted.

Side by side we plunged down the slope, heads bent, our skis sizzling through the snow, thrusting the powdery top surface up like bow waves on either side of the up-curved points.

Ahead of us the two tiny figures swung further left. The leading figure turned still more. He was close by the railway now where it ran through a long cutting. He paused and half-turned his head. Dahler's smaller figure was gaining on him. Farnell swung away suddenly to the right, his skis throwing the snow up in a huge wave as he turned at speed. A moment later he was running parallel with the line directly below us.

I glanced once more over my shoulder. The train was moving steadily out of Finse. Jill saw it too and, without speaking, we turned and went headlong down the slope towards Farnell. Jill shouted to him. He must have heard, for I saw him look up. Dahler, too, had turned. He passed directly below us, a black speck hurtling down towards the railway.

Jill, in the lead again, swung away to the right, following Farnell's movements. Finse was hidden from us now by a long shoulder round which the line curved in a snowshed. Farnell was disappearing round the corner, Dahler close behind him. Then they vanished from sight. Faintly came the siren sound of the train as it went into the first of the snowsheds after Finse.

A moment later, and we had turned the point of the shoulder. We were right over the line now, skiing along the roof of one of the snowsheds. It ended just round the bend. Here the line made a convex curve to another shoulder of hill where it entered the next snowshed. Farnell was climbing now up the side of the shoulder of land nearest Finse. Dahler came hurtling down the slope of the bend. He was making for the railway, clearly with the idea of getting between Farnell and the line.

It all happened very quickly then. The slope was steep

where Dahler was coming down. At the bottom, just above the line, he did a jump Christi. Either he was tired or he was handicapped by his withered arm. At any rate, he muffed the Christi and went slithering down on his side. The next instant he had fallen down the sheer side of the cutting on to the lines.

Jill stopped then and I stemmed. We were standing at the end of the snowshed. Below us was the wooden tunnel over the line holding off the snow that poured like an avalanche slope down the shoulder of the hills. In places the wooden boards showed through the snow, which was blackened by smoke. Curving round the farther headland was the next snowshed, its entrance gaping black like a tunnel. Between the two snowsheds was the convex curve of the snow-ploughed cutting, with the lines showing black through the tight-packed snow. The walls of the cutting were quite sheer, the snow packed hard and tight. Its width was the width of a train. And in that cutting Dahler struggled to his feet and brushed the snow off his ski suit.

Beyond the headland the train hooted as it entered another snowshed. Jill clutched my arm. Her fingers bit into my flesh. For the moment I couldn't understand her agitation. Then I saw Dahler trying to scale the sheer snow walls of the cutting and I realised the danger of his position.

I glanced quickly up the shoulder ahead of us. Farnell was still climbing, glancing over his left shoulder as though measuring the distance to the line below. He was directly above the next snowshed now. Then I looked down towards Dahler. He was scrabbling frenziedly at the snow with his hands, trying to get a purchase for his skis. Round the headland I could hear the heavy panting and rumbling of the approaching train. " Mr. Dahler ! " Jill screamed. " This way. Under the snowshed." Her fingers dug at my arm. " Doesn't he know there's room for him to get off the track in these snowsheds ? " she breathed. " Mr. Dahler ! "

But the man was panic-stricken. Where he was, he could probably feel the trembling of the rails under his feet as the giant locomotive came down the track beyond the headland.

" Dahler ! " I shouted. " This way ! "

But he was frenziedly tearing at the wall of snow as though he would burrow through it. Every now and then, where he had made it crumble a bit, he tried to climb with his skis.

" Dahler ! " I yelled.

He looked up.

I waved to him. " This way, for God's sake. Get under the shed here."

He seemed to take it in at last, for he straightened up. The engine hooted again. The sound of the siren was very clear now. It was hooting for the entrance to the snowshed on the other side of the headland. Dahler half turned and looked at the black, gaping hole of the snowshed. Then he started to ski towards us. But his skis caught in the sleepers and he fell. " Take your skis off and run for it," I shouted.

He bent down and worked like a madman at his ski bindings.

Jill pulled at my arm. She was pointing to where George Farnell stood poised high up on the slope of the headland. He was watching the track below, his body bent forward as though about to start the run for a ski jump. " What's he going to do ? " Jill whispered.

" I don't know," I said.

The sound of the train was loud now, the noise of it magnified by the snow-arched tunnel. Dahler had at last got rid of his skis. He was running down the track towards us. Above the snowshed I saw Farnell do a half-jump turn and come hurtling down the slope. And suddenly I knew what he was going to do. He was going to do a ski jump from the lip of the snowshed entrance on to the top of the moving train as it came out of the tunnel. Jill had understood too, for her grip on my arm tightened.

The rumble of the train grew louder. Here and there on the outer side of the shed little puffs of smoke seaped out into the cold air. Farnell was just above the snowshed now, his body bent forward, his sticks poised ready. A perfect jump turn in a welter of snow and he was coming straight towards us along the very top of the shed. My hands were gripped around my sticks so that it hurt. Suppose he reached the edge of the shed before the engine emerged? But he was stemming now. The blunt, cow-catchered front of the engine burst out of the tunnel in a roar of smoke, its headlight blazing dully in the sunshine. The tender and then the first carriage appeared. In that instant Farnell reached the end of the snow-shed and jumped. And in that instant I realised with horror that the forward carriage had no snow on it. The smoke from the engine must have melted it. He had gauged it perfectly and for a moment I thought he was going to make it. He had skied on to the train at the exact speed the train was moving. And for one instant he stood erect on his skis, steady on the very top of the carriage.

Then his skis caught something, slipped and threw him. He folded at the knees in a proper fall and clutched at one of the ventilating cones. I think he gripped it. But one of his skis caught the snow that was on a level with the top of the carriage and in a second he was dragged sickeningly back along the carriage top, ground down between the moving carriages and the snow wall at the side and then spewed up again on to the snow above the cutting.

I felt Jill tense. I looked down at her. She had her hands over her eyes. Then she relaxed and looked up again. But in a moment she had stiffened with renewed horror. The train was on the curve now. Below us, in the cutting, Dahler was running towards us. Behind him, the engine panted and rumbled round the curve. I saw him glance over his shoulder. Then his face was turned towards us again and I saw that it was a mask of fear, his eyes wide and his teeth bared with the effort of running. He wasn't a young man and he'd been ski-ing all morning. He ran incredibly slowly, it seemed.

The engine rounded the bend of the cutting until its headlight shone straight at us. The noise of it shook the snow-clad hills. And Dahler ran—ran for his life. The driver saw him and the brakes squealed as he applied them. But the heavy train was on the down-grade. Dahler turned his head again. He was about twenty yards from us. I could see the sweat glistening on his face. The engine was bearing straight down on him. He hadn't a hope. I took hold of Jill and pressed her to me, so that she couldn't see what happened.

It was all over in a second. Realising that the iron monster was on top of him, Dahler flung himself against the sheer snow wall, squeezing himself against it in the hope that there would just be room between the snow and the train. It was the worst thing he could have done. There just wasn't enough room for his small body. I stood there, helpless, and saw the iron edge of the loco-motive cut into him, mangling him to a bloody pulp against the ice hard wall of the snow. His thin, high-pitched scream like the cry of a trapped rabbit merged and was lost in the squealing of the train's brakes. With a roar and hiss of hot smoke in our faces the engine thundered into the snowshed, rumbling heavily in the snow under our feet and shaking the buried wood structure. Then the sound of it was drowned by the metallic clatter of the buffers as the carriages overran each other.

" Oh, God ! " Jill muttered. " How horrible ! " Her face was buried against my wind-breaker and she was shuddering. In that moment she was thinking of Dahler and not of Farnell. Then she stopped shuddering and straightened herself. " What about—George ? " she asked and peered through the smoke towards the far side of the curve where George Farnell's body lay in a dark heap on the snow above the cutting.

"We'll go and see," I said. Anything for action. To stand there waiting for Dahler's mangled body to emerge from the other end of the train was unthinkable.

We started forward then, leaving the top of the snow-shed and moving along above the cutting. Below and to the left of us the last carriages were moving slower and slower into the dark tunnel entrance of the snowshed.

The last coach moved sluggishly past me and stopped, with just half of it protruding from the tunnel to show that a train was standing there beneath the snow. I glanced hurriedly into the cutting. The farther wall, directly below me, was broken and scarred with crimson as though some political agitator with more ardour than education had tried to daub a slogan. Of Dahler himself there was no sign. Somewhere along the train they would find his remains caught up between two carriages. I did not like to think what his body would look like.

I turned my head away and trudged on as fast as I could. It was Farnell I had to reach—Farnell, who might be still alive. But I could not get the thought of Dahler out of my mind. I'd liked the man. There had been something sinister and unreliable about him. And yet, remembering his past, it was all so understandable. I was sorry he was dead. But perhaps it was as well.

"Bill! I think I saw him move." Jill's voice was small and tight as though she were fighting to keep control of herself.

I peered ahead. The brilliance of the sunlight on the snow played tricks. My eyes were tired. I couldn't focus properly. "Maybe he's not dead," I said, and pressed on, my skis crunching in the frosty snow.

When we reached Farnell he was lying quite still, his body curled up in a tight ball. His ski points were dug deep in the snow and there were smears of blood along the broken lip of the cutting. Jill lifted his head. It was all bloody. I loosened the bindings of his skis and cleared them from his boots. One leg was horribly broken. As I eased it round so that it was less twisted he gave a slight groan. I looked up and, as I did so, I saw his eyes open. Jill was wiping the blood from his face. His skin beneath the stubble was ivory against the pure white of the snow.

"Water," he whispered. His voice rattled in his throat. Neither of us had our packs. Jill smoothed his forehead. He stirred and tried to sit up. His face twisted with pain and he lay back again, his head cradled in her lap. His teeth were clenched. But when he looked up into her face and saw who it was, he seemed to relax. "I nearly made it," he whispered. "No—snow. I'd have done it if——" He stopped and coughed up a gob of blood.

"Don't talk," Jill said, wiping his face again. Then to me, "See if there's a doctor on that train."

I started to get to my feet. But Farnell stopped me. "No use," he said.

"You'll be all right," I said.

But I knew he wouldn't. I could see it in his eyes. He knew too. He looked up at Jill. "I'm sorry "—his voice was barely audible—"I've been a poor husband, haven't I?"

Husband? I glanced from him to Jill. And then I understood—all the things that had puzzled me were suddenly clear.

He had closed his eyes and for a moment I thought he had gone. But his grip on Jill's hand was tight and suddenly he looked up at me. His glance moved from me to Jill. Without a word he put her hand in mine. Then he said, "Bill—you must take over where I left off. The thorite deposits——" He gritted his teeth and raised himself. Jill supported his back. His eyes were narrowed against the light as he gazed out across the valley. "The *Blaaisen*," he murmured.

I turned and followed the direction of his gaze. He was looking across to the Jökulen, to the flank of the mountain where the glacier ice shone a brilliant blue. When I looked

back at him he had relaxed and closed his eyes. Jill bent
and kissed his lips. He tried to say something, but he
hadn't the strength. A moment later his head lolled over
and the thin blood trickle of a hæmorrhage started from
his open mouth.

Jill laid him back in the snow as a shadow fell across us.
I looked up. Jorgensen was standing over us. I became
conscious of many voices from the direction of the snowshed. The half coach was still protruding from the tunnel
and in the cutting police and officials mingled with a mob
of excited passengers.

I glanced at Jill. She was dry-eyed and staring at
nothing. " Dead ? " Jorgensen asked.

I nodded.

" But he told you before he died ? "

" Yes," I said.

I stood up, conscious again of the aching of my limbs,
and I turned and stared across the valley to the Jökulen.
At my feet lay the remains of George Farnell. But out
there, under the Blue Ice, lay all that he had lived and
worked for, all that was best in him. That was the sum
total of his life. Nothing visible—nothing that has not
been visible since the Ice Age first elected to make the
ice on the flank of the Jökulen blue. But an idea—something born of a lifetime's study and work, backed by the
solid presence of mineral wealth under the rock and ice.
And I swore then and there that I'd stay up here at Finse
and build an industrial monument to George Farnell,
who died there in the snow—ex-convict, swindler, forger,
deserter, murderer—but for all that a great man who
subordinated everything to one idea.

And now, here it is, half completed. When I began this
story the days were shortening and Finse was in the grip
of ice. It is still in the grip of ice. But now the days are
drawing out. Spring is coming. All through the long
winter months Jill and I have been living up here and the
work has gone steadily forward. We have done all the

exploratory work. We have proved that George Farnell did not die for nothing. Soon now we shall mine the first ore. Soon these sprawling, wooden buildings will be humming with activity. Finse will be a small town, centre of the life blood of one of the world's greatest industrial plants.

Open the window now and look out across the snow. I can see from here the spot where Farnell died. And away to the right, its icy jaws seeming to grin back at me, is the Blue Ice and all he lived for.

THE END